lal
1-26

NO REST FOR THE WICKED

A Pirates of King's Landing - Book 1

LAUREN SMITH

This book is a work of fiction. Names, characters, places, and incidents are the product of the author's imagination or are used fictitiously. Any resemblance to actual events, locales, or persons, living or dead, is coincidental.

ISBN: 978-1-952063-78-7 (e-book edition)

ISBN: 978-1-952063-79-4 (trade paperback edition)

For Amanda Pereira, my writing/editing goddess of a friend, for Aimee Harvey and her lovely ideas and support, for Deborah Camden who named the dashing quartermaster Reese and Kym Young who named the sweet-hearted cabin boy Griffin.

PIRATES
OF
KING'S LANDING

PROLOGUE

CORNWALL, ENGLAND 1727

"Hit 'em harder!"

Fourteen-year-old Dominic Greyville swung a fist at the large lout of a boy and snarled like a badger as he bared his teeth. There was nothing more exciting than fighting on a dirt road with a bastard who deserved a good punch or two.

"Look out, Dom!" Another warning sent Dominic diving out of the way. The lad he was fighting struggled and staggered back after his looming fist just missed Dominic's face.

Dominic kept his eyes on the boy but listened for his best friend, Nicholas Flynn, to warn him of another tricky move.

"You bastard!" His opponent lunged for Dominic, and the pair of them hit the dirt with a heavy thud. His ribs ached beneath the weight of the bigger boy. Dominic swung wildly, catching the other boy's jaw, and he grunted as pain shot up his hand and into his arm.

The boy slumped over onto his side, and Dominic rolled up onto the balls of his feet. His ears rang from the blows he'd already taken, and blood coated his split lip, but Dominic laughed in delight. Perhaps it was his mother's wild Spanish blood, but he couldn't resist a good fight, especially when a boy like this had been slapping a pretty young tavern girl around. Dominic had taken one look at her tear-stained face and launched himself at the wrongdoer. The lad had to be sixteen or seventeen, and his meaty fists were capable of great damage, but it was worth the risk to do what was right.

"Oi!" A deep bellow sent the small crowd of boys who had been watching the fight scattering away. Only his friend Nicholas dared to remain behind.

A burly man with gray-black hair marched up the lane toward them. "What'd I tell you about fighting, eh?" Judging by the looks of his apron and the overpowering stench of mead rolling off him, he had come from the tavern down the road.

Dominic's opponent got to his feet, one hand clamped over his gushing nose.

"Little shitter hit me, Pa!" The lad pointed at Dominic with a bloody hand.

The lad's father slapped a paw of a fist on his chest. "I said, if you fight, you better finish it. Go on! Kill the little rat." The man pointed to Dominic, urging his son to kill him. For a second Dominic was shocked that a man would urge his son to kill another boy, but the hateful look in the man's eyes warned him that he meant it. There was no way around it—Dominic would have to win the fight because the stakes were suddenly higher.

The lad eyed Dominic with open hatred that mirrored his father's. He lunged for him. Dominic danced sideways and swept one foot out, tripping the boy. He fell face first so hard into the ground that he groaned and went limp.

"Bloody useless fool." The rotund man spat on the boy's prone body and glowered at Dominic and Nicholas. "Off with ye, brats!"

Dominic didn't need any further urging. He and Nicholas took off running down the road and only stopped when their lungs were burning for air. Pressing his palms to his thighs, he bent over double and let loose a surprising laugh, and Nicholas did the same. In that moment he felt invincible, as though he could conquer the world.

His eyes caught his friend's, and Nick grinned through his panting, as though he too sensed the magic of the moment. There was something about this time of day when the sun was not quite set and the world glowed a soft burnished gold. It was Dominic's favorite time of day, when he felt anything was possible, and yet a hint of the evening's melancholy floated in the air, making the moment almost bittersweet.

"That was a close one," Nicholas said once they caught

their breath. “I thought he had you for a minute there. I was about to jump in and help.”

“I was doing just fine,” Dominic replied.

Nicholas snorted in clear disagreement.

Nicholas was the better behaved of the two and rarely fought, unless it was clear Dominic was about to have his arse beaten. As the son of the Earl of Camden, Dominic’s behavior ought to be above reproach, but he had a knack for getting him into scrapes. Those scrapes had the tendency to drag his best friend into the problem. Nick was a squire’s son and legitimately tried his best to be properly behaved, but Dominic often lured him into temptation.

“You and your pretty skirts, Dom. Always ready to throw a punch for a dainty ankle or a sparkling smile.” Nicholas shook his head, his sandy-blond hair tousled by the wind as he climbed the short stone wall near where they stood.

Dominic joined him, and they studied the fields and distant woods. The roof of a manor house, built when Henry Tudor ruled England, was barely visible above the tops of the trees. Camden House. Home. He adored it and yet wanted to escape it at all costs. Whenever he was home, his father constantly reminded him of his duties as the future earl.

Home was a short distance away, beckoning him, but Dominic couldn’t help but cast his gaze back toward the tavern and beyond, toward the dockyards and the sea. The clouds towered above the distant water, promising storms, but it didn't scare Dominic. His hands itched to curl around the rigging of a vast frigate or a sleek sloop. For as long as he could remember, he'd listened to stories of pirates braving the wild seas. It was even rumored that back in the fifteenth century, the Duke of Cornwall, whose estate was not too far from Camden House, had been a great and fierce pirate.

"Nick, you ever think of going to sea? Buying a commission, I mean?" The thought of going to sea had always intrigued Dominic, and on more than one occasion he'd threatened to run away and board a ship whenever he and his father fought.

Nicholas's gaze moved toward the ocean behind them. "Out there? Not unless you went. I'd go anywhere with you. Even the farthest horizon."

Nicholas's words made Dominic flush. They'd grown up side by side, getting into mischief all their lives. They'd become blood brothers long ago, having spit upon their cut palms and clasped them together, swearing undying loyalty to each other under the harvest moon. He couldn't imagine going anywhere without Nicholas either.

"You'd truly go to sea with me?" he asked, watching Nicholas's face closely.

"Of course. Someone would have to keep you out of trouble, or else you might become a pirate. Your father wouldn't like that one bit."

"Well, there's pirates and there's *pirates*. Some pirates

have a letter of marque giving them permission to harass the enemies of England, you know." Dominic had always liked the idea of being a noble pirate like Sir Francis Drake.

"Those are called privateers."

"Still, a privateer is just a pirate with a license," Dominic replied with a wicked grin.

"And that still wouldn't sit well with your father. God help us if we ever have to go to sea."

They both laughed and then fell into a pleasant silence. The wind whistled through the trees ahead of them, and Dominic dropped down into the meadow with a heavy sigh.

"Time to go home?" Nicholas asked, and Dominic answered with a sad nod.

He shoved his hands into his trousers, trying to tuck his shirt back in. He knew he looked a fright. His mother would be furious at his ripped pants and bloodied shirt as well as his dirt-covered waistcoat.

"See you tomorrow?" Nicholas asked.

"Definitely." Dominic watched his friend head down the road before he crossed the field into the woods. He took his time getting to the house, knowing full well he would pay for getting into a fight.

When he reached the front gates, one of the servants saw him and rushed over to speak to the tall dark-haired woman in a gold sack-back gown as she examined a row of

English rosebushes. His mother lived for her gardens, especially the roses.

"Dom!" His mother called his name, and he quickened his pace until he stood before her. Lucia Greyville was still every bit the Spanish beauty she'd been as a girl of eighteen when she married his father. Now, at two and thirty years, she'd become an excellent countess and a fiercely protective mother.

"Come. Let me see you," Lucia demanded as she cupped his face, examining his bruises and split lip. "What happened to you?"

"Just a tussle, that's all, I swear," he promised.

His mother's cinnamon-brown eyes narrowed. "A *tussle*? That's the third one in a week. Your papa will"

"Please don't tell him, Mother." He grasped one of her hands. They were of an equal height now, both five foot seven inches, and it made him feel more protective of his mother than ever. Soon he would be taller than her if his father's height of six foot four was any indication.

"Even if I keep my silence, dear boy, he will see the bruises himself."

"Please, Mother. It will be our secret."

Lucia sighed, though her lips twitched as she fought off a smile. "Run along. Wash up and change for dinner." She kissed his cheek and nudged him toward the door.

Dominic raced up the steps and into the house. He caught the lingering scent of cigar smoke, which meant his father must still be in his study. There might yet be time to hide the worst of the damage. Dashing up the grand staircase, he reached his room without being discovered. He washed and changed, pausing only a moment to examine the purpling bruises on his cheek and jaw. His father would notice those, but what could he do? He'd tried clever lies in the past, and his father never believed them. He could always read Dominic's face too easily.

By the time he came down for dinner, his mother was kissing the twins good night. Josephine and Adrian, his little sister and little brother, were only two years old and spent much of the day in or near the nursery. Adrian favored their father in looks, with lighter brown hair and gray eyes, unlike Dominic, who looked more like his mother. Josephine—or Josie, as Dominic liked to call her—favored their mother, but everyone could see their father in her eyes.

Dominic smoothed a hand over his dark hair as he watched his mother give each child a tiny hug before the nurse carried them upstairs. A moment later, his father strode into the hall. Aaron Greyville went straight to Lucia, embracing her with a passionate kiss that made Dominic blush and turn away in embarrassment. His parents were forever kissing and whispering in alcoves when they thought they were alone. It was unsettling. People like his parents should never be kissing. He turned away, but his single step to leave caused a floorboard to creak, which caught his father's attention.

"Dominic." The tone made it clear he was in trouble.

"Yes, Father?"

"Come here, please."

Dominic reluctantly trudged over, keeping his head down. Aaron frowned, his mustache wilting as he studied his son.

"Fighting again?"

"Yes, but"

"Dominic, you know how I feel about that. Good men need not resolve disputes with their fists. It isn't civilized to beat another man like that."

"But this bloody oaf was hitting a sweet little wench, and"

"Wench?" his mother cut in sharply.

"A young lady," he corrected quickly. "She was crying, Father. You taught me never to strike a woman."

"I did," Aaron agreed. "But I also expect you to act with honor. Striking some foolish boy from the dockyards is cowardly. I won't have a coward for a son. Do you understand?" His father's eyes were hard. "I think a night without supper will give you a chance to think upon your actions. Off to bed with you." His father's order made him grit his teeth. He hadn't been there—he hadn't seen the girl crying. Any honorable man would have fought the other lad.

"Perhaps *you* are the coward," he snapped.

Aaron stared at him with a heavy sigh of frustration that hit Dominic deep in the chest.

"Someday you will understand that choosing not to

fight in certain circumstances is the right course. A noble-hearted man cannot face difficult situations by raising his fists at every turn."

"Not fighting still makes you a coward," Dominic retorted.

His father's scowl deepened. "If you truly think that, you haven't grown up like I thought you had. I never once said don't fight—I merely said you don't always have to fight with physical violence."

His black look only infuriated Dominic, but he didn't respond. Instead, he rushed upstairs, desperate to get away from his father and the disappointment in his eyes.

Dominic passed by the nursery and froze as he heard the nursemaid, Mary, singing a soft lullaby to the twins. Bitter tears stung his eyes, which only brought more shame upon him. He wiped the back of his hand across his face, trying to rid himself of the evidence of his crying.

No one understood him, except his mother. She used to whisper tales of her life aboard a ship on the Spanish Main. Her father had been a Spanish naval captain and had spent many years fighting off pirates. Dominic loved to hear his mother spin yarns of her carefree childhood on the high seas. It had often been his only escape from his boring life in Cornwall. Far too often, he was locked up here in this stuffy manor house, studying tedious lessons on history, mathematics, and sciences under the guidance of a tutor. It was no fun at all.

As he stepped into his room, anger and shame still

warred inside him, making his stomach knot and his head pound. The thought of spending time in his bedchamber alone and hungry sounded dreadful. He kicked the heavy trunk at the foot of his bed and threw himself down in the chair beside it.

He grinned as an idea flashed across his mind. He went to his armoire and retrieved a rope ladder that he had made a few months ago. He carried it to the wide bay windows of his bedchamber, secured the rope at the base of his bed, and opened the window. Then he carefully scaled down the makeshift ladder and dropped into the flowerbeds.

Dusk stretched along the ground from the topiaries in the gardens, casting unsettling shadows on the usually cheery shrubbery. Dominic ducked between the shadows until he reached the woods. As he ran in the direction of the small dockyards at the end of Boscastle's main port, he hummed a colorful tune. His pockets jingled with a few coins, and he knew that lovely girl from the tavern would see his hunger and take care of him with a meat pie, a pint of ale, and perhaps even a kiss for protecting her honor. Dominic was still smiling as he reached the street that led to the tavern.

A few streetlamps offered no real light against the now heavy gloom. The hairs on the back of Dominic's neck rose as he had the eerie sense of being watched. Perhaps this hadn't been the best idea after all...

He spun to face the darkness behind him but saw

nothing. The shadows seemed to thicken as the fog rolled in from the sea. Dominic shivered and straightened his shoulders. He wasn't a child. He shouldn't be afraid of a little fog. He took a step toward the tavern, and just then a hand clamped over his mouth. He was hauled back into the alley, his screams muffled by his captor. He kicked his legs and rammed an elbow back into whoever held him.

"Little bastard!" a man snarled.

Something hard struck his temple, and he knew no more.

A LONG WHILE LATER, DOMINIC AWOKE TO THE rocking of a ship. He blinked, trying to focus in the dim light. A lantern swayed above him, casting a flickering light on the room. The sensation of the ship pitching and rolling made his stomach churn. He tried to move, but pain cut into his wrists and ankles. He stared down in horror at the iron manacles that restrained him. A dozen other boys his age or close to it were shackled beside him. Many had faces the shade of puce. Some had recently vomited. Several wept for their mothers.

A bitter taste filled Dominic's mouth as he too wanted to cry out for his mother. But she wasn't here and wouldn't be able to save him.

Dominic looked to one of the boys sitting close to him. "Where are we?"

The boy had a distant, almost dead look in his eyes. After a moment, he responded. "We're being taken to the West Indies...to work as servants."

"What? But they can't do that. We're not slaves. We..." Dominic looked around, seeing that he was indeed bound next to several healthy-looking dark-skinned men. They gave him a pitying look as he seemed to realize he was in the same helpless position as them.

"We won't survive. Most likely we'll die during the voyage," the first boy said. "And from what I hear, that will be a blessing. The captain of this ship...they say he has unnatural tastes." The boy nodded toward the other young boys beside them. "Before you were here, another boy died, and before he did, he told me to pray for death."

Fear filled Dominic's mouth with a strange taste, almost like blood, and his ears started to ring. In that moment, he realized that he would never see home again. He would never see the little twins or his mother and father ever again.

All because he was a hotheaded fool, just like his father had said.

I

PORT OF CÁDIZ, SPAIN, 1741

Captain Dominic Greyville was in a *most* compromising position.

This particular position involved a buxom Spanish lady sitting astride him, her skirts hiked up past her hips, moaning his name as she rocked her body against his. The wide windows of the woman's bedchamber were open, the filmy white curtains blowing gently with the evening breeze as he placed deep kisses to the swells of her breasts.

"Oh, Dominic, *mi amor*," she whimpered, her nails digging into his shirt. He was still fully clothed, but soon enough he would use her passion to get the answers he needed. He kissed up her throat to her lips, chuckling as she released a feminine growl of frustration.

"Why must you tease me so?" she huffed, her husky tone making his body ache with arousal. "Diego will be back any minute!" She tugged on Dominic's hair, trying to get his attention away from her neck.

"Patience," he murmured as he slipped one hand up her red silk skirts and beneath the petticoats. She hissed as he eased a finger inside her, and he chuckled as he played with her, delaying her pleasure. He kept one ear cocked toward the bedroom door, making sure her husband didn't surprise them.

Dominic didn't mind if he was discovered with this woman. The man would try to kill him, which was half the fun—the thrill of discovery and a quick escape. He pulled her face to his, tasting her plump lips.

"When must you return to your ship?" The woman's words were layered heavily with her seductive Spanish accent.

"Soon." He moaned as she ground her hips against his.

"Will you be gone long?" she asked, her hands running through his long dark hair. He usually kept it tied back with a leather thong, but she'd pulled it loose when he'd first arrived.

"One never knows. I'm at the mercy of the winds and tides." Dominic's lips lowered to the woman's breasts again as he nibbled her olive skin.

She arched her back in pleasure. "Don't make it too long."

"What have you heard from the ports, my love?" he asked as he played with her beneath her skirts.

"The ports?" she whimpered.

"Yes, what has your husband been telling you?"

She moved back to look down at him. "If I tell you, *mi amor*, what will you do for me?"

"Anything you wish, my love. Anything at all." He ran his gaze over her voluptuous body, knowing it wouldn't be a hardship to take her to bed. She was very lovely, but a bit too unimaginative for his tastes. He liked his women to have wits as sharp as his cutlass. There was no fun in bedding a woman when he couldn't spar with her with words—it kept things interesting.

"Diego said he heard the English are sending a merchant ship, the *Fortune*, to the Caribbean. It left port yesterday on its way to Port Royal. Apparently, the merchant ship is carrying precious cargo."

"Precious cargo?"

"Precious enough that they're sending an admiral with it."

Dominic's blood heated in excitement as he considered what *precious cargo* might mean. Money? Jewels? Whatever it was, he and his crew could intercept the *Fortune* and relieve the ship of its precious cargo.

"You're quite sure you heard the cargo was valuable?" he pressed again. It was unusual for an admiral to be accompanying cargo which meant the value must be great.

"*Sí*, very precious. Diego was most curious, but he didn't know what it was. I think it is jewels." The woman's eyes gleamed. "Don't you think I would look beautiful covered in jewels, *mi amor*? Jewels and nothing else?" She slid her hands down his chest as she spoke, but Dominic's thoughts were leagues away from her.

Dominic used his hands to give her the pleasure she sought, and once she had come, he slid her off his lap. She reached for him, still wanting more, but he slipped free. He didn't care to finish with her—she'd lost her allure, like all the other women he'd ever had. Whenever a woman started to show signs of missing him, he cut ties and sailed his ship permanently out of that amorous port. It created too many complications if they were to ever cross paths again out in the streets.

"Where are you going?" the woman snapped.

"My dear, it's been lovely, but I must go. Until then, Francesca..."

"*Maria!*" she corrected sharply. She rose from the bed and slapped him hard across the face. When she made to slap him again, he caught her wrist, squeezing just hard enough not to hurt her but enough to remind her who was in control.

"Fine then, go, you heartless pig!" she spat at him.

He released her and gathered his coat, cutlass, and pistol, and without a second glance at the scowling Spanish lady, he ducked out of the open window and eased along the building's second-story ledge.

Dominic at age twenty-eight was captain of a named called the *Emerald Dragon*. Maria had found him enticing because he was a rogue. There was nothing more enchanting for a married woman who was tired of a neglectful husband who drank too much than to sleep with a man like him. Bringing a seafaring rogue to one's bed—one whose skin was darkened by years in the sun, his palms rough from climbing seawater-hardened ropes was something ladies in Spain liked to boast about. He was exotic to such women, and he didn't mind at all that it gained him entry into some of the finest beds in Spain, France, and the Caribbean. The one place he would not make berth was England.

He'd turned his back on his old life. He'd had no choice at first, a surviving heartless indentured servitude in the West Indies after he'd been kidnapped from Cornwall. By the time he was eighteen he'd won his freedom by killing the man who'd enslaved him. He'd been pirating along the American coasts and the West Indies for four years now.

His father's harsh words and disappointment still cut deep in Dominic's memory. He'd comforted himself with the thought that his little brother, Adrian, would be his father's heir to the earldom, and he would no doubt be better at it than Dominic ever would have been. So he'd embraced his new life and remained a pirate, on his own terms, with his own ship, his own crew, and a code of honor.

Pirate was such a harsh word, though. He much preferred to be called an enterprising man, like the privateers a hundred years before. But the truth was, he was simply too fond of breaking the rules to pass up the opportunity to strike at the Spanish, French, and English alike. They were all equal prey in a pirate's conquest. When Dominic and his crew weren't chasing merchant ships, they often targeted slave ships, freeing the men and women at the first opportunity. After his own years in slavery, he swore never to let a slave ship get past him.

Dominic slid down the wall of the hacienda, catching his hands and feet against the rough stones to slow his way before he dropped onto the street below. Dawn was a few hours off, and he would be back on his ship soon. He'd gotten what he needed from Maria. She'd happily breathed word of a British merchant ship, the *Fortune*, on its way to Port Royal, bearing precious cargo. Dominic planned to be there first, before any pirate ships prowling the Caribbean might try to intercept it. It had been a while since he'd chased something of great value, and his mind buzzed with a dozen ideas of what the cargo might be.

When Dominic strode up the *Dragon*'s gangplank, he was met by his bosun, Jon Chibbs, a stout Englishman in his late forties.

"Cap'n." Jon tipped an invisible cap at Dominic.

"Chibbs. Are we ready to make sail?" Dominic asked.

"Just waitin' on you, Cap'n. Reese is in your cabin, ready to set the course," Chibbs added.

"Any problems while I was gone?"

Jon chuckled and shook his head. "Not a one, Cap'n,

not a one, except maybe Mr. Lee. He's fussing quite a bit since he had to take over for Mr. Bolton."

Lee was the new cook, after Bolton had been shot and killed in Tortuga a few weeks prior when he'd cheated another man at cards.

"Lee's not happy?"

"Not so much, Cap'n. He says he ain't no proper cook, an' my stomach agrees. My pa used to say, a crew is only as good as its cook."

"Tell him to be patient awhile longer. I'll find a cook soon." He was tempted to stop in Port Royal and acquire someone there. It was possible, after all, to land his ship at a private bit of beach in Jamaica.

Lee, like Chibbs and Reese, was a loyal man, loyal to the death for Dominic. Most of his crew were. Pirates tended to lack loyalty to all but the codes to which they agreed when entering the secretive brethren. Dominic had asked each and every man on his ship to be loyal to him, and if that loyalty waned, they had the freedom to walk away, no hard feelings betwixt Dominic or the crew member choosing to leave. He kept his men well fed and well compensated for injuries, and their share of profits was always fair, even among the officers like himself and Reese.

"I'll be in my cabin if you need me, Chibbs." Dominic left his bosun to handle the deck.

Dominic descended to the quarterdeck, greeting some of his crew in the hall as he passed them on the way to his cabin. The musical mix of French, English, Jamaican, and Spanish always made Dominic smile. He took men on his ship no matter their station in life. If they worked hard and didn't mind the dangers of life aboard his vessel, they were welcome.

Inside Dominic's cabin, his quartermaster, Reese Belishaw, leaned over the ornate desk. Maps spilled over the surface, weighed down at the corners with books. A compass sat open, the arrow pointing north along the coast where Reese was mapping a route with a sextant. Reese was eight years younger than him with hazel eyes that lit up when he was planning a course route as he was doing now. His blond hair wasn't as dark as Dominic's but it fell into his eyes and he brushed it away in frustration before focusing on the charts again.

"How was Francesca?" Reese asked without looking up.

"Maria, apparently," Dominic said with a chuckle, which made his friend look up in confusion. "Francesca must be some other wench here in port."

"Which means we'll be avoiding this place for some time, I assume."

"Most definitely." Dominic strode over to the desk and threw himself into the chair behind it, propping his feet up on the desk's edge.

Reese shifted the maps away from Dominic's boots before studying the coastline again. "Good God, man, we'll run out of places to resupply if you keep up with your women this way." Reese's hazel eyes glinted with mischief as he laughed. He too was a favorite among the ladies like Dominic but he kept his liaisons strictly limited to the brothels and taverns in the ports.

"That's because you're still wet behind the ears," Dominic teased, knowing that Reese being only twenty left him defensive as to his tender age compared to Dominic.

Reese's hazel eyes flashed. "So...what did *Maria* have to report, then?"

"Precious cargo...headed to the West Indies by way of a British merchant ship, the *Fortune*."

"Coin, do you think? Or perhaps goods? The lads love it when we land a prize with goods."

Dominic remembered the last prize his ship had taken, a merchant ship packed to the gills with tea, coffee, tobacco, and silks. They'd sold off all the cargo within a few hours of docking in Kingston, knowing more than one buyer who wouldn't ask too many questions. The coin that had lined their pockets had allowed them all to fill the taverns and brothels for an entire week.

"Maria didn't say what kind of cargo, only that it was to be guarded by a small naval guard on board the merchant ship. An admiral will be on board the ship, or so she heard."

"An admiral?" Reese puzzled over that.

Dominic was less concerned with the nature of the cargo, given that he wasn't dependent on it for his livelihood. He'd earned a place in Jamaica long ago, carving out a small bit of land for himself. Anything he did now was merely to keep his crew satisfied and to entertain himself.

"Lord knows what a stuffy old goat like that would be doing out on the high seas. They prefer to stay on dry land and give orders to their subordinates," Dominic chuckled.

Reese set the sextant down and rolled up the maps, binding them with a bit of blue silk ribbon and setting them in the map chest.

"Rather interesting. Sounds like one of the rare merchant ships that belongs to His Majesty."

Dominic shrugged. It was rare but not unheard of for a merchant vessel to be commanded by a set of naval officers if the goods on board were related to the crown.

"Whatever is on board will likely be worth the trouble then," Dominic replied.

"When do we leave?" Reese adjusted the gun tucked into his belt as he headed for the door of the cabin.

"Straightaway. Go and ready the ship."

"Aye, Captain." Reese left the chamber.

Dominic picked up the compass, flipping open the lid. He watched the arrow spin slowly and stop, pointing north. It was an old, battered bit of brass, but it had never failed him in ten years. He'd earned the compass fighting another boy for it while under his old captain's orders. A compass, a pistol, and a loaf of weevil-infested bread. Only the strongest survived. He'd proven his strength that day by shooting his captain through the heart with the very same pistol.

He stared at the compass a moment longer, and his thoughts drifted deeper into the past, beyond the days of hunger, pain, and misery.

He gave his head a shake. The past was just that—the past. A man could not beat against the tides, no matter how much he might wish to. There was only the next horizon, the next golden dawn to chase in search of treasure and glory. Dominic clamped the compass shut, and a grinned as he hummed a little tune and listened to the sounds of the men making ready to sail.

2

Roberta Harcourt leaned on the railing of the royal navy merchant ship, the *Fortune*, scowling at the rolling blue sea before her. She loved the ocean, but she did not love the reason she was crossing it.

Her father, Rear Admiral Charles Harcourt, was moving to Port Royal to run a naval office from the port, and she was being dragged along with him. It wasn't that she disliked Port Royal—she'd always longed to visit the West Indies. But she was quite certain her father had dubious intentions upon his mind when he'd decided she was to come with him rather than remain in London.

She'd spent the last two weeks listening to him describe the eligible, titled men whom they would likely meet upon reaching Port Royal. The list of gentlemen and their estate holdings had nearly put Roberta to sleep the previous evening. She'd caught herself just before her face landed in a bowl of soup. The cabin boy attending them had snickered, and she'd almost joined in laughing at herself, but her father's stern glare had killed any amusement from the moment. The truth of the matter was, she was being put on the market like a prized cow.

"Roberta, my dear," her father greeted as he joined her at the ship's railing. "I should like to speak to you."

"Papa," she answered quietly. "If it's about last night, I was tired. The crossing has been more than I'm used to, with the tossing waves." That part was most certainly a lie. She'd slept quite soundly; the rocking of the sea was something she'd grown used to. Her mother had died when she was five, and her father, unsure what to do with his dearly loved child yet couldn't abandon her to a governess's care, had simply taken her and the governess along with him on every voyage. She had better sea legs than half his crew.

"Oh no, it isn't that, my dear. But there is something important that I must speak to you about. I've just spoken to Captain Huntington, and he's requested a private audience with you. I believe the captain has finally worked up the courage to ask for your hand in marriage. I've assured him that you will be most receptive, and I have given him my blessing." Her father's chest puffed out with pride. At fifty-nine he was still a handsome man, even if out of his prime, but there was a weariness to his face that showed his time at sea and his years as a single father were weighing heavily upon him.

"I...Papa, I really don't..."

"Please, Roberta, think of it. A captain for a son-in-law. I would be most proud of you. You would travel the world with him as you've done with me. Wouldn't that be lovely?"

She wished she could agree, but she knew what her father did not—that most men loathed to take their wives or daughters upon voyages or move them to foreign lands. No, they kept their wives in pretty cages at home in London whilst they conducted affairs far away. That was not a fate she wished to resign herself to.

Her father's scrutiny fell upon her, and he sighed heavily. "You truly don't like him?"

"I don't *dislike* him, Papa. But he's like all the other gentlemen I've met—pompous and arrogant in their belief that a woman is incapable of anything besides twittering about gowns and producing children. I don't believe he would even let me stay with him aboard ship."

Her father suddenly chuckled. "I saw you only yesterday twittering about the very gown you're wearing now. You love a pretty dress as any other lady does, and you've told me often that you wish for children."

"But that isn't all that I am, Papa. I've helped fix the navigational charts when your navigator was ill. I know more about loading guns on a ship than most cabin boys learn in their first few years. I can tie any knot just as well as your men. I can name all of His Majesty's ships of the line—"

"I yield, my dear, I yield." Charles laughed softly. "I

cannot help but fear I've put you at a great disadvantage by letting you live as freely as you have, if the idea of marrying Captain Huntington has frightened you so."

Roberta wanted to disagree, to argue that she wasn't afraid of Captain Huntington or his marriage proposal, but she *was* frightened. It would mean the end of everything that mattered in her life.

"Very well, then. Hear the man out and then let him down gently." Her father patted her cheek, his eyes twinkling. "I believe we may yet find a husband for you in Port Royal. A good tea planter, perhaps? Or a successful merchantman who does business in England? Those sort of men might be more open to a wife involved in their affairs. I shan't give up hope to see you happily wed."

She gripped his hand and gave it a tender squeeze. "I'd rather you see me simply happy, in whatever way that may be."

"I do, my dear, I do. But when I'm gone, you will need a force to stand between you and the wolves of this world. I owe your mother that much, God rest her." He leaned in and kissed her forehead before walking back down the deck and vanishing inside a doorway.

And what if I am the force between myself and the world, Papa? She asked the question silently, allowing the sea to catch her thoughts as the winds buffeted her pale-blue silk skirts around her ankles. A smile escaped her lips as she thought back to how she had indeed twittered in excitement over the gown she now wore. The blue silk was gathered at the waist and flowed down over the large side pannier hoops she wore beneath her petticoats, and the bodice was a rich gold embroidered with tiny seahorses. She'd asked the seamstress to make it for the voyage. The poor woman had stared at the sketches of the marine animal and then muttered something about mad young ladies and their fancies.

Roberta glanced over her shoulder, watching men scale the riggings as they worked the ropes. So often she felt torn between the glittering world of balls and this world, the one where the winds and tides drove a person's destiny. The crew called out orders to one another, all corresponding to the orders from the officers who stood at the back of the ship near the helm. Two men stood out more clearly, their white breeches and blue frock coats adorned with gold trim and shiny gold buttons marking them as officers.

Captain Huntington and his second in command, Lieutenant Flynn. It was uncommon for navy officers to be in charge of a ship like the *Fortune*, but in this case, her father had wanted a light sloop that could outrun most pirates if they encountered any. Bigger ships from the royal navy would be able to fight, but their maneuverability was slow and her father never trusted a slow ship. Thus they'd ended up with Huntington and Flynn on board a merchant ship rather than a civilian captain and his crew.

Huntington was a nice man, a polite man, handsome

even. But he was forty years old, while she was barely even twenty, and those two decades between them felt more like a hundred years. She was ready to discover life, not end it, and marriage to him would be just that. She'd be pregnant within the year and never free to see the world again. Her passion for knowledge and adventure would be crushed the moment she spoke her vows.

If any man on this ship caught her interest, it was the quiet, intense Lieutenant Nicholas Flynn. He'd seen her eyeing the set of sea charts one evening after dinner and sat with her for more than an hour, showing her their course from southern England down the coast of Spain before they would set out across the Atlantic. Flynn had become a friend to her during the voyage. They'd spent many an evening talking over a glass of sherry about life at sea, the various ports they'd both visited, and the latest updates on the maps provided to the Royal Navy.

His stormy blue eyes and dark-blond hair, accompanied by his classically handsome features, were accented by his patient manner and his quiet, unspoken interest in her. Yet there was a sorrow in his eyes that seemed to create a chasm between them, as though he was afraid to let anyone get close to him, even her. But they had become friends during the long voyage, much to Captain Huntington displeasure.

She turned her focus back to the sea, a mistress she loved, respected, and feared at the appropriate times. The water was that spectacular shade of blue that prevented her from seeing deeper than a few feet, yet she could sense its endless depths as the ship cut through it on their voyage. The afternoon light flashed across the water's edge where the whitecaps formed, sending a diamond-like spray into the air, enchanting her. She had spent hours watching the water, and she never tired of the sight.

A smudge of gray beneath the water caught her eye, and a moment later a dolphin broke through the surface. Roberta lifted the hem of her gown to climb up on the first wooden ledge to get a closer look. Her gown was in the style of a *robe à la française* with its sack back split into two pale-blue pleats flowing away from her shoulders in the ocean breeze. She knew if she closed her eyes, it would feel as though she could take flight upon the winds themselves.

"You look lovely today, Miss Harcourt," Huntington said from behind her.

Her eyes shot open, and she clutched the railing securely as she stepped back down onto the deck. She continued to watch the dolphin as it broke through the surface for air and then disappeared again.

"Thank you, Captain," she said softly.

"I had hoped you might call me Thomas now. We've spent much time together on the voyage. Port Royal is only a few days away." Huntington moved to stand next to her.

"If the wind stays at our backs," Roberta agreed.

His brown eyes gazed upon her with the slightest hint

of possessive hope. She wondered what he saw when he looked at her. Did he see a petite but fiery red-haired beauty? Did he mind the faint smattering of freckles on her nose and cheeks because she refused to wear hats in the sun? Or perhaps he was lost in her jade-green eyes framed by smoky dark lashes that batted slowly as she gazed at the sea. She knew she was considered a beauty by some, yet she didn't think she was half so lovely as the fair-skinned blonde-haired women who were favored in the assembly halls of London.

Roberta was more spry than dainty, in her opinion, and the gowns she wore concealed the smooth muscles and curves of her body. She lacked that delicate, frail appearance that men seemed to desire. Her slightly tanned face had created gossip among the *ton*, and she knew well enough that she was called ugly names behind her back. But she supposed she was pretty enough to attract men like Huntington, with her heart-shaped face with its upturned nose and sweeping brows that made her look as if she was always up to mischief. Her father used to call her his little water sprite because she often created trouble aboard any ship she was on, usually to the amusement of the crew, proving that women weren't all unlucky upon the sea.

"Do you like the sea?" Huntington asked. His right hand fell very lightly on her own, which rested on the smooth wooden railing.

She felt no warmth, no spark, no life; what she was

looking for was simply not there. Shouldn't there be fire or explosions of heat? She'd heard the men belowdecks talk of the passion a lady could inspire in a man's heart and his loins—though they always phrased such things in far cruder terms. Surely it could be the same for a woman, to feel that passion at the touch of the right man? If that was so, then the captain was not the right man for her.

"I love the sea," she replied, her gaze still plunging into the sapphire depths. How she longed to join the dolphin, to have no concerns above the water's surface. She'd often wished that the old legends of mermaids were true and that she could trade places with a princess of the sea and never again worry about what lay on land.

"Once we marry, I can bring you with me," he suggested.

Roberta could not hide the enthusiasm that was triggered by this idea. If she had misjudged him, she would own up to it and give him a chance to catch her interest again.

"You would let me join you?" Her face brightened in the wake of this small hope. Huntington seemed surprised that this, of all things he was willing to offer, seemed to be what excited her.

"Some captains are allowed to bring their wives...on short voyages, in safe waters," he clarified. "A trip around the bay or up and down the coast for a day."

Roberta deflated. "Is that all?"

Huntington straightened as he gazed upon the sea, as

if remembering his duty. "It would be against protocol. It's simply too dangerous for a delicate young lady. Surely you are more comfortable in a drawing room enjoying tea with other ladies."

Had the captain read that from some book entitled *How to Infuriate Free and Independent Women*? Perhaps he had written it.

A small sigh escaped her lips. It was better to be at sea —however boring the voyage—than not at all, she supposed. For once in her life, she wished she could see a sea battle. Even the distant crack and thunder of cannons and the haze of gun smoke on the horizon would be enough for her. She'd witnessed such things up close only in military maneuvers and gunnery drills. A real battle would be something entirely different and far more thrilling. She just wanted to *live*, to feel her heart racing wildly as she joined the men upon the ropes and prepared for a boarding party.

But she wasn't a fool. A sea battle meant danger and death, and she knew just how dangerous life upon the water was. Women didn't fare well. Pirates were notorious for raping women before tossing their bodies overboard. There was no glory in that violence, but her heart still hammered at the thought of chasing down a pirate sloop and bringing its black-hearted crew to justice.

"I have spoken to your father, of course, and he has given his blessing. He was most excited for our marriage."

"Captain, please, trouble yourself no further. I have

decided not to marry, though I am most honored by your offer." *Better to cut him off before he can start naming our future children,* she thought.

"What?" Huntington's mouth opened in shock as he sputtered. "But...your father said..."

"My father was mistaken. He forgets how much I love the sea. If he mistook my excitement for hopes of an intended proposal from you, I'm most apologetic. But you see, I do not wish to marry."

"Whyever not?" the captain demanded, his tone frosty now.

"Because..." She struggled for an excuse and realized there was no better one than the truth. "Because I'm simply far too much trouble, Captain Huntington. One month of marriage to me would drive you utterly mad."

"Well...I don't see how a pretty young lady like you could—"

"Allow me to be plain for a moment, Captain. I would insist on accompanying you on all voyages, no matter the duration. I would rather not be stuck in a parlor with other ladies. In fact, I'd rather face the gallows alongside the vilest of pirates than spend one minute listening to women gossip over tea."

Huntington's face began to turn a concerning shade of red. "But that's your place. As a woman, you should—"

She cut him off again. "And that's *exactly* why you and I would quarrel endlessly. I don't believe in where you think I belong. There are plenty of young ladies who would be happy to marry you but I am not one of them."

For a long second he stared at her, shock widening his eyes. No doubt he'd never encountered a woman who spoke her mind like that, and it would take him a minute, or possibly several, to catch up with her in order to respond.

"I hope that you don't take offense or mistake my rejection of your offer of marriage as an attempt to play coy. I simply desire to be honest. You would not be happy with me, Captain, and I would not be with you, so we need not trouble ourselves further."

Huntington opened his mouth to say something more, but the sharp, piercing whistle of the ship's bosun cut him off.

"Sail to the south!" a man in the crow's nest cried out. Suddenly the deck was swarming with men. Roberta stayed by the rail, keeping out of the way. She knew better than to disrupt the flow of the men to their stations.

"What colors does she fly?" Huntington yelled up to the man in the nest. His voice was surprisingly loud—she'd never heard him speak above a conversational tone before. The sea captain in him had taken over.

"No colors, Captain, but there is a flag," the man shouted back down. "White with some sort of black shape on it."

Huntington's face paled. He glanced at Roberta before he turned his gaze southward and pulled out a brass spyglass from his breast pocket. Roberta followed the direction his spyglass was pointing. Her eyesight was good, but she could only just make out a vague rippling insignia. If she'd been closer, she might have sworn it looked like...

"The *Emerald Dragon*. Damn him!" Huntington hissed and crushed the spyglass back into his breast pocket. Roberta's face was afire with excitement.

"The *Emerald Dragon*? The ship captained by the infamous Captain Grey?" Her heart skittered inside her chest in a mixture of excitement and fear. Huntington's face darkened with displeasure.

"You've heard of him?"

"I am the daughter of a rear admiral. I hear things, even during those dreadful hours spent in parlors over tea." She found it insulting that he assumed she didn't know the latest naval scandals. The *Dragon*'s captain was the talk of Spain. He never ventured close to England—his hunting grounds were the West Indies and the coasts of Spain and Portugal. It was rumored that he was part Spanish and part English. Some said he was handsome enough that the devil himself was jealous of the pirate's good looks. That sort of gossip had been the only thing worth listening to when she'd been trapped in the Spanish parlors before they'd left port.

"He's no man you should put your mind to. He's a bloody pirate." Huntington looked as mad as a spitting cat. "Get below deck with your lady's maid, now! And stay there. The deck is no place for a woman, especially during a battle," Huntington snapped.

Roberta's gaze bored into his enraged face, but at last she turned on her heel and descended below deck. Her heart was pounding so hard against her chest that it hurt to breathe. She had to find her maid and, more importantly, her pistols and her dagger. If they were boarded, she would need to defend herself and her servant.

The *Emerald Dragon*...it was as if by simply dreaming of pirates, she had summoned one of the fiercest since Captain Morgan.

She only hoped she would not live to regret it.

3

"We're coming up on 'em, Cap'n!" Chibbs bellowed from the quarterdeck of the *Emerald Dragon*.

"Keep the sails open. I want to come up on her starboard side. Ready the round shots in the swivel cannons!" Dominic ordered from where he stood on the forecastle deck. Reese stood one deck below and repeated the order.

"Man the cannons!" Reese raised his cutlass, and the cannon crew rushed to their stations.

Dominic leaned against the railing on the bow, grinning wickedly as he watched the *Fortune* try to outrun him. The *Dragon* was three hundred yards away from her prey, and the royal merchant ship had almost reached Port Royal unscathed.

The *Dragon* had followed it for the last few weeks, keeping the *Fortune*'s masts just visible above the horizon.

If there was one thing his crew and the ship itself were good at, it was vanishing from view, like a wolf edging behind trees as it watched a rabbit nibbling on grass in an open meadow. The ship could go unseen until it was ready and then catch up with little warning. That was one of the many benefits of using a sloop. The *Dragon* had outrun every ship that had ever chased it.

Dominic's men were armed and ready for the battle ahead, but they needed to cripple the *Fortune*. Reese, at the helm, had managed to pull the *Dragon* up so her hull avoided direct fire from the *Fortune*'s cannons. Then Reese rushed to the deck below to see to their own cannons. Dominic kept his gaze on the other ship, raising his spyglass, watching the crew of the *Fortune* rush to ready themselves. Their captain was shouting, his face red as he ordered his men to load.

"Reese! Chain shot to the mainmast!" Dominic shouted over his shoulder.

"Aye aye, Captain!" Reese changed his orders for the middle gun crew. "We're going to cripple her, men!"

Dominic collapsed his scope and tucked it into his leather waistcoat as he rushed down to the waist of the ship.

"Cast loose your gun!" Reese barked. "Level and prime your gun!"

The first explosion of sound came from the *Fortune* as their cannons unleashed half a dozen shots simultaneously.

The round shots whizzed overhead, ripping through one mainsail.

"Run out your guns! Aim at the mainmast!" Reese cried out. While they were reloading their guns, the *Dragon* would try to bring down their mainmast.

"Point and fire!" Dominic and Reese shouted together.

The thunderous boom accompanied by the blast of shot from three of the *Dragon*'s cannons wreaked devastation on the mast. Each cannon fired two cannonballs, chained together, that flew between the ships and struck the *Fortune*'s mainmast with such force that the mast snapped in half. Men on the *Fortune* screamed and dove out of the way as the mast crashed down onto the deck, its white canvas sail fluttering like the wings of a dying seabird.

The *Dragon*'s crew broke into cheers that were abruptly cut off as the *Fortune* unleashed a fresh volley, one ripping through his crew on the quarterdeck. Dominic's vision blurred as the ship's doctor rush to the injured. Dominic held his breath, the sounds of his injured men crying out in pain drilling into his head. He waited for the pronouncement from the doctor.

"Two dead!" Abel confirmed over the screams.

Dominic's body went cold, his mind whiplashing as he trained his gaze on the *Fortune*.

"Aim for the decks!" Dominic ordered. "Grapeshot on all cannons!"

The *Dragon* waged war on the *Fortune* for another fifteen minutes, but their prey refused to give up easily.

Chibbs rushed to Dominic on the quarterdeck. "They won't surrender!"

"Then we board and make them reconsider. I'll wager we've taken the fight out of them. I want the officers restrained and the crew detained belowdecks until we see what cargo they're carrying."

The boarding party lined the port side of the *Dragon*, their weapons ready as the ships drifted close enough for the men to swing across on ropes. Smoke billowed up from the guns of both ships, and the cries of battle-ready men echoed across the open water. The *Dragon* nudged her prey, creaking in wooden groans as the ships collided. Dominic put a dagger between his teeth, tucked his cutlass into his waistband, and leapt from his vessel to the merchant ship.

He landed with a thud midway on the *Fortune*'s upper deck. Two of the merchant ship's crew rushed him, swords raised. He pulled out his cutlass, knocking one man back with the force of his blow while the other man swung at his waist. Dominic leapt back, narrowly avoiding the deadly strike. Reese suddenly appeared behind him, and they charged toward the waist of the ship, the crew of the *Dragon* following at their backs. Gunfire cracked about him as he and his men battled through the throngs of sailors.

In half an hour the fighting had died down, and

Dominic's men were celebrating victory. The captain and his lieutenant, along with a rear admiral, were bound and tied to the remnants of the mainmast while the remainder of the survivors of the *Fortune*'s crew were confined belowdecks.

"Ready to parley, Cap'n?" Chibbs asked as Dominic shot a glance toward the three officers. "As my pa used to say, when a man's beat, ya shouldn't give 'im time to catch his breath."

"I suppose you're right," Dominic muttered. Dealing with officers was his least favorite part of taking a ship. They were always arrogant sods, and they reminded him of home. It was why he usually avoided English ships, but the lure of whatever their cargo might be had him going against his usual behavior.

He strode to where the officers were tied down, Reese at his back. Giving the men a once-over, his eyes snagged on something familiar about the lieutenant. Blond hair, cut in the popular fashion, framed an aristocratic face with blue eyesblue eyes Dominic knew on sight but hadn't seen in more than a decade. There was no mistaking him. The years may have changed his boyish looks, but Dominic would know that face anywhere. A well of emotion he'd thought long dead inside him rose in his chest.

"You!" Dominic growled as he tried to comprehend that fact that he was facing Nicholas after all this time.

The lieutenant's furious gaze shot to his, his anger

replaced by unspeakable pain as recognition flashed in Nicholas Flynn's eyes. For an instant, it was as though they'd parted ways only yesterday, that Dominic had never been kidnapped, and that his childhood hadn't come to a crushing end as he lost his family, his best friend, and his freedom all at once.

"You know this blackguard?" the captain of the *Fortune* demanded, his face flushed.

Nicholas, his face ashen, gave a bare shake of his head to Dominic, who understood it immediately. The bonds of their friendship hadn't changed in all the years spent apart.

"No, he doesn't know me. He just reminds me of someone I once knew...someone from a long time ago," Dominic answered calmly, then turned to the captain. "Now, you're in charge, I presume? Or should I be speaking to the admiral here?"

The admiral tensed. He seemed ready to fight, despite his predicament, but blood trickled down the side of his head, and he looked a little too pale to be a threat.

"I'm in charge," the captain said. "The admiral is a guest, and I was escorting him and—" The captain suddenly closed his mouth.

"And the admiral's precious cargo," Dominic finished. "Well, that's exactly what my crew and I would like to help you with. Now, Captain..." He allowed the title to linger.

"Huntington." The captain added his name with a glower.

"Huntington. Tell me what sort of cargo it is you have, and then my lads and I will be on our way."

"Silks...it's silks," Flynn cut in hastily. "Free me and I'll take you to the cargo hold."

Dominic stared at his old friend. He was lying. The tension in his lips and the way his eyes narrowed, that was the Flynn he remembered, the Flynn who'd been able to fool almost anyone but him when they were boys.

"Silks, is it, Captain Huntington?" Dominic asked. He watched the man nod slowly in agreement, but the admiral's expression revealed the truth. The desperation in the man's eyes told him that whatever was belowdecks was indeed far more precious than any of the men wished for Dominic to know.

"Silks, yes," Huntington growled.

Dominic stroked his chin and then looked to Reese and Chibbs, who awaited their orders. "Please escort the captain and his crew to the longboats. Any man who wishes to join my crew is welcome to. The lieutenant shall remain behind as collateral until we reach port, at which point he will be set free."

"No! You cannot do this!" the admiral gasped, but his breathless words were accompanied by his struggle to stay conscious.

Dominic looked toward Flynn. "You have a doctor on board?"

Flynn nodded. "Yes, Dr. Frankston."

"Chibbs, have their doctor take a look at the admiral

once you get them in the longboat. Make sure they have a compass and any supplies they need before we cast off. I want all of the valuable cargo transferred immediately over to the *Dragon*, along with the lieutenant. Take him below and throw him in one of the cells."

"You cannot do this to us!" Huntington shouted. "We'll die out there."

Dominic turned to Huntington. "You're two days of easy rowing from Port Royal, due west. Unless you're daft, you'll be just fine. You're lucky you didn't meet with another pirate crew. We're one of the few who leaves survivors."

Then he turned to assess the *Fortune*. It was damaged beyond saving, and in less than an hour it would be at the bottom of the ocean.

Out of the corner of his eye, he watched the crew of the *Fortune* settle into the longboats, the doctor tending to the injured admiral. Flynn was released from the mast, and his hands were bound behind him before Reese shoved him toward Dominic.

"Give me a minute with him before you take him to the *Dragon*," Dominic told Reese. His quartermaster stepped back and walked a short distance away.

For a moment neither of them spoke. Dominic was torn between wanting to embrace his old friend and hit him for being on the opposite side of him in a battle.

"Dominic," Flynn whispered. "It's really you?"

Dominic's throat tightened as he tried not to look at

the man who'd once been as close as a true blood brother to him.

"I doubt I'm anything like the boy you remember," he answered softly, his gaze drifting to the sea.

"What happened to you? You went missing, and we searched for months. Your father"

"Is probably glad I'm dead. Listen to me, Nick—I'll not harm you, so long as you don't cause trouble. The moment we make port, I'll let you go, a free man. You understand?"

Flynn nodded. "I'll likely be cast into irons once Huntington catches up to me. He'll see my being captured as joining you rather than being a prisoner."

"You could always join us," Dominic offered, knowing Nick would turn him down. Of the pair of them, Nicholas had always been the one with the noble heart.

"You know I couldn't, Dom. You know I don't have the..." He trailed off.

"The black heart required to be a pirate? No, you certainly don't. Reese! Take him to the *Dragon*." Nicholas's refusal to join him hurt worse than he'd expected. Their childhood vows to always stay together, to be loyal to one another to the end, were clearly just a hazy memory now between them. Nicholas would never side with him, not with a pirate. It likely wouldn't matter that Dominic had made a point to sink Spanish slaver ships in order to free slaves. He was still a pirate. It shouldn't have surprised him that Nicholas had gone and done the respectable thing by joining the bloody Royal Navy.

"Dom! Wait!" Flynn struggled against Reese's hold, trying to break free. Reese knocked him hard in the temple with the hand guard of his sword, and Flynn went down with a heavy thud on the deck.

Reese's face fell. "Sorry, Captain, I didn't know how else to stop him."

"It's all right, Reese. Just see that he's not hurt. The man was...a friend once. A long time ago."

The young quartermaster nodded solemnly. "Understood." Then he hoisted Flynn up and headed for the gangplank that now stretched between the two ships.

Chibbs ran over, panting. "Cap'n, we have a problem."

"What is it?" Dominic's hand tightened instinctively on the hilt of his cutlass.

"It's two cabin boys—found 'em cowering in the wardrobe of the captain's cabin."

"Oh?" Dominic felt a twinge of guilt. Those boys should be on the longboats, not stuck here. They'd be forced into a life of piracy if Dominic didn't have a chance to get them to shore soon, and he wasn't about to put any more young men into the life that had been forced upon him.

"Bring them up here, Chibbs. And where are the silks?"

"We're loading them now, Cap'n. Looks to be a set of trunks, not much at all. Must be damn fine silks if that's all they have. But as my pa used to say, a fortune is a fortune, whether 'tis bars of gold or a handful of diamonds, but one is certainly easier to carry. Silks are damned heavy. Wish we'd found jewels instead."

Chibbs waved an arm to two wavering shadows near the stairs leading below deck. The boys were both short. One had bright-red hair pulled back into a ponytail at the nape of his neck, while the other was a brown-haired little creature with wide, scared eyes. The red-haired boy eyed Dominic with open curiosity. He wasn't used to young lads eyeing him like...what? Something was off about the boy, and it made Dominic shift restlessly on his feet.

"What are your names?" he demanded gruffly. The brown-haired boy stifled a terrified gasp and clutched the sleeve of his braver companion.

"I'm...Robbie, and this is Luke," the red-haired boy announced. His voice was rather high, and it seemed that neither of these boys was near manhood. They couldn't have been more than twelve or thirteen, with their small hands, high voices, and delicate features. They reminded him far too much of the younger lads he'd served with during those first few years. Most hadn't been strong enough to survive on board the same ship as the infamous French pirate Gerard La Roux.

"Well, lads, I'm sorry we did not find you earlier, otherwise you'd be with the captain and his men on the longboats. You find yourselves passengers aboard my ship. I'm Captain Dominic Grey."

"What of the admiral? Was he with them?" the red-haired boy demanded. Dominic was rather surprised. What interest could this boy have in his fate? More importantly, what sort of cabin boy had the bravado to demand answers of a pirate captain?

"He is with them. He suffered an injury, but he was loaded into the boat with care. The ship's doctor was tending to him."

Tears glistened in the corners of the boy's green eyes. The last thing Dominic needed on board the *Dragon* was a pair of weeping children. They wouldn't last the first major storm or battle.

"Buck up, boys, all will be well. You must come with me to my ship now."

The red-haired boy looked ready to protest, so Dominic continued. "This ship will be below the sea soon. Unless you want to be visiting Davy Jones, you'll not be staying here a moment longer." His declaration of the ship's ultimate fate caught Robbie's attention.

"She's truly sinking, Captain?" The boy looked about the ship in a knowing way that promised the lad was perhaps a better seaman than Dominic had originally assumed.

"Aye, so you'd best get moving."

Robbie studied him for a long moment. Then he seemed to decide he could in fact trust Dominic and took his companion by the arm and marched over to the edge of the ship, where they jumped onto the gangplank that led to the *Dragon*. Dominic watched them disappear below the deck before he turned back to Chibbs. There was something about them that didn't quite seem right, but he didn't have time to determine what it was that was bothering him. Perhaps it was that they both were so young. He wasn't used to that.

"What other cargo did you find?" he asked quietly so as to not be overheard.

Chibbs shrugged. "Not much, Cap'n, only a few trunks of fine ladies' gowns."

"*Gowns?* Did they look special in any way? Expensive silks?"

"I can't say for sure if they are special, Cap'n, but they are pretty things," Chibbs said. "Silk for sure."

Dominic frowned and rubbed the heel of his palm over the butt of his pistol as he considered it.

"Maybe they hold value. Have the men bring the trunks aboard. If nothing else, we can sell them when we reach Tortuga. Strip the ship of anything of value before we cast off." While Tortuga was not usually a place for business trading, given the nature of the men who made berth there, Dominic had managed to sell quite a bit of his stolen wares there for a tidy profit over the years.

"Aye aye, Cap'n." Chibbs hurried off to do his bidding.

Dominic abandoned the *Fortune* to its fate and boarded the *Dragon*, his mind mulling over the new cabin boys. He'd seen lads shake like that before, when it was their first voyage. And he'd given this pair quite the memory.

Bitter memories of his own first voyage at fourteen set his teeth on edge. He didn't want to remember the bite of the cat-o'-nine-tails lashing his back, or the feel of a meaty fist pummeling him into silence when he spoke back, or the groping hands in the dark stealing his food and water because he wasn't strong enough to stop them. He'd learned quickly how long a man could last without food and water before dying, and he'd also learned just what he was willing to do when facing his own death.

Dominic shook his head and tried to rid himself of the dark memories that churned inside his head like the treacherous waters. The past, much like reefs hugging the shorelines, could sink a man.

He turned his attention back to the matter of the cargo and Flynn's attempt to convince him that the precious cargo was a few useless trunks of silks. Was it really just dresses? Or perhaps the dresses themselves were a clue. He'd heard of jewels and coins being sewn into gowns before to hide wealth. Something tugged at his mind, but he couldn't figure out what was bothering him.

He climbed the ladder up to the forecastle deck, where Reese stood waiting at the helm.

"Cast off from the *Fortune*. Hoist the mainsails and the topsails. Heading north by northeast. I want us chasing the horizon all the way to Tortuga."

"Aye aye, Cap'n!" The cheers went 'round the ship, and Dominic leaned against the railing overlooking the top deck.

There would be rum for every man tonight to celebrate their victory. And whilst they were distracted with drink, he would get to the bottom of this matter of "precious cargo" and figure out just what it was that Flynn was hiding.

4

"Get control of yourself, Lucy!" Roberta hissed at her sniffling maid. The young woman was on the verge of sobbing. "If you don't stop crying, they'll hear you and come to see what's the matter. Cabin boys don't cry."

"My lady...we are among the worst sort of men!" Lucy wailed. "What happens when they find out about us?"

Roberta stifled a groan of impatience. They were in a dangerous predicament, and if they weren't careful, Lucy's sobs would surely expose them. She'd thought for a moment that the captain would see through their charade, but he'd been preoccupied. Luck was with them, but only for so long if they didn't perfect their act as young men.

"They won't, if you keep your wits about you. Lucy, listen to me—you must become Luke, a cabin boy. Do as they ask, and they shouldn't harm you. Just follow my lead." They were currently in the captain's cabin, where a grizzled-looking man named Jon Chibbs had informed them before he left that they would be assigned duties by the captain once they were underway.

Lucy's face pinched up in fear. "But I don't know anything about ships, my lady. I cannot possibly pretend to be a cabin boy."

"I do, Lucy. Just do what I tell you, and no one will guess what you and I really are," Roberta advised.

"And just what *are* you, exactly?" A deep voice chuckled with amusement from behind them.

Roberta's heart stuttered to a stop for several long seconds. She hadn't heard the cabin door open, which meant they could have been overheard for Lord knew how long.

She took a deep breath and turned around, putting Lucy safely behind her. Captain Grey leaned against the doorjamb, lips quirked up in a crooked smile. Masculine power radiated off his body, his tan skin showing off his smooth, taut muscles. His dark eyes and long dark hair made her wonder if he was indeed Spanish, as the rumors said. But his accent was perfectly English—too perfect for a rough pirate, in fact. He sounded far more like Captain Huntington or Lieutenant Flynn.

His shoulders were broad enough to almost entirely block the doorway, leaving no chance of an escape. And where would they escape to, even if they could? Roberta's skin flushed with an unexplainable fire as she noted how his body went from his large muscled shoulders to his trim tapered waist and the way his lean but muscled legs were outlined in the short breeches he wore, and how the leather vest was so dark against his white lawn shirt. A mustache accompanied a very trim beard and he wore a single gold earring in his right ear. Roberta had known few men who could look so well after neglecting their razor. The captain made that beard on his jawline both fascinating and unbearably attractive.

"You are not cabin boys, that much is clear." He crossed his arms and settled in further against the door, indicating he would not move until they explained themselves.

"Tell him, my lady," Lucy whispered fearfully.

Dominic didn't take his eyes off Roberta. "My *lady*? Yes, do tell me." Dominic's dark-brown eyes sparkled. He seemed far too amused by their exchange of panic-stricken glances. Foolish Lucy had revealed they weren't boys, and now Roberta would have to bargain with whatever she could to protect her maid and herself. She still had her pistols safely tucked inside the loose coat she wore, as well as her dagger in her boot, but she didn't think she'd get to use any of them, unless she could find a safe chance to pull them on the captain.

"I will tell you, then. But I want your word as an Englishman that we shall have safe passage to the nearest neutral port." Roberta crossed her arms, trying to mimic his stubborn bearing. But she was so short that it seemed far less effective.

The captain barked out a sharp laugh. "I fear that my word as an Englishman holds no value. Perhaps I should swear on the beauty of your eyes? Or the luscious curve of your lips?"

He was mocking her! Roberta stamped her little booted foot, catching his attention.

"Control your tongue, sir. You are in the presence of Miss Roberta Harcourt!" Lucy snapped with surprising courage, before she ducked her head behind Roberta again. The captain grinned at hearing this.

"Harcourt, you say? As in the daughter of Rear Admiral Harcourt, who I just tossed into a longboat? I am honored indeed." He offered her a mocking bow, and Roberta wished that the sound of his laughter didn't warm her body, laughter that was dark and rich at the same time. Under other circumstances, she would have quite enjoyed it. But at that moment, she'd rather be able to swiftly raise one knee into the man's bollocks to silence him.

"If any harm befalls us, you will answer to my father and Captain Thomas Huntington. We are betrothed." Roberta had no intention of marrying Huntington, of course, but the claim might make him reconsider whatever actions that had crossed his mind.

The captain's eyes widened. "You're betrothed to that pigheaded fool?" He wasn't laughing anymore, and a hint of anger tinged his tone. She shivered and wondered if that particular lie had been a mistake.

"Yes." Her voice sounded less sure than it should have been.

"Would you give us a minute, *Luke*, is it? I need to have a word with your friend here." The captain gestured that Lucy should pass by him and wait outside the cabin, but Lucy refused to budge.

"Go ahead, I'll be fine," Roberta assured her maid, though she wasn't sure, judging by the dark gleam in the pirate's eyes.

Once Lucy was outside, the captain shut the door and slid the latch, locking them both in. Roberta's heartbeat quickened as he closed the short distance between them. She tried to back up, but she tripped over a wooden box near the desk and started to fall. He caught her by the waist, pulling her up against him.

She wanted to scream, but he covered her mouth with his hand. Roberta reacted instinctively, biting him. He lifted her off the floor and dropped her down on top of the desk so her hips were level with his. She struggled, reaching for one of the pistols while he shook his hand in pain. She got it all the way out from her coat and halfway pointed at him before he realized what was happening.

He knocked the gun from her hand, but not without effort. "Bloody Christ, woman!" Then he roughly searched her, finding the second pistol, which he tossed to the floor at his feet.

"Now listen here, *Robbie*—you have two choices on my ship. You can warm my bed and have full protection from my crew, or you can take your chances as a cabin boy and play your silly charade. I won't reveal your secret, but I doubt you'll last a day before it comes out on its own."

"I..." For the first time in her life, Roberta was speechless. Sleep with a pirate or take her chances with the crew as a cabin boy? Well, it was obvious it was no choice at all.

"Well?" He gripped her chin, and their gazes locked, fire clashing with fire.

"I'd rather swab the bloody poop deck with my tongue than spend one minute in your bed." Even as she said it, her mind flashed with traitorous images of her body trapped beneath his, his muscled body overpowering hers as he fiercely claimed her. It was every woman's nightmare...yet it was also a fantasy she had regrettably indulged in a time or two over the last few years. But this wasn't some silly dream, and the man holding her at that moment was no hero. He was a pirate, one who had killed some of the *Fortune*'s crew and injured her father, sending him helpless into a longboat with the remaining crew. He was a heartless, cold monster, not some misunderstood hero from a novel.

"Are you quite sure?" he asked, his voice low and dangerous.

The scent of leather mixed with sweat enveloped her as he forced her legs apart and pulled her body tighter against his. She struggled, throwing her arms out to strike his chest, but the shock of his body touching hers terrified her. His arms wrapped around her lower back, squeezing her skin through the fabric of her breeches. She gave a little moan as a flush of heat shot through her. Her head tilted back so she could stare up at him, and she gasped in shock and surprise as he bent to kiss her.

This was no delicate caressing of lips, just a powerful ravaging of her mouth with his tongue. She writhed, desperate to escape the foreign feel of his mouth on hers. Exhausted, she shuddered and softened, regretfully yielding to him. The moment she surrendered in his arms, his lips gentled and the kiss turned almost tender. He laughed, not mockingly as before but more as though he was pleased with her decision. It sent a zinging sensation from her lower belly clear down to her toes.

"If you stop fighting me for one minute, little minx, you might find you like this," he murmured against her lips.

"I might still shoot you," she warned before letting him kiss her again. She arched her back, pressing herself against him. She was swept away by the first masculine physical possession she'd ever encountered. She was new to these sensations, her body shivering in long-awaited anticipation of what might come next. He released her lips slowly, smoothly smiling as she leaned forward when he pulled back.

What the bloody hell had happened to her? She wasn't supposed to *like* being kissed by him. Her first kiss with a man was certainly not supposed to be from a pirate, either. Lord, what a rotten mess...what a *dangerous* mess.

"Now that you are being reasonable, we shall have a little talk." His body was still touching hers, and she was mesmerized by the movement of his lips. "I am not taking you to a neutral port, I am sailing for Tortuga, but once you're there you'll be free to leave. I can even arrange to have a message sent to Port Royal to assure your father of your imminent return to him. I would greatly enjoy a spitfire in my bed, but as I've said, you have a choice. I don't force women."

"You forced that kiss," she argued.

He smirked. "You *needed* that kiss, Robbie. Needed it more than your next breath. Besides, I had to know how a sweet, innocent English lady tastes, in case you don't change your mind before we reach port, but I think you will. All ladies come to my bed in time."

She scoffed. "You believe you're that irresistible, Captain Grey?"

His hearty laugh rankled her. "Call me Grey, if you please, or Dominic—or Dom, if you're feeling particularly affectionate, my dove." He brushed a stray wisp of hair back from her face, and she resisted the urge to bite at him like an angry cat.

"You are not irresistible, Captain Grey. You're a bully, an overgrown oaf of a man who will never"

He pressed a finger to her lips, silencing her. "Best to hold your tongue, my dove, someone might hear us. We wouldn't want the men knowing we have ladies running about. They're good lads, but they aren't saints, if you take my meaning."

She did take his meaning, and it filled her with fresh dread.

"I advise that you and your 'Luke' behave as decent cabin boys, or you might run into trouble. I will speak to the three men from the *Fortune* who joined me today and have them swear silence on the matter of your identities. It will make for a unique loyalty test, if nothing else. Can you agree to these terms?"

His hands tightened again, sliding lower to cup her bottom, keeping her close to him. It fogged her senses. The feel of his hands gripping her so fiercely was both terrifying and exhilarating. But with the exhilaration came shame. Something had to be wrong with her to find excitement in this moment.

"Well?" he asked, his lips dangerously close to hers again, still smiling. He knew just how his actions were affecting her.

"I...agree," she said at last, trying not to think about how thrilling his kisses had been, or how she'd desperately wanted more, or how she hated herself for that desire.

"Good. Now, about your duties while on board—I assume at least one of you can cook?"

Roberta nodded. "Lucy...er, Luke can. Her mother was the cook at my home back in London."

"Good. We lost our last cook, and our current one..."

Dominic shook his head. “Let me simply say that a change in recipes would be most welcome to me and my men. I’ll have Luke assigned to assist the cook.”

“And what about me?” Roberta wished she could join Lucy in the galley, not that she had any experience cooking whatsoever.

“You’ll be attending to me and a few other duties. My cabin boy, Griffin, has grown old enough to join the men on deck and will be glad for the unexpected promotion.”

Roberta managed a nod. Yes, she could be a cabin boy. That was an easy enough duty. She’d run errands around the ship, keep the captain’s quarters tidy, serve the officers their meals. Did pirate ships have officers? The captain, surely, and perhaps Chibbs and that other handsome fellow, Reese? They likely dined together, and she wouldn’t mind serving them. Handing out plates of food and refilling glasses of wine wasn’t at all taxing.

“Good, I’m glad that’s settled. Now, as to your sleeping arrangements. The cabin boys typically sleep with the men.”

Roberta gazed up at him, suddenly frightened. He still held her close, and his eyes narrowed at the sudden tension in her.

“Calm yourself, Robbie. I can have a storeroom cleared out, and Luke can stay there. As for you...” Those dark-brown eyes swept over her, appraising her in a way that made every feminine instinct come screaming to life in warning. The captain lusted for her, that was obvious, but what she didn't know was how long he would resist his urges and respect her demand to be left alone.

"What about me?" She couldn't summon the strength to sound as brave as she'd like.

"I suppose you would be fine in a hammock with the rest of the men?" he suggested. A merry twinkle in his eyes banished her fear and brought a fresh wave of anger to the surface.

"A hammock with the rest of those pirates? Are you mad?" She shoved at his body and leapt off the desk, scowling at him as she smoothed her shirt and waistcoat.

"Don't tell me you are as 'delicate' as your friend outside?" Dominic watched her try to puzzle out how to secure a safer sleeping arrangement. She didn't want to be with the men, nor did she wish to admit she was as frightened as Lucy.

"Couldn't I share the room with my maid?" she asked.

"I'm afraid that would be unfair to your friend, because it is so small already. If you must sleep away from the others, I suppose you could sleep in my cabin." He sighed, the resigned sound making it clear he wasn't amused at the idea of giving up his bed for her. No captain would wish to relinquish the spacious quarters of his cabin to go sleep with his crew in an uncomfortable hammock.

Roberta smiled. He was sacrificing his space for her? *A true gentleman!*

"That will suit me very well," she declared, pleased that the sleeping arrangements were finally settled.

"It will suit me as well," Dominic said with a slow smile, which Roberta did not understand. "Now, get yourselves to work. I am far too busy to play nursemaid to the pair of you. Chibbs will see Luke settled with the cook, and he'll explain your duties as well." He strode over to unlock the cabin door. Lucy came back in, passing the captain warily as he departed.

"What are we to do, my lady?" she asked, her hands wringing together fretfully.

Roberta covered the maid's hands. "All will be well. Mr. Chibbs will be here in a moment to introduce you to the cook. Apparently, they are in desperate need of a man who can prepare decent meals. You'll spend most of your day attending to the food in the galley."

The young servant gave a relieved sigh. "If there's one thing I know well, mistress, it's food. So long as they have decent stores, I'll be able to bake Mama's biscuits and her rosemary chicken and..." Lucy's face turned dreamy as she was instantly lost in thoughts of her mother's fine cooking.

Mr. Chibbs's gruff voice announced his presence a few seconds later as the cabin door opened again. "You boys ready?"

"Yes, Mr. Chibbs," they answered in unison.

"Very good, then. This way." He nodded toward the hall, and they followed behind.

Roberta couldn't stop grinning. She and Lucy were starting out on the grandest adventure she could ever hope to have, living aboard a pirate ship. Yes, it was dangerous, and Dominic filled her belly with butterflies, but she wasn't about to let him ruin such an experience. Once she and Lucy were free and safely in Port Royal, she would be trapped again in a world of balls, parlor teas, and the rigid life of a caged bird waiting for marriage to a man who would never understand her. If this was her one chance to live wildly, she would take it for as long as it would last.

5

Dominic entered the empty storeroom that he'd had converted into a temporary holding cell for his other guest. Flynn sat on an overturned crate, chin resting in his palm as he gazed at the wall. The other hand was bound in an iron manacle that was secured to the wall. He had enough freedom to move about and climb into the hammock slung across the back part of the storeroom, but he couldn't escape. Reese had the only set of keys, and he kept them in Dominic's cabin two decks above.

"Flynn," Dominic greeted quietly as he closed the door, sealing them alone inside the room. He kept his tone low, not wanting any of his crew to overhear them.

"Dom." Nicholas slowly rose to his feet. "We have to talk."

"We certainly do. I want to know where the hell this

precious cargo is. My crew was not pleased to find a trunk of silk gowns as our plunder."

Nicholas stared at him for a moment, then chuckled. "Precious cargo? Is that what you heard?"

"Yes. Why the bloody hell are you laughing?" Dominic's blood burned with fury. He didn't like to be laughed at, and they weren't boys anymore.

"We didn't have any cargo. Yes, the *Fortune* is a merchant ship, but she was on her way to Port Royal to *retrieve* cargo. Captain Huntington and I were assigned to escort Rear Admiral Harcourt to Jamaica. Once we arrived there, we would be assigned a new vessel and the *Fortune* would be turned over to a civilian captain. The only *precious cargo* I can think of is the admiral's daughter."

"Ah yes, the admiral's daughter. When were you planning on telling me I was to play host to her and her lady's maid?" Dominic asked.

Nicholas's chuckling immediately died, and he gazed at Dominic with worry. "Miss Harcourt is here? I had hoped she would have been sent aboard the longboat with her father."

"Alas, she and her maid were discovered aboard the *Fortune* too late. The pair of them tried to pass themselves off as cabin boys." Dominic braced a foot on a wooden crate and leaned on his knee as he studied his friend. "And she's the last thing I need aboard this ship, the fiancée of a damned English officer. That red-faced buffoon will be chasing us from port to port so he can bloody well hang me."

"I wanted to warn you about her, but you didn't give me a chance." Nicholas scraped a hand over his jaw, pausing a long moment. "Dom, what happened to you?"

"What happened?" Dominic's tone turned icy as an ancient rage returned. "I ran away to sea, just like I said I would." He wasn't sure why he lied to Nicholas, but the thought of admitting to his old friend that he'd been kidnapped and sold into indentured servitude made his stomach churn.

Nicholas gave his head a little shake, his tone softening. "But you didn't take me with you. I said I would go with you *wherever* you went, even to the farthest horizon."

"To the farthest horizon," Dominic echoed, pangs of childhood longing striking his heart like a cutlass. In a flash, he was back on that stone wall sitting beside Nicholas and dreaming about the future, a bright, sunny future where they would have been friends their entire lives. A future that had been ripped away from him—from them both.

"Dom, tell me what really happened. *Please*." Nicholas reached out to touch him, but the manacle kept him short of reaching Dominic's shoulders.

Suddenly unable to breathe, Dominic stepped back, his hand touching the door handle. "I...I can't, Nick. I just...not now." The horrors he'd suffered were dark shadows in the back of his mind on the best of days, but seeing his old friend, remembering for a brief instant his former life, the boy he'd been, the family he'd lost, remembering what might have been, dragged those dangling skeletons into the light. He turned the door handle and started to pull it open.

"Fine, don't tell me," Nicholas said. "But please, take care with the lady and her maid. She's undeserving of whatever fate your crew may have in store for her."

Something inside Dominic twisted with pain and made him speak cruelly. "Whatever use I find for her is my decision. The wench is pretty enough and will warm my bed if I so desire. If I share her with the crew, that's also my decision."

"Dom," Nicholas growled. "The boy I knew would never harm a lady or any kind of innocent."

He wanted so desperately to tell Nick that he was still that boy who defended those who couldn't stand up for themselves. Nicholas's eyes filled with hope, but Dominic couldn't let him believe in something that was no longer true.

"That boy is dead. You have his ghost to thank for your generous conditions." Then Dominic left the makeshift prison cell, slamming the door behind him. Nicholas shouted for him to come back, but Dominic ignored him, letting the sounds of the sea hitting the wooden hull of the ship drown out his old friend's cries.

Now in a black mood, he stalked up the stairs and out onto the upper deck to find something to better occupy his mind. He spent the remainder of the day far away from the women, which proved more difficult than he had expected. It seemed that everywhere he turned, there was Roberta, underfoot. She seemed to delight in running messages about the ship from him to Reese and Chibbs.

She'd skid to a stop right in front of him and salute him in the most cheeky way and shout, "Message for you from Mr. Chibbs." And each time, Dominic would be tempted to curl an arm around her waist and drag her to him for a kiss or perhaps spank her for enjoying herself a little too much. She wasn't supposed to be amusing herself playing the part of a cabin boy. She was supposed to be exhausted, irritated from working, and ready to give herself to him in passion, where he might spoil her rotten as any lovely lady deserved.

Until then he'd content himself with watching her move a mop around the decks, splashing soapy water about. He'd have a chance to see her hips sway, and his body would stiffen with arousal as he pictured bending her over the nearest barrel and taking what she was tempting him with. More than once he'd had to turn and face the sea to hide his very clear state of arousal, like some untried youth who'd never glimpsed a woman before.

But the thing that truly puzzled him—no, rather, it fascinated him—was the way Roberta would pause, only briefly, in her duties to stare out at the sea, the wind tugging at the bright-red hair she'd pulled back with a black ribbon. Her eyes would light up, and her lips would curve in a smile of pure joy. That was something he recognized. The serenity and peace that gazing upon the sea could bring. Not everyone understood it, but Dominic could see Roberta understood the sea just as he did, and that earned his respect more than anything else.

She wants to be here. She wants this life of freedom as much as I do.

As if hearing his silent thoughts, Roberta set aside her mop and wooden bucket and came over.

"What's our heading, Captain? I've been taking measurements, and it seems the tides are pushing us farther north. Should I tell Mr. Reese to adjust course?"

"What do you know of tides?" he asked, genuinely curious. Most people assumed tides existed only close to shore. But tides out in deep water adjusted every minute and could push a ship far off course, confusing even the most seasoned sailors if they didn't continuously monitor their position.

"I know enough. You aren't an admiral's daughter without learning something about the sea."

He replied with a soft hum, sensing that she knew a fair amount more than that about the ocean, but he'd discover just how much at a later time. "Go and tell Reese to adjust our course."

"Yes, Captain." And off she sprinted, nimble as a rabbit. Dominic tilted his head to the side, both amused and aroused. He'd never seen a woman move like that, jumping and sliding and dodging all manner of things on deck, from cannons being cleaned to sailors bent over fishing nets they were fixing.

For the most part, the crew seemed content to let her run about all over the place. Most young lads would have been clumsy, still growing into their bigger hands and bigger feet, but Roberta was used to her size and completely comfortable in her own skin. There was nothing clumsy about her at all. More importantly, she seemed to know exactly what she was doing. He was glad none of his crew had figured out they had two women running about on board. And if it was up to Roberta's performance alone, they probably never would.

Things were going smoothly, even though some of the men grumbled about the lack of plunder as well as the risk they'd taken by sinking a merchant ship and casting its captain and an admiral into a longboat. He'd promised them another prize soon, and they trusted him. He would have to find another ship to take, or those grumbles might grow a bit too loud for his comfort. He'd never had a mutiny before, and he certainly didn't want one now.

Chibbs joined Dominic after a while, both watching the rolling blue waves turn dark as the sun sank in the sky.

"How are the men? Furious?" he asked Chibbs, half teasing. The other man nodded curtly, his dark beard casting extra shadows on his face as the sun began to kiss the horizon. The red sky was a welcome sight, and the absence of clouds put him at ease that they would have an easy night of sailing.

"Cap'n, I'm not the first to be saying it, but the men were hoping for a fair bit more than some silk gowns."

Lord, how was it that even when in private councils with Reese, the word of the ships they intended to target always passed along the ship faster than rats fleeing a sinking vessel?

"Tell the men we'll rest a bit in Tortuga before we chase down another prize."

"Aye, Cap'n." Chibbs wandered off down the deck, hollering orders to switch the tack on certain sails to catch a better angle upon the ever-changing Caribbean winds.

Dominic leaned back against the railing as Roberta and her maid appeared on the waist deck. Chibbs was behind them, shooing them along like a pair of pigeons he was trying to roust from a nest. The bosun pointed to the mainsails and issued an order, but Dominic couldn't hear from where he stood by the helm. Content to watch whatever was to happen play itself out, he chuckled.

Roberta attempted to coax Lucy into climbing up the rigging of the mainmast. Dominic hid his smile as he watched the admiral's daughter scale the rigging with ease and come back down, showing her maid how it was done. Lucy showed a little hesitation and slipped on the rigging a few times before she got her footing straightened out. The shoes both girls wore were a tad large, no doubt because they'd stolen them from the *Fortune*'s cabin boy. But one thing was clear—the girl was a natural on the ropes.

"The sea is in your blood, isn't it?" he murmured to himself.

If she hadn't been an admiral's daughter, but some little urchin he'd found on the streets, he'd consider forcing her to stay on the *Dragon*. He could tell she loved the ship's activity and the adventure that this life brought. Her smile, even from a good distance away, was somehow brighter than the setting sun behind her.

His thoughts now drifted into dangerous waters. This little sprite of a woman was engaged to that oaf Huntington. Anger boiled his blood. Men like Huntington hunted pirates like him. Many pirates like him had been in similar circumstances and had never been given the choice to leave a life of piracy. By the time he'd earned his freedom, he carried a price upon his head that ensured he could never go home. If he hadn't been taken, hadn't been foolish enough to leave the safety of his home that night, he would have become the Earl of Camden, a respectable gentleman, a man who could have properly courted a woman like Roberta.

For the first time in ages, Dominic's mind painted a picture of what that life might have been like. Balls and dinners, feasts and hunting parties, Christmas with his family, and trapping a lovely beauty like Roberta in an alcove where he might steal more than just a kiss beneath a kissing bough. She would have looked beautiful decked out in her finest silks, her bodice tight enough to press her breasts up, displaying them so that a hungry man like him might lavish soft, hot kisses upon them. He would slip a hand up under those soft skirts, making them whisper against her skin as he found her center, stroking her until she screamed his name against his lips. He would have swallowed that cry of pleasure and been forever enchanted by a woman like her.

But he would never have a moment like that. Because he was a pirate. The earldom of Camden would fall to his younger brother, Adrian, who would be sixteen by now. Any life he might have had as the earl was a dream now, nothing more. Dreams only hurt a man, so it was best not to dwell on them.

"Cap'n, might I have a word?" Chibbs broke through Dominic's dark thoughts.

"What is it, Chibbs?"

"Those new boys...there's something funny about 'em."

Dominic bit his lip to keep from laughing. "Oh?"

Chibbs stroked his beard. "They...well, I can't quite put my finger on it, but it ain't right." Chibbs watched a frightened Lucy take a few tentative steps up onto the ropes of the rigging.

Dominic glanced around, assuring himself they were alone before he spoke. "Chibbs, those boys...aren't boys. It's the admiral's daughter and her maid."

Chibbs blinked and then turned seriously to Dominic.

"*Ladies* aboard the ship? That's bad luck, that is. And two of them? Double the curse, double the danger, that's what me father would say."

Dominic tried not to laugh. The list of Chibbs's father's sayings was extensive, and Dominic was quite certain the man had said none of them.

"What do you mean to do with them?" Chibbs asked.

"I suppose I'm going to be honorable and try to keep them out of harm's way. We'll see them safely to Tortuga, perhaps even find them a ship bound for Port Royal."

Chibbs seemed to realize there was far more on his mind than that. "Oh aye, Cap'n, sure, and you plan to have a go at one of the pretty lasses before long. It's written all over your face. Well, that's a danger I wouldn't risk, Cap'n, not if I was you." But they both knew Chibbs's warning had fallen on deaf ears.

If Dominic desired a lady, he would find a way to have her. He hadn't earned his reputation in Spain as a master seducer for nothing. But he would take his time with Roberta, enjoy the merry chase before she finally succumbed to him.

6

By nightfall, Roberta had returned to Dominic's cabin. She was exhausted, every muscle, every bone had been stretched to its breaking point after a long day of work. Roberta winced as she sank down onto the captain's bed and examined the red blisters on her palms. If she didn't find some salve, the skin would soon crack and bleed. It was a good thing she'd only allowed Lucy to climb a few feet up and down before she let the other woman return to the galley. Lucy would not have handled the pain of blisters well at all. For a servant, she was rather delicate.

Trying to distract herself from her exhaustion and the pain in her hands, she turned to the stack of clothes that Lucy had managed to secretly retrieve from Roberta's trunks in the hold earlier that day, which thankfully included her new gown with the seahorse embroidered bodice. A long, gossamer-thin nightgown was among the items Lucy had set on the bed for her. She picked it up, tracing her fingers along the fine lace on the neckline. A long, heavy sigh escaped her. It would be a relief to put on something soft and go to sleep.

Today had been challenging, but good. Better than expected, given that she and Lucy were prisoners, along with poor Lieutenant Flynn. When she'd discovered Flynn was aboard, she'd asked if she might see him, but both of the *Dragon*'s senior officers had denied her. She didn't ask Captain Grey, however. She had a feeling he would be the last person who would let her see Nicholas.

She'd also bothered the captain enough today with her messages. The wild look he gave her whenever she got too close had begun to frighten her. She couldn't tell if he wanted to kiss her or throw her overboard. She and Lucy would have to continue to be careful. Women aboard a ship were certainly in peril of ravishment and molestation, and cabin boys weren't entirely safe either. Young men and women were both known to be victimized aboard ships, even ships of His Majesty's navy.

Despite her fears about being trapped aboard a pirate ship, Roberta had enjoyed her day. She was getting used to the freedom of breeches and loose shirts. Having her breasts lightly bound with cloth rather than being trapped in a fully confining corset was a far more comfortable choice, and having her legs free to run around the ship's decks had been wonderful. Unfortunately, the thought of breeches reminded her of the captain spreading her legs and standing between them.

Dominic... She knew she shouldn't think of him so intimately, but his name was such a lovely, dark...*seductive* name. Just like him.

She put a hand to her abdomen as she felt a sudden ache. His kiss and the way he'd held her trapped in his arms as he'd ravaged her mouth, the feel of his body pressed against hers, leaving no room for even air between them...

Roberta trembled. Dominic was dangerous in so many ways.

A soft knock at the cabin door jolted her from her thoughts. She went over to open it, puzzled as to what Lucy might need. She'd already bid Roberta good night.

She cracked the door open and saw Dominic's handsome face looking down upon her.

"What are you?"

Dominic pushed the door open, forcing her back as he strode in without so much as a polite greeting or any explanation. He locked the door and surveyed the room.

"I trust you find the lodging to your liking?" he asked, smiling.

She did indeed like the cabin. There was a decent-sized bed and a large desk and a window looking out over the sea. Roberta had been unable to resist taking a peek at the charts covering the desk to get a sense of their bearings.

"Yes, it is quite comfortable," she said. Her eyes flicked

to the locked door, and she wondered what he meant by this rather late disruption in her bedchamber. Surely he didn't mean to...

As enjoyable as kissing him had been, that behavior could not be tolerated because it could lead to other things that would deprive her of her innocence and, frankly, her good sense. Her governess had taught her to be wary of men and their desires. If a lady wasn't careful, she could lose her head and her heart to a man who would use her and discard her. Ruination was a fear even for a woman like Roberta.

"Good. Glad to hear that you've settled in. Now, if you'll excuse me..." He brushed past her to open the small wardrobe door.

He pulled off his shirt, folded it, and tossed it on the small shelf in the wardrobe. Roberta stood rooted to the floor, unable to look away from the surface of his well-muscled bronze back. She had the sudden desire to touch it, to see if his skin felt as warm as it looked—and it looked very, very warm. Then she regained her self-control and realized that a half-naked pirate captain was standing in the room that was supposed to be her only safe haven aboard this vessel.

"What are you doing, Captain Grey? These are my quarters, and I will not be treated in such a familiar fashion." She crossed her arms, hiding a wince as her injured palms scraped the fabric of her waistcoat.

Dominic turned around, revealing an equally sculpted chest that heated her body from within.

"You are mistaken, Robbie. These are my chambers —*you* are merely a guest. I was kind enough to share my room with you, not sacrifice it." He grinned wickedly.

Roberta's hand itched to slap him for his deception. Instead, she snatched her nightclothes and stalked off toward the door. If he was going to be this way, she refused to stay here.

He threw out an arm, barring her way. She nearly ran into his muscled arm. She glared at him, but her fury began to waver as she realized how close she was to him. The heat of his half-naked body radiated into hers, warming her chilled skin.

"I don't think it would be wise for the men to see that you are not Robbie but Roberta. They might be less civil than I." He stated this matter-of-factly, but she knew he did not exaggerate the possible danger she could find herself in.

Better to fight off one handsome devil than thirty foul ones, she thought darkly.

"Fine, but you will sleep on the floor," she said and moved toward his bed.

Dominic laughed, catching her by the waist. She reacted instantly and stepped hard on his booted foot. He grunted, and she stumbled free. Dominic arched a brow in challenge, but rather than come after her, he walked over to his bed and stretched out upon it in the most leisurely fashion, making a show of settling in as he kicked off his boots and folded his hands behind his head on the pillow.

"*You* may sleep on the floor, but I wouldn't recommend it." Dominic shut his eyes. "One pitch on a wave and you'll roll right into that desk."

"I'd rather risk that than the alternative, which I suspect would involve the loss of my virtue." She reached for the spare pillow trapped just below one of his elbows, struggling for a moment before he smirked and lifted his arm the slightest bit. She freed the pillow and dropped it on the floor.

"Blanket?" he offered.

His eyes were still closed, but he held out a dark-blue blanket, and she tried to snatch it from him. They had a brief tug-of-war over it, to the point where she almost toppled into the bed on top of him, which she suspected was his intention. She dug her heels into the floor. Her balance being quite good, finally succeeded in jerking it free of his hand. It hadn't escaped her that he'd easily held the blanket with one hand, almost lazily, while she'd had a deathlike grip on her end with both hands. The man was too strong, and just thinking about that sent wild flutters through her body.

The idea of sleeping on the floor sounded dreadful, but sleeping beside him in that bed, which was barely large enough for two bodies if they lay right up against each other—that was a far greater danger to her.

Roberta glowered at Dominic, but he didn't see her

face since his eyes were still shut. She looked once more at the door, then back at him, and turned her back to change, praying he'd keep his eyes shut. She peered over her shoulder once to check and almost shrieked when she saw him peep an eye open. Frantically dropping her nightgown down over her body, she muttered a string of curse words that would have made her father blush.

"Learn those from a fancy ball?" Dominic asked.

"No, I learned them from the men on my father's ships."

The captain laughed softly, the rich sound making her body flush. "I had wondered about your seamless transition into the role of cabin boy. Far better than that of your friend. How much time have you spent at sea?"

His interest in her past surprised her, and for a moment she wasn't sure what to say. Could one simply have a pleasant conversation with a pirate?

"I...well, quite a bit. My father took me to sea every summer. We traveled to France, Spain, Portugal, Italy, even America, although I wasn't fond of the North Atlantic crossing. The storms..." She shuddered at the memory of how cold the water had felt whenever the wind whipped it up over the decks, even in July.

"The northern crossing storms are treacherous most of the year," Dominic agreed. "The Caribbean is less vengeful a mistress to her sailors, but the spring and fall bring hurricanes like you've never seen. I swear, whole islands can vanish for weeks until the water recedes.

Entire towns have been wiped out, with everyone drowned." His eyes were open again, and he stared at the ceiling, not her, a mix of longing and pain stretched over his features. He looked like the tragic hero of an ancient Greek play.

"My father said the sea has her secrets and that we mortals will never know her well enough to fully trust her." Her soft reply drew his attention. The few candles that lit the cabin created shadows on the walls.

"Your father is a smart man."

"He is." She hesitated before speaking again. "Captain, was my father badly hurt when you last saw him?"

"He wasn't mortally wounded, but his head wound wasn't a mere scratch. Rest assured, he will pull through with a bit of tending to. I made sure the doctor from the *Fortune* had his supplies before I put them in the longboat. They were only two days east of Port Royal. I expect they'll land tomorrow, and that fool Huntington will launch a thousand ships to try to rescue you."

Roberta bit her lip. She'd almost forgotten she'd told him that she was engaged to Huntington.

"Yes, I'm sure he will," she added quietly. The sudden spike in tension between them was almost tangible. Dominic seemed to truly despise the *Fortune*'s captain.

"And what will you do with me? Will you let me go as you promised?" she asked, her voice barely above a whisper. She was almost afraid to hear his answer.

Dominic's dark eyes fixed on her. "Let you go? I

honestly don't know. I rather like you right where you are for now."

"As your prisoner?"

"Or my guest, if you prefer it." His intense gaze was softened somewhat by his wolfish grin. "Rest assured, little Robbie, I'll not touch you tonight, not even if you beg me to." He looked back to the ceiling and closed his eyes again.

She stalked toward to the bed and jabbed a finger into his bare chest, prodding him awake. "Not good enough. I want your word that you will not try anything that will threaten my honor."

"I thought we agreed my word held little value." He smirked, looking up into her face. "Be at ease, Roberta. I'll not 'threaten your honor,'" he said.

With that, she eased down onto the floor as far away from his bed as she could manage and put her pillow beneath her head. She curled into a ball and pulled the blanket up over her body, preserving as much heat as she could stave off the icy planks beneath her.

She rubbed her face into the pillow, inhaling the heavy scent of leather and a hint of spice on it, not the sweaty scent she was accustomed to encountering from sailors. She briefly imagined what it might be like to be surrounded by that scent and the heat of the body it came from. It was a pity the man was a pirate. Why couldn't she have met him at a ball or a dinner party? Things could have been so different. He would cut a fine figure in a dashing waistcoat and breeches with his hair cut and pulled back, perhaps without his beard and mustache. She wished she could picture him without them, but she couldn't seem to draw up any images.

Would he have asked her to dance? Or would he have been focused on prettier women? Would he have been a good dancer? She could almost picture them swirling around a gilded ballroom, the glow of candlelight and the strains of music filling the air around them. His hand at the small of her back would have made her blush, and she would have stretched to reach his shoulder…

"Floor comfortable enough for you?" Dominic's voice shattered her silly, girlish dreams and made her shiver with frustration and the chill of the room. At least her anger heated her blood, keeping her warmer for a moment.

"It's quite comfortable," she lied and closed her eyes tight, wishing she could fall asleep. It was going to be a very long night.

7

Dominic lay still, scarcely breathing as he listened to Roberta shift and struggle. He couldn't believe she'd actually taken the floor. He had expected her to cry, or beg and plead to have his bed. He was willing to give in, depending on how pretty she was with tears in her eyes.

But it turned out the little minx was made of iron. She sniffled a few times and muttered some delightfully foul curses, then after a time, her breathing evened out. Unable to resist his curiosity, he rolled to the edge of the bed and peered down at her.

She lay on her side facing him, her body curled like a nautilus shell. The blanket covered most of her, but one hand extended out, palm up. A gash marred the flesh of her palm. Rope burns. The woman had gone and hurt herself by climbing the rigging. Her pretty, smooth skin had been rubbed raw by the ropes. And knowing ropes as he did, he knew they'd be hardened from the salt as they'd been at sea for a long time. Her wounds had to be stinging something fierce with the salt rubbed deep into them.

Yet she hadn't made even a peep of protest all day. He was impressed—he would give the lady that. As much as he was tempted to leave her undisturbed, he did not want her hands healing the wrong way. The moment she opened her palms up tomorrow, the wounds would crack open and start to bleed again. Dominic slipped out of his bed and stepped over her body before he pulled his shirt and boots back on. Then he silently left his cabin. He moved through the ship, hearing the clang of the bells counting the hours on the watch, and knocked lightly on the infirmary door.

Dr. Abel Maynard was an older gentleman who had joined the *Dragon* a year ago from the colonies. "Captain?" He squinted at the now open door as he held a lantern aloft.

"Sorry to wake you, Abel, but I need the salve jar, the one you use for rope burns. One of the cabin boys has some wounds on his palms."

The doctor's brow knit, and he turned to his cupboard, shining light on the collections of bottles and jars, all with labels written in scrawling ink.

"Salve...," he muttered, moving bottles this way and that as he searched. "Ah!" He found a green glass jar and handed it to Dominic. "Apply this and bind the boy's hands with these. If it's deep, keep him off the ropes for a few days until he can heal." He held up a few strips of clean white bandages.

"Thank you." Dominic left the doctor in peace and carried the jar back to his cabin. Roberta was right where he'd left her, sleeping soundly on the floor.

He knelt beside her and carefully lifted one hand up, peering at it in the dim light. Then he slipped a finger full of salve onto the wound. Her fingers curled slightly, but she didn't wake. He rubbed it in a little more, and then he bound her palm with the bandages. Then he repeated the actions with her other palm.

She whimpered in her sleep and pulled her injured palms closer to her chest, her brow wrinkled and worried. Something about seeing another person hurting, one unused to pain, brought back such dark memories of his own. Flynn was right. Roberta was a sweet, innocent young woman, the sort of woman he would have bled for or even died to protect as a lad.

But the person he once was he could never be again. That realization burned deep within him, making his chest ache. One could never reclaim innocence. Once lost, it was lost forever. Yet he had a second chance of sorts—he could protect Roberta and her maid until he got them safely to Port Royal, though the thought of letting such a unique creature go set his teeth on edge.

He stood back up, putting some distance between himself and her sleeping form. The temptation to touch and take what didn't belong to him was almost a siren's call. With a heavy sigh, he backed out of his cabin and headed up to the forecastle, where he stood watch.

"Captain," Reese greeted, his eyes glowing almost gold in the light of the lamps.

Dominic leaned against the railing that looked down over the rest of the ship. "Quiet tonight?"

"Aye, quiet and calm. We have a good breeze. Should reach Tortuga in a day or two if the wind stays fair, but..."

Dominic didn't like the hesitation in his quartermaster. "But?"

"I smell a storm coming, a nasty one. I fear we may be too far out to reach land before it hits." Reese had a sense about these things and had never been wrong before. Even the most seasoned sailors on board deferred to his judgment. He could tell when the winds would make the slightest change and how they'd need to correct their course to stay afloat.

"Which way will it come from?" he asked.

"From the east. I would recommend we race as far north as we can and then turn to face it when it comes."

"Take the necessary precautions to ensure the safety of the ship and the crew."

"And the ladies? What of them?" Reese inquired.

Dominic shouldn't have been surprised. Of course Reese would have figured out their secret.

"How did you know?"

Reese chuckled, the sound more ancient than befitting a man of his young age.

"It was the way you were watching them today. You seemed patient, almost amused. Normally new cabin boys draw your ire and frustration. Not these two. You were tender when you looked upon them." Reese flashed him a wicked smile. "Besides, one of them smelled of rosewater."

Dominic laughed and shook his head. "I should've known better than to keep it from you."

Reese's lips curved as he watched the moonlight play upon the black waters. "I suppose you claimed the red-haired woman for your bed already?"

"Actually, no. The lady doth protest too much," he snorted. "The damnable little minx is sleeping on my floor. Wouldn't have me."

"Truly? She must be a clever lady indeed to resist the likes of you."

"Indeed, she is too smart for her own good." Dominic listened to the sounds of his ship, hearing the creaks and groans of the water against the wooden hull as the night breeze carried them closer to Tortuga. He didn't want to think about the coming storm and the last few hours of calm he and his crew had on board.

"Wake me when the storm comes."

"Yes, Captain."

Dominic returned below deck to his quarters and eyed the woman sleeping on his floor. If a storm came, she could be tossed about and hurt, and he didn't want that.

So he risked the little minx's wrath and placed her on his bed. She stirred a little, but only to sigh and burrow deeper into his blankets as she wrapped them around her body, leaving none for him.

"Little thief," he snickered and then lay down beside her. He faced her, pulling her back against him, cradling her to him. It felt good to hold a woman so close and breathe in that sweet rosewater scent.

He shouldn't let himself sleep too deeply, because he needed to keep his mind half-alert in case the storm arrived early. It was a trick he'd learned long ago, the ability to wake and run if needed, and it had served him well over many years. But the feel of Roberta's warm little body tucked against his pulled him deeper and deeper into a dangerously full sleep.

Black waves rolled beneath Dominic, and a cold, heartless laugh followed him as he plunged beneath the waves.

"Stay still, boy. Stop struggling." The captain's vicious snarl was as violent as the hands upon Dominic's bound limbs. Ropes cut deep, and he moaned in agony as the man took what he wanted. Dominic could only whimper against the rag stuffed down his throat. Tears stung his eyes as he tried to find a secret place inside his head. Trees full of gold as the sun sank toward the horizon, the bell-like sound of his mother's laugh, the giggling chatter of the twins, the smell of his father's cigars and the rare

smile he'd cast Dominic's way. Nicholas, the lad who had vowed to follow him to the farthest horizon...

"Dom!" Nicholas's voice jolted through him. The sunny memories began to bleed in at the edges like ink splashed on parchment.

"No!" Dominic cried, wanting to retreat back into that safe, secret world. But the black waves were back and the sea was angry, her howling winds a stark reminder that she was always in control.

"Dom!" A different voice, not Nicholas's, shook him awake.

Reese stood over him, a lantern raised in the darkness of the cabin. "She's coming," he whispered urgently. "She comes *now*."

The storm had arrived. Dominic gently shook the woman in bed beside him. "Robbie, wake up." He shook her more sternly as she tried to shrug him off.

"Robbie, wake the bloody hell up. A storm's coming."

Roberta's eyes flashed open, and she sat up. Her momentary confusion at finding herself in his bed would have had him laughing any other time, but not now.

"Get dressed and find your maid. Bring her to my cabin and stay here. Don't go on deck unless I send for you, and don't go deeper into the ship. If we start to sink, I want you close to the top deck. Do you understand?" He held her gaze, even as the *Dragon* pitched deep into the trough of a mighty wave.

"Yes, Captain," she whispered, her eyes now wide with terror. She knew the sea, knew it better than any woman he had known except a few pirate wenches he had crossed paths with over the years.

"Go, get dressed." He released her, even though he had the strangest urge to drag her close to him and not let her out of his sight. He had to get above deck.

He followed Reese up on deck, his sole focus now on his ship and the lives of his crew.

"Bind the sails, batten down every hatch, and wake every man," he ordered Reese. Then he joined Chibbs at the helm.

"Put her face in the wind, Chibbs."

"Aye, Cap'n."

Dominic blinked away the rain as the skies opened and a deluge was unleashed upon them. Straight ahead, the skies were black and the clouds churned as violently as the seas below. Dominic could barely make out the difference —he saw only the rage of nature before him.

"God have mercy on us. It's worse than Reese predicted!" Chibbs bellowed into the howling wind as he gripped the helm with all his might. Dominic gripped two more of the spindles, helping hold the wheel in place as the sea tried to toss it about. They would be lucky to survive the night.

Please, my lady, Dominic prayed to the sea. *Please, have pity on us poor souls...*

❄

Roberta scrambled to get dressed, stumbling on awkward feet as the ship dove and rose into the peaks and valleys of waves. Her stomach twisted in knots, but she didn't toss the contents of her stomach. The moment she was clothed, she used her hands to brace herself to walk down the hallway to Lucy's storeroom-turned-cabin. Her maid was bent over a bucket, retching.

Roberta knelt beside her maid, using a leather thong to tie her hair back from her face. "Oh, Lucy. Try to breathe, dear, just breathe." She stroked Lucy's back and comforted her over the howling winds.

"My lady, are we going to die?" Lucy asked between panting breaths.

"No. Captain Grey is an expert seaman. He won't let anything befall his ship or its passengers." She believed in her own words, but she also knew that the seas could overpower even the strongest ship and its bravest captain. The fear she'd seen in Dominic's eyes had struck her with terror. If a man like him was worried, she should be as well. But she couldn't fall to pieces in front of her maid. She had to be strong, just like her father taught her.

Once Lucy felt able, Roberta helped her back onto her cot. "Lie still and rest. I'll see if the doctor has anything that might help you." She tucked Lucy into her blankets.

"I should be helping you," Lucy said with a sniffle.

"Nonsense. We take care of each other." Roberta checked the wick of the candle in the swinging lantern hanging above Lucy's bed. She didn't want her maid to grow panicked if the candle burned out while the storm still raged outside. She stepped into the corridor. The ship pitched unexpectedly, and she smacked hard into the wall. Pain radiated from her shoulder where it struck the wood. She righted herself and used her arms, keeping them spread wide to catch herself from falling again as she headed to the doctor's quarters.

Dr. Maynard was wide awake, his infirmary full of patients. There were three men stretched out on cots, one sick, one with a broken arm, and one with a large wooden splinter lodged in his calf muscle. The last man was hollering in pain.

"Stop that screaming," Dr. Maynard shouted at the sailor. He noticed Roberta lingering in the doorway. "You, boy. Fetch the sleeping draft in the dark-blue bottle with the twin circles on it." He nodded at the cupboards. Roberta swayed on her way over to the cabinet and fumbled until she found it. She brought it back and handed it to him. He uncorked the bottle and pressed it to the sailor's mouth.

"Drink now, one big swallow."

The sailor gulped once and cursed before he handed the doctor back the bottle. As Maynard corked it again, the sailor heaved and slumped back, unconscious on his cot.

"Don't just stand there, lad. Get in here and help!" Maynard snapped.

Roberta closed the door, trying to ignore the panic

filling the room, which smelled of blood and seawater. Her boots slid on water rushing in from the waves that were cascading over the ship's sides one deck above. She reached the table, and Maynard nodded at the unconscious sailor's leg.

"Help me tie him down. We need to get the splinter out and tie it off, or he'll bleed to death." Maynard tossed several leather straps across the sailor's body, and Roberta helped to secure the man. The doctor then used pliers to pull the large splinter out. Blood oozed from the open wound. Roberta's stomach clenched at the sight, and bile rose in her throat.

"Turn your head, lad." The doctor's voice gentled, and she did as he commanded. The doctor cinched a belt above the man's wound just below the knee. When Roberta mustered control of her stomach, she faced the doctor, and he nodded toward the man holding his broken arm.

"Right. Let's set the bone on this one."

Half an hour later, Roberta leaned back against the infirmary wall, her clothes splattered with blood, sweat, and seawater. Maynard surveyed the three sailors, all treated and resting now.

"Go back to your room, lad. I appreciate the help."

"Thank you, Doctor." Roberta started back into the hall. She returned to the captain's cabin and changed into a fresh shirt that Dominic's old cabin boy had lent her earlier that day. Then she headed back into the hall to check on Lucy again.

Flashes of lightning illuminated the stairs leading to the main deck above her. Figures danced in a macabre silhouette as the sailors on deck tried to secure the rigging to the masts. She clung to the railing off the stairs, unable to tear her gaze away from the scene. Griffin, Captain Grey's previous cabin boy who had been promoted to work with the rest of the men, was trying and failing to tie down a line to the mainmast. A wave washed over the side, and Griffin slipped on the deck and headed toward the railing. Roberta acted without thought. She sprinted up the stairs and intercepted Griffin as he slid past her on the deck, reaching out for him.

Their arms locked, his hooking around hers at the elbow. Pain tore through her, and something popped in her shoulder. She choked down the pain but didn't let go. More water surged past them.

"Hang on!" she gasped. Griffin's eyes widened, and he tried to keep his grip, but they were both sliding. If they didn't get to safety, they would be washed over the side.

Lightning ripped across the sky overhead, and the force of the thunder rumbled deep into her chest. Roberta bent her legs tightly around the crevice between the stairs on the deck, but it wouldn't last. They were going to be washed overboard.

"Let go, Robbie, or else we'll both die!" Griffin's shout was barely audible over the storm.

She refused to let him die, but her fingers began to loosen and the pain in her arm and shoulder was almost too much to bear. Black dots danced around the edges of her vision as her arms began to fail her.

Just as Griffin began to slip free, Dominic and Reese were there. Reese grabbed Griffin by the scruff of his neck like a pup and hauled him to the base of the forecastle, where he couldn't wash overboard. Roberta was scooped up by Dominic and carried to the opposite side of the deck and tucked into another corner, her body twisting in a mix of relief and pain. The captain used his legs to brace them into the corner, and he kept one arm banded around her waist.

"You damned fool," Dominic growled in her ear as lightning illuminated his face. She didn't have the strength to move or even argue. He held her close to his chest, their bodies in a tight, desperate embrace as the ship was tossed about. She burrowed into him, holding on with her uninjured arm, terror coursing through her veins. The ship pitched down and surged, and water splashed over them hard enough and long enough that she feared they might drown more than once.

"Hold on, Robbie," Dominic shouted in her ear. "Don't let go."

She didn't, not until there was a momentary break in the thrashing waves and the ship was even-keeled for a brief few moments. Dominic bent and lifted her uninjured arm around his neck to help her walk, and they descended below deck, heading toward his cabin.

Dominic muttered a string of curses as he helped lower her onto his bed. “Don’t move. I’ll fetch the doctor.”

Roberta held her cries inside as he left her. It seemed like hours before he returned with Maynard.

“Little fool hurt himself. Risked his damn neck to save Griffin from going overboard.”

Maynard brushed Dominic aside and knelt by the bed. “Let me take a look.” He gripped her left arm and tried to move it. She screamed in pain—she couldn’t help it.

“Dislocated shoulder,” Maynard told Dominic. “I need you to help me lift him into a sitting position and keep him still while I adjust the arm.”

“Christ,” Dominic hissed and helped Roberta sit up. She wanted to shout at him, but some of her pain eased when she leaned back into the hard warmth of his body.

“Bite on this, boy.” The doctor slipped a scrap of thick leather between her teeth. She sank her teeth down into the leather band and tried to focus on anything but the pain as Maynard lifted her arm upward and began to bend it. Every tendon in her arm and shoulder were on fire.

“Robbie.” Maynard’s voice was dim as though from a distance, beneath a vast ocean. “We’re almost done.”

“Look at the sea,” Dominic’s seductive voice whispered intimately in her ear. She stared at the cabin windows, out toward the black swells rising and falling as the waves thrashed in every direction.

"We're in the eye of the storm now." Dominic pointed to the swirling clouds that seemed to have been spat out of hell itself.

"Now!" Dominic hissed, not to her but to the doctor.

Maynard moved her arm swiftly in toward her body, and something popped again. She screamed against the leather strap. A few seconds later the agonizing pain ebbed, drawing out of her like a retreating tide. Only aching soreness remained.

"He's a tough lad," Maynard said. "I've seen grown men piss themselves when I set a shoulder like that." Maynard clucked and fussed like an old hen as he fashioned a sling for Roberta's arm and tied it securely around her neck.

"No lifting, no hard work, Captain. Not if you want the boy to heal properly."

"A useless cabin boy," Dominic grumbled.

"An *alive* cabin boy. You should be grateful. I had the lad in the infirmary with me not half an hour ago."

"Seasick, was he?" Dominic's bitter tone broke through some of Roberta's pain. She wanted to kick him, sink her teeth into him, but her shoulder leeched most of her energy.

"No, not in the least. He helped me with Jennings, Schaefer, and Colton. The boy kept his head on his shoulders when most men wouldn't have. A lot of blood was involved."

Dominic stiffened beneath her slightly. "Well, I'm glad to know he's not useless."

"Certainly not," Maynard said. "He's just young. Give him a chance, and he'll be as good a man on board as any of the rest." Maynard patted Roberta's knee and then looked up at Dominic. "Let him rest out the storm. If you need another crewman, pull the captive lieutenant out on deck. He may be a Royal Navy man, but he'll want to see land again as much as any of us."

Dominic answered the doctor with a grunt, and then Maynard left them alone.

"I still think you're a fool," he growled, but the words had less bite to them than before. "You disobeyed a direct order. There will be consequences."

He held on to her for a moment longer, and she closed her eyes. She would hate herself in the morning for relishing his warmth and the support of his arms. Right now, she hurt too much to think of anything else.

Dominic gently eased her down onto his bed. "Sleep now. We'll talk in the morning."

She mumbled something drowsily and sank deep into an exhausted slumber. Not even the rolling waves of the wild storm playing with the *Emerald Dragon* could wake her.

8

"How is Robbie?" Reese asked.

Dominic shut the door behind him as he stepped out into the hall. "Dislocated shoulder."

Reese winced. "Christ, that must hurt. A young lady enduring that pain... She must be very strong."

"And stubborn. How's Griffin?" Dominic braced himself as the *Dragon* crested another large wave.

"Berating himself for putting Robbie in danger. You know how he is, Captain. You should give the boy a nod the next time you see him, cheer him up. Otherwise he'll think he's disappointed you."

"Very well," Dominic said. He liked Griffin a lot. The boy was a good worker. Dominic had rescued him from another pirate ship by buying off his debt. Ever since, Griffin had followed him about like a young pup, eager to please. Dominic couldn't blame him. He knew what life was like on a ship where a man owned you.

Looking to his quartermaster, he spoke again. "How much longer will the storm be on us?"

"Another hour, I think." Reese sniffed the air. "We need help on deck, though. Someone who knows the sea. We should use the *Fortune*'s lieutenant."

"Maynard said the same thing. I might as well go fetch him." Dominic held out his hand, and Reese passed him the keys to the cell. "I'll meet you on deck."

Dominic took the stairs down two at a time to the cell where Nicholas was. As soon as he opened the door, the man was on his feet.

"About bloody time, Dom. Get this off me so I can help." He shook his manacled wrist.

Dominic unlocked the iron manacle from Nicholas's wrist. "This is only temporary. Once we are in calmer waters, you go back down here."

"Anything's better than waiting to drown in here." It was clear from the state of the cell that Nicholas had been battered about during the storm. Heavy wooden storage crates lay in disarray all around him.

Nicholas flexed his arm and touched the raw skin from where the manacle had rubbed too hard, but he made no show of discomfort. There was a cut on his forehead, and he limped as he followed Dominic through the door.

"How bad is the wind?"

"Bad," Dominic grunted. "Coming down from the northeast."

"Northeast? That's unusual for this time of year in these parts." Nicholas trailed close behind as they stumbled up on deck.

"'Bout bleeding time, Cap'n!" Chibbs, soaked to the bone, had wrapped his stout body around the helm as they reached him on the forecastle deck.

"Reese!" Dominic bellowed. The young quartermaster was one deck below with twenty men who were pulling the ropes tight to secure the masts.

"Dom!" Nicholas pointed to the mizzenmast, which was starting to bend from the force of the wind.

"Reese, out of the way!" Dominic tried to warn his quartermaster just as the mast nearest him and the crew snapped and came right toward them. Nicholas and Dom leapt over the railing, landing and rolling on the deck before they scrambled up. They raced into the storm together and leapt across fallen timbers to see to the crew.

Dominic forgot about the past, forgot the pain, forgot everything but Nicholas and the joy he'd had as a boy with his closest friend. Even in the face of danger, he took pleasure in this unexpected reunion. All the years that had hardened them both into men had not dimmed that instinctive trust when it mattered most.

"To the farthest horizon!" he called out to Nicholas as they sprinted on the slippery decks as the ship rolled on a fresh wave.

Lightning lit up the ship, and he had but a moment to see Nicholas's familiar grin as he dared to laugh as they ran headlong into danger.

ROBERTA CAME AWAKE, BITS AND PIECES OF SCATTERED dreams tangled like English vines growing outside her old home in England. She tried to clear her head as soft light illuminated the backs of her eyelids.

Such strange dreams. Ones of black seas and white flags, of splintered wood and blood mixing with seawater until her stomach...

She rolled over and threw up on the floor with a pained whimper. Her left arm and shoulder throbbed with an intense aching pain. Not a dream after all.

"We have chamber pots for that." A rough voice from behind her made her wince as she took in her surroundings.

"Griffin!" She tried to get out of bed, but a tan, muscled arm thumped down over her body, dragging her back into the narrow bed.

"Stay put. The boy is fine. Just a little bruised," Dominic said. "Now stay still and let me get back to sleep. I was up all night on deck."

She ceased her struggling to free herself of his hold as she heard the weariness of his tone. He wasn't going to do anything to her. Not right now.

"That's better. Now sleep."

Roberta would have bristled in indignation at being ordered about, but she was honestly glad to get the chance to rest. Everything hurt. She felt like she had collided with every wall on the ship twice over. Being gently caged back against Dominic's body felt comforting in a way that worried her greatly. She felt...*safe*. With a pirate. That wasn't good.

"Was anyone lost?" she asked after a moment. Dark memories of the sea and how she had seen the wall of water higher than the ship's mast while Dominic held her close to him were seared in her brain.

"Not one life was lost, though most of us have seen better days." Dominic's voice was muffled, and she dared to shift a little on the bed to see him. He lay on his back, his head turned away on his pillow. His bronzed body was a thing of beauty, with carved hills and valleys of pure muscle. But the scars...there were too many along his back to count. She shuddered at the thought of how he'd gotten them, the pain he had endured for every lash.

She struggled to return to their conversation so she wouldn't ask about his scars. "Thank heavens. I thought surely someone would've..." She let the tragic thought go unfinished.

She tried to lie back and not think about the fact that she was in bed with a pirate who was holding her very inappropriately, or that one of her own arms was tucked in a sling.

"I can hear you thinking, Robbie," he growled. "Sleep, for God's sake."

She closed her eyes, swearing she wouldn't, but she knew that was a battle she would eventually lose. Not more than ten minutes later, Dominic's breath evened out, and she rested her chin on his chest. She made a silent catalogue of the scars she could see, wondering how he'd acquired each. Some looked older than others.

He was still a vision of masculine perfection, but the scars…they made her want to bury her face in his neck and hold him close, whispering soft apologies for how he'd suffered. She wasn't a tender woman, and she'd never had much occasion for such sentimentality when there was work to be done, but knowing this man who'd saved her life had been hurt so deeply made her want to care for him, just as he'd done for her. She realized he'd even treated her rope burns sometime during the night.

Unable to resist the temptation, she kissed the nearest scar, just a faint brush of her lips before she gazed at his face again, the hard lines of his handsome features softened only slightly by sleep. Then she nestled back down in the bed, tucking her cheek against the cradle of his arm before she fell asleep.

DOMINIC HELD VERY STILL WHILE ROBERTA EXPLORED his chest, making sure to keep his breathing even and his muscles relaxed. He wasn't sure what she intended until she started tracing his old scars, ones he'd forgotten about because they had been on his body for so long they'd become part of him.

She made a soft sound of distress when she found a particularly deep scar that ran across one of his ribs. He'd earned that slash from a cutlass when he'd thought to argue with his captain when he'd been only fifteen. Gerard La Roux had held him down on top of a table in Tortuga and sliced his chest as a warning not to disagree with him ever again.

Dominic's heart began to race at the horrible memory, as he remembered how his blood had dripped down onto the dirt floor of the tavern they'd stopped in for a bit of rum, but then he felt Roberta's lips replace her fingertips, and the light kiss she gave his scar wasn't sensual, though it did drive his body to the brink of his self-control. It was the tenderness, the reverent sweetness in her kiss that puzzled him. Why did the woman care? He'd captured her and forced her to work on his ship with barely a word of appreciation. Most women would hate him for that. Yet she seemed almost...thankful?

Well, he supposed she damned better be, given how he'd almost died last night saving her and Reese had almost died saving Griffin. As fond as he was of Griffin, there were cold equations to be considered at sea, and the choice between losing one crew member and four, as hard as it was, was often no choice at all.

Fresh anger boiled up inside him, but he kept still until he felt her fall asleep. Did Roberta think she was in control? That she could run about his ship, risking the lives of his men and her own, without a thought to consequences? If she did, he'd bloody well remind her who was in command of this vessel and what the price was for disobeying orders. Not when lives depended on it. No one was going to make him feel like a young lad again, broken and deprived of control. Never again.

WHEN ROBERTA WOKE AGAIN IT HAD TO BE WELL AFTER midday, given the shadows in the room from the window. The bed was empty except for her. She leaned over to examine the floor, but the evidence of her queasy stomach had been cleared away. Had Dominic done that? She couldn't imagine him doing anything like that, but she also couldn't see him ordering someone else to do it while she was still in his bed.

The door to the cabin swung open, and Lucy walked in. "Morning, miss!" she greeted and muttered a curse she must've learned from the cook. "Robbie, I mean." Though they were alone, one never knew when someone might come within earshot of their conversation.

"Luke, how are you feeling? I never came back with any tinctures for you." Roberta pushed herself up into a seated position, wincing at the flare of fresh pain.

"Oh, I'm fine. I slept most of the night after you left. But how are you?"

"Me?"

"Yes?" Her maid set a small plate of food down on the captain's table. "The whole ship is abuzz with your rescue of Griffin. You're something of a hero."

Roberta bit back a whimper of pain. "I certainly don't feel like one."

"Come and eat a bit of tea and biscuits. Some food will have you feeling better in no time."

She perked up at the thought of a good cup of tea.

"It's a bit bland, but it's drinkable," Lucy assured her.

Roberta seated herself at the table, trying to ignore the unpleasant smell of her clothes, the saltwater and sweat from last night still embedded into the fabric. Careful not to hurt her arm, she nibbled on the fresh biscuits. Lucy had made them, judging by the taste. They were definitely not the hardtack biscuits served to the crew on most ships. Lucy leaned against the large windows while Roberta ate.

"How is your work in the galley? Is Mr. Lee treating you well?"

Lucy turned her way, blushing. The temporary cook on the *Dragon* was a tall, intimidating, dark-skinned man, a former African slave who had been freed by Dominic, and also quite attractive. Lucy had all but trembled when she'd first approached him, but it hadn't been from fear, Roberta could tell that much.

"Mr. Lee is very kind," Lucy replied carefully. "He was so gruff at first, but now we talk. He has traveled much of the world while serving Captain Grey. He told me about this tiny island they visited last year that was full of parrots. Can you imagine? Thousands of colorful birds as far as the eye can see?"

"It sounds magnificent." Roberta wished she could see that. She wondered if Dominic would take his ship there while she and Lucy were still aboard.

After she finished her breakfast, Lucy left her to return to the galley to help Lee prepare the next meal for the crew. Roberta was at a loss of what to do, but she couldn't stay in the cabin a moment longer. She left the quarters and climbed the stairs up to the quarterdeck. She halted at the sight of Lieutenant Flynn. He was tending to the ropes of the mainmast, along with six other men. She started toward him, but a hand came down on her uninjured shoulder.

"Been wondering when you'd surface on deck." Dominic's voice made her jump.

She spun around to find the tall, dark-haired captain glaring down at her. Had she truly spent all night in this man's bed and even kissed his scarred, muscular body? Each time she came face-to-face with him, she was reminded of how large and powerful he was. His broad stance on the deck accented the strong thighs outlined by his knee-length trousers and the slender hips that gave way to a broad torso and a fine pair of shoulders.

Roberta couldn't help but compare him to a man like Huntington. Huntington was fit, like any captain of his age, but with Dominic there was a force, a presence of power and movement, even when he stood very still, as though at a moment's notice he could burst into action.

He reminded her of the tiger she'd seen once as a child when she and her father had visited the king. Dignitaries from India had presented the wild beast to the court, and everyone had watched the mighty creature prowling on the length of his large chain. Its natural beauty and the gleaming striped fur and gold eyes had lured one foolish courtier to venture too close, and he had been mauled. A powerful blunt swipe of the tiger's claws and the man had been rushed to the doctor. Roberta had clung to her father's neck as they both stared in awe at the beast.

Dominic was like that tiger. Handsome, alluring, and deadly.

"I told you to stay below deck last night." His tone was soft, but there was an underlying edge, which sparked tension inside her. She slid backward a step, her body bumping into the railing overlooking the waist deck below.

"I was...I did," she protested.

"Yet you risked your pretty little neck for a boy like Griffin?" Dominic shot the young man an almost murderous glare where he was working on deck next to Flynn.

"I saw a chance to help," she hissed. "If you're upset about that, then you are a fool, Captain Grey."

"I'm tempted to have you flogged," he muttered back.

She stared at him. "Flogged? You wouldn't *dare*!"

He grabbed her good arm, pinning her to the railing with his body.

"I would do more than dare, darling. Don't forget, you had a choice: share my bed as a lady or work as a man aboard this ship. You chose the latter, and then you disobeyed my orders. Three other lives could have been lost, not just Griffin's. You, Griffin, Reese, and I could all be dead at the bottom of the bloody ocean, feeding the sharks because of your actions. One life on this ship is always better to lose in order to save others."

Roberta couldn't help it—her temper was stoked by his. She had never been coolheaded when she was forced to deal with fools.

"I *saved* a man's life. If you want to flay me for that and risk the rage of your crew, then go ahead." She was calling his bluff. He wouldn't dare punish her, not when she held the crew's esteem for saving one of their own. Dominic's mouth hardened into a cold smile.

"You've been on my ship all of a few days, and you think in that short time you've earned the loyalty of my men over me? Now that is worth testing, wouldn't you say?"

Roberta swallowed hard. *Oh Lord, I've done it now...*

He dragged her down to the waist deck.

"Reese, come here," Dominic bellowed. The young quartermaster left his post overseeing the repairs from last night's storm.

"Captain?" Reese's hazel eyes moved carefully between her and Dominic. Roberta jerked hard on her arm, struggling to free herself from Dominic's hand.

"Bring the barrel."

Reese's eyes widened. "Surely you don't want to—"

"The barrel, Reese. Now. Gather the crew on deck. I want everyone to witness this."

"Aye, Captain." Reese's eyes were filled with regret as he crossed the deck and enlisted two of the crew to help him bring a large barrel to the middle of the ship. They turned it on its side and roped it into hooks on the deck floor, securing it in place.

"Please... Please don't," Roberta begged him in a whisper. She wasn't strong enough to take a lashing. The cat-o'-nine-tails would rip her to pieces. Memories of Dominic's back, covered in scars, made her body shake. She wasn't strong enough to survive that.

"You had your choice, Robbie." He spoke in such a soft whisper, almost sweet. "I'll offer it one last time. My bed or the barrel."

"You black-hearted monster!" She refused to hand over her virtue like that simply to avoid punishment. She was many things, but she wasn't a coward. She struggled now, dragging her heels along the deck, but he pulled her to the barrel. He nearly had to carry her.

Lucy appeared on deck just then and started to run to her, but Mr. Lee threw an arm around her waist and held her back.

"Captain?" Griffin stepped forward, as well as Lieutenant Flynn behind him. "Something wrong?" Everyone had gathered on deck, and nearly a hundred men in total were watching wide-eyed. The only sound on deck was the wind flapping through the canvas sails. Their free, glorious sound seemed to mock her.

"Robbie disobeyed orders last night and put his life and the lives of others at risk. He will take five lashes for it."

"Captain!" Griffin's gray eyes bulged out with fear. "Captain, he rescued me. He didn't—"

"Silence," Dominic said. He didn't need to shout. The word was strong enough to cut across the deck like the crack of a pistol.

"I'll take the lashes." Griffin stepped forward, but Lieutenant Flynn nudged him back.

"No, I'll take them. Robbie's too small. It could kill him." Flynn looked to Roberta, and she saw the noble blond man step forward, pulling his waistcoat and shirt off. Dominic was silent for a heartbeat too long, giving Roberta a tiny bit of hope that he had changed his mind. Then he turned to face her.

"Would you let another man take the punishment for your recklessness and disobedience?"

The challenge was there. She could almost hear him

speaking to her in her head. *Are you a coward, Roberta? Would you let an innocent man take your punishment for you?*

"No, I will take it." She was startled by how firm her voice was because the rest of her was shaking violently. She looked at the heavy oak barrel.

"Dom!" Flynn shouted. "Don't!"

"Silence him!" Dominic shouted. Several crewmen grabbed Flynn's arms, and one man bound him with a gag as they dragged him back into the crowd of pirates. He almost threw them off, but he was outnumbered. Their eyes met, and she gave a little shake of her head. If he kept this up, he'd only be punished alongside her.

Young Griffin looked torn, and she warned him off with a wave of her hand. She was not going to let Dominic win this battle of wills. She had wanted this, to be a sailor like all the others. And he was right—she had disobeyed a direct order from the captain and had put lives in danger to save hers. Four lives potentially lost: hers, Reese's, Griffin's, and Dominic's. If she hadn't gone on deck, only Griffin would have gone overboard. One life to four. She understood Dominic's fury, but if she could reverse time, she would not change a thing. She saw it as one life now for five lashes. A fair price to pay. Her father would have been proud.

"Ready?" Dominic asked, his sable eyes dark and impossible to read.

"Ready," she said, the word sending her heart into a panic as she stepped forward toward the barrel.

9

Roberta approached the barrel and carefully removed the sling around her shoulder. Her shoulder still ached, but she had no choice. She had seen this done before on other ships. The sailor was to grip the edges of the barrel and hold on while he took his punishment. If he couldn't stay down, they would tie him down. The thought created a bitter taste in her mouth, and her blood began to pound inside her ears, making it difficult to think.

She would leave her shirt on—she had to, or else she would betray her gender. With a deep breath, she bent over the barrel, stretching out her arms, holding back the cry of pain the movement caused her shoulder. Reese stepped into her line of vision, uncoiling a flogger. It did not have spikes embedded in the tails. It was merely a set of leather strips. That was one small mercy, she supposed, but her relief didn't last long. Dominic leaned in close to whisper something to Reese, who nodded his understanding. The bastard was probably telling Reese to hit her extra hard. When Reese moved out of sight behind her, her fear spiked and her breath started coming in pants as she waited for the first blow.

Roberta tensed, and her fingers slipped on the barrel as she tried to grasp at the metal rings around the ends of the barrel. Dominic suddenly appeared in front of her as he knelt down on the opposite side of the barrel on one knee. He gripped her forearms, pinning them to the oak barrel, preventing her from slipping. But his hold was surprisingly gentle. Their gazes locked.

"Normally, we strap men down," he whispered. "But not you." His eyes were stark with a strange intensity. The feel of the heat of his hands on her arms, even through the fabric, was a welcome relief. It gave her another sensation to think about before—

Crack! The flogger snapped across her upper back. She jolted in shock and terror, crying out, an animalistic sound of fear escaping her rather than a ladylike scream.

"Steady," Dominic growled. "That's one."

Roberta blinked, sweat beading on her skin as she tried not to thrash against the barrel in panic.

Crack! The second blow hit her bottom, and the stinging forced her body to jerk harder into the barrel. The pain was...bearable, she suddenly realized. The stinging was hard, true, but it faded quicker than she'd expected. This was not the excruciating pain she'd anticipated. Rather, it felt like the time her governess had taken a switch to her bottom for trying to climb out a window during a lesson. Feeling braver, she raised her gaze to Dominic's, keenly aware that she was suffering a humiliation like this in front of the entire ship.

The feel of so many eyes upon her, watching her punishment, choked her with humiliation, but she didn't cry, wouldn't cry no matter what came next. Dominic's eyes held hers as the next blow landed, locking her focus onto him when she would otherwise have looked around at the other men.

"That's three, Robbie. You can handle this, can't you?" He whispered the words so only she could hear. "You're as tough as any man on this ship, aren't you?" He was forcing her to realize that this wasn't about pain. It was about reminding her that his orders were the law and that she'd broken them. The next sting she felt wasn't anywhere near the torture she'd expected.

"Four," Dominic said, his fingers tightening around her wrists, which helped ground her in the moment with him. His voice seemed to mix with the waves against the ship, and the wind stirred his long dark hair. The sun made his eyes a warmer, lighter brown than she'd ever seen.

"Four," she repeated back, feeling the need to acknowledge that she was completely focused on him.

Dominic never looked away from her, and by the fifth blow something strange happened. The pain seemed to almost fade completely, and a sweet, dizzying hum took its place as she stared back at the fierce pirate in front of her. The warmth of her skin, heated from the flogger, seemed to carry her mind to a faraway place where only she and Dominic existed. His lovely dark eyes shimmered with hidden pain, an echo of her own. Was he hurting along with her?

"Five!" Dominic's shout jerked her back into herself, and she slumped against the barrel as he released her arms and stood. "That's enough!" The pain from the blows seeped slowly into her body, and she couldn't help but let out a small moan. This definitely felt like a good switching from her childhood. She'd have trouble sitting down for a few days. But she also knew this couldn't have been a proper flogging, either. She'd seen the damage those left behind.

"All of you, back to work."

Roberta struggled to breathe. Her back and bottom felt *hot*. And not like the time she'd been switched. This felt...different. She was covered in a layer of sweat.

Booted steps came up behind her. "Captain?" Reese's soft, uncertain voice made her wonder if she was more badly injured than she thought.

"Give Robbie a minute," Dominic said as he released her arms. She slid down the barrel to land on her knees. Every muscle in her body was weak, shaking. She couldn't even stand. Her legs were as wobbly as a newborn foal's.

"Best to stand and move," Dominic told her, but she

shook her head, not out of any desire to defy him, but because standing was simply impossible.

"I'm not sure the boy can," Reese whispered. "You'll be all right, Robbie. Give me your hand." She placed her trembling palm in his. Reese lifted her swiftly to her feet. Before she could react, Dom had a firm grip on her good arm, pulling her away.

"Walk, or I'll have to answer questions about why I'm carrying my cabin boy like he's a damsel in distress," Dominic warned, but the bite of his tone was gone.

He took her back to his cabin, and she collapsed onto the bed, uncaring if that upset him. What more could he do to her?

"How bad is it?" she asked when it became clear he wouldn't leave her alone. She opened one eye to peer up at his looming form beside the bed.

"How bad?" He raised his brows in confusion.

"The blood... Will my scars be deep like yours?" The heat she still felt had to be from warm blood—there wasn't any other explanation.

Something flashed in his eyes. A moment of pain from the past, perhaps.

"Blood? There isn't any blood. You'd be surprised the amount of control a skilled man can have with a whip. He gave you nothing more than the spanking a misbehaving child would have received. It will be tender for a few days, but I assure you, you're perfectly unmarked for your future husband." He crossed his arms and scowled.

But as his words sank in, rage exploded through Roberta.

"*Spanking?* That hurt!"

"Spankings are supposed to."

She leapt off the bed, ignoring the painful throb of her injured arm as she stood toe to toe with Dominic. "And I'm not a misbehaving child!" She punched a finger into his chest, but he didn't move.

His dark eyes flashed with fire, and he clamped a hand on her bottom, squeezing. Not hard, but the pressure where his palm was felt raw and far too sensitive. "You are not really hurt." A flood of fresh heat rolled through her, and she was shocked by the way her body responded to him and that purely carnal hold he had on her bottom. "And you really were misbehaving. You're an admiral's daughter; you know that challenging the captain's authority in front of the crew cannot be tolerated."

"Let go of me," she growled back at him.

"Is that what you really want?" he asked. His voice was almost sweet, but she sensed the sensual danger lurking in his tone.

"Yes." She didn't move, didn't pull away. Instead she gripped his shirt by the collar and glared up at him, their faces inches apart.

"I think you're lying," the captain said. "I think that light punishment awakened something in you, Robbie, something that was buried beneath all your fine manners and silk dresses. Believe me, I've seen it before."

"And what is that?" she demanded. Her heart beat wildly as something flared between her and Dominic. He disturbed her in every way, upsetting what she thought she knew about men, and it both scared and thrilled her.

"It awakened your passion. You've tasted the edge, my lady." Dominic's whisper tickled her skin, making it break out in gooseflesh.

"The edge?" She didn't understand what he meant.

His palm on her bottom moved to her lower back, and she felt the light sting of pain from the flogger's blows. He was right, damn him. The blows hadn't truly hurt, not the way she'd expected, and the panic and the excitement of the unknown had stirred something new to life inside her. She felt like she could face anything now.

"The edge where a gentleman becomes a pirate, where an innocent lady becomes a woman who seeks her own pleasure. You're tasting life, *true* life, Robbie. You're free of that pretty cage you were born into. The question is, what will you do with that freedom?"

He let the question linger like a single note plucked on a harp, vibrating in the air between them. He lowered his head to hers.

She didn't fight him on the kiss. She welcomed it. His eyes, an almost sable color now, were the last thing she saw as she closed her own eyes and gave in to the feelings that consumed her. Shivers ran beneath her skin as she clutched his shoulder with her good arm and kissed him back. His trim beard and mustache tickled her, and she moaned as he moved her back, pinning her against the wall by his bed. The feel of his body trapping hers only heightened the excitement she felt.

Emotions and sensations swirled in eddies around her. Her blood beat a steady pulse in her ears as she struggled for breath. The second her lips parted, his tongue swept inside, conquering hers in a dance that made wetness pool between her thighs. She barely noticed the dull throb of her injured arm anymore.

She was lost in the taste of Dominic's slightly salty lips mixed with the natural sweetness of his mouth. His calloused palms explored her bottom and back in sweeping strokes. He was rough enough to remind her that she was with a dangerous man, but gentle enough that she didn't think he would truly harm her. He nibbled at her lips, chin, and neck, and she winced as he tried to pull her shirt off.

"Ouch!" She tugged her arm back down, cradling it against her chest. He stepped back with a curse.

"I shouldn't have..." He shook his head as though to clear it of the fog of their shared passion. Disappointment hit her harder than the blows from the flogger. She hadn't wanted the moment to stop. She wanted more, and *more* was such a dangerous word. More kisses, more roving hands, more pleasure. Her body was still attuned to him, still eager for his touch.

"I need to get back on deck," Dominic said after a moment.

Without a backward glance, he left her alone in the cabin. She bit back a sob, hating the strange, sudden, and unbearable need to cry. She never cried. She was tougher than that. But despite this, fat tears rolled down her cheeks as she sank down onto the bed.

What was happening to her? The pirate captain had gotten under her skin. She had to remember who she was, not who she wanted to be, no matter how tempting it might be to follow the edge, as Dominic said. But deep down, she sensed that the edge was too close and she was already falling.

DOMINIC'S HANDS SHOOK AS HE REACHED THE UPPER deck. His crew paused to stare at him. Some with respect, others with disbelief. He hadn't had anyone flogged on his ship in nearly six months, and he almost never flogged boys. The *Dragon* was full of men who were loyal to him and to their purpose, and anyone who needed constant discipline was sent on his way at the nearest port with a full purse of coins to buy his happiness while he searched for a new crew.

Reese joined him on the forecastle deck. "Captain, a word?"

Reese rolled up his sleeves; his tan arms were covered with faint scars like Dominic's. Reese had never shared the story of his scars or his past. He'd simply appeared on deck one day, asking for work. He had won Dominic over, and in less than two years had been promoted to quartermaster. Dominic trusted the man with his life.

"What's on your mind?"

Reese looked out at sea; the waves were still so powerful, despite the storm having long since passed.

"Is she—I mean, is Robbie all right?"

The worry in his eyes startled Dominic. "She is. You did well. She's tender, but 'tis more her pride hurt than anything else."

"Good." Reese was quiet for a long while. Then he drew in a deep breath. "Don't ever make me do that again. Deserving or not, I'll not do that to her or any other woman. If it means you flog me, then so be it."

Dominic stared down at the toes of his boots, the truth, as painful and twisted as it was, on the tip of his tongue.

"I didn't mean to go through with it, but she almost got us both killed last night. People die in storms—you know that as well as I do. She risked her neck for that lad. I saw them both sliding toward the edge, and I just lost my bloody mind." The terror of seeing Roberta almost washed into the raging black waters had filled him with a fear he'd only felt once before—the moment he'd realized he would never see his home in Cornwall again.

"I mean it, Captain. I won't do it. Whatever else she's doing to you, sort it out in private—don't put me in the middle of it. It's clear you want her, and I would wager she wants you too, fine lady or no. If that's the case, then take her. Once she's been taken, her allure will fade, and you can focus on the ship and crew again."

Dominic didn't reply. How could he tell Reese the truth? He'd found a passionate creature like Roberta, one who fit both sides of him, the earl he would have become in Cornwall and the pirate he was now. He didn't know what to do, and he didn't trust his instincts anymore.

He'd held her arms, keeping her steady over that barrel. Dominic had seen her fear and bravery duel one another, and her bravery had won out. In that moment he had bonded a part of himself to her, the part of him that remembered fear and pain when that language of lashes and beatings was still new to him. Now he crushed his fears with his fists and lived in the shadow of mountainous pain.

Sailors spoke of death as an old friend, but for Dominic, death was a reaper, a wraith cloaked in darkness. He'd grown so used to being hurt that he had become numb to causing it. But somehow, Roberta had dragged those early years of light and life back into his soul, leaving him feeling raw and blinded.

No, he would never again hurt Roberta like he had today, even as mild as that punishment had been, because he didn't want to become like Gerard La Roux, the man who had caused him so much suffering. Seeing Nicholas try to rush to Roberta's defense had reminded him of the man he used to be.

Dominic Greyville had been born to defend the weak and helpless, not hurt them. He'd let his pirate life blacken his heart. Even though he and his crew spent much of their time chasing down slaver ships and freeing men and women, he never felt absolved of his early sins, even the ones he'd been forced to commit to survive. He knew he was not worthy of redemption, but he would start this very day reminding himself that he could still act with some nobility. His innocence might be long gone, but he could and would protect Roberta from himself at any cost. He still wanted her, but he had to woo her as a gentleman, not a pirate. It would be damned near impossible, but he would do everything in his power to act more like Nicholas.

He studied the horizon and the way the sun sat heavy in the skies. It would be evening soon, and he owed Nicholas a talk. He headed below to the lower deck where Nicholas had been returned after the flogging. His friend had been left unshackled this time, and when Dominic entered the room, he found Nicholas pacing. A track had been worn into the dust on the floorboards, showing how long the other man had been walking back and forth.

Nicholas froze at the sight of Dominic, his hands curled into tight fists. There was a moment of silence before Nicholas charged him with a roar, shoving Dominic against the wall. Nicholas had him pinned by the throat before he even had a chance to raise his arms.

"Bloody hell, when did you learn to move like that?" Dominic choked out as his friend squeezed his windpipe.

"You bastard! You whipped a woman. A defenseless woman!"

Black dots danced in Dominic's vision, but he could feel where Nick had left himself open. He swung low, punching Nicholas's side below his rib cage. Nicholas's hold on his throat loosened, and Dominic punched him again, harder. His old friend stumbled back, clutching his side and wheezing.

"My quartermaster barely hit her, Nick. On my honor. I just saw to her myself, and she's on her feet and showing a fine temper."

Nicholas caught his breath and braced himself against the back wall of the cell.

"You let me think... But she screamed." His blue eyes burned in open challenge.

"She was startled. Anyone would yell at that first blow, no matter how light." Dominic couldn't believe he was defending himself to Nicholas, and he couldn't believe Nicholas didn't trust him. But then, he was a pirate after all. "I'll send her to you if you don't believe me."

A flash of something other than worry appeared in Nicholas's eyes. "Yes, I want to see her."

Had Nicholas and Roberta...? No, she was engaged to Huntington. Perhaps Nicholas was in love with her but was hiding it the way any honorable man would.

"What is she to you?" Dominic asked, uncaring of the

bluntness of the question. All the manners and civility he had been raised with had perished long ago.

Nicholas met his gaze evenly. “She is a friend. We became acquainted on the voyage. She’s brilliant, Dom. Absolutely brilliant. She’s a better navigator than I am.” Nicholas’s lips twitched in a ghost of a smile. “She even ran circles around Huntington. It made the shipboard dinners quite entertaining.”

“More intelligent than her betrothed? Entertaining indeed,” Dominic mused. What on earth did she even see in that oaf?

“Betrothed? She and Huntington aren’t…” Nicholas’s words died off. “She told you they were?”

“Yes.” Dominic caught on to Nicholas’s unspoken thoughts. “But she isn’t, is she? A woman like that wouldn’t tie herself to that fool.”

“No. I knew he was proposing to her, he boasted of it, but I also knew she wouldn’t say yes.”

“So the little minx wanted me to believe he was her betrothed so I would treat her well.” Dominic couldn’t help but laugh.

“Dom,” Nick warned. “Don’t harm her. For the sake of what was once between us as friends, I’m begging you.”

They stared at each other—the pirate and the gentleman—for a moment before Dominic nodded.

“I told you before that the man I used to be is gone, but I was wrong. A part of me was buried, not dead. The lady is safe with me.”

"Good. May I see her?" Nicholas asked.

"Why?" Suspicion flattened Dominic's tone.

"I want to reassure her that her father will be well. She did not see him loaded onto the longboat."

"Very well. I will send her to you." When he started to leave, Nicholas spoke again.

"Your father never gave up looking for you, you know. Nor your mother. My last letter from them was two months ago. Your father has ships still looking for you in the colonies and Spain. The last I heard he was sending men to the coast of Africa and here to the West Indies. You can..." Nicholas's voice roughened. "You can go home."

Dominic's throat tightened. "After what I've seen, what I've done? No, I can never go home." He closed the cell door, hoping to leave the wounds of the past far behind him.

10

Nicholas gazed at the wall of his cell, his mind strangely blank. He still couldn't believe Dominic was alive after all these years. When Dominic had disappeared, it had destroyed him. He'd gone to the docks, asking everyone if they had seen Dominic, hoping to learn if Dom had joined a merchant crew. But his inquiries had been met with stoic silence. Only a girl from the tavern by the docks, the one Dominic had fought for all those years ago, had sworn in urgent whispers that she'd seen him being carried away to a ship.

No one else would say a word, assuming they had seen anything. Dominic's parents had been frantic with worry, hiring men to question the townsfolk, and they sent other men riding down every major road looking for Dom. But it was as though he had vanished into the night, like a wraith or a ghost.

Dom wasn't dead. The realization was in some ways still sinking in. Nicholas had never given up hope, not quite, not even after all these years. It was partly why he'd joined the navy. He had thought, perhaps foolishly, that he would come across Dom on another ship, that maybe he'd escaped and then decided to run away to sea after all.

It was common enough, but horrifying. Young lads stolen, some even from their own beds, and sold into slavery in the West Indies or the colonies, where they had to work to earn their freedom over a couple of decades. Some had been forced into lives of piracy, and they were unable to go home because they risked being hung for their past crimes. The thought made Nicholas's stomach turn.

Poor Dom, at the mercy of pirates. Any man in Dom's place would have gone through hell itself, and Nicholas hadn't been there to protect him. He buried his face in his hands and bent over his knees as he sat on one of the empty crates. And now he was a captain of them. Perhaps he was too far gone to ever come back.

He wasn't sure how much time had passed when he heard keys jangling in the lock. He looked up, not surprised to see the man called Reese, the quartermaster, standing there. But he stepped aside and allowed what appeared to be a thin slip of a boy into the room. Nicholas rose to his feet as Miss Harcourt entered the room, still wearing her cabin boy disguise.

"Lieutenant," she said quietly and cast a questioning

glance over her shoulder. Reese answered with a silent nod and closed the door behind her, leaving her alone with Nicholas.

"Miss Harcourt, I'm sorry. I have failed to protect you."

She held up a hand. "I wouldn't say that. We're both prisoners, aren't we? You've done your best, as have I, but our circumstances were such that we never stood a chance. So let us not forget that." She stepped closer to him, looking him over in concern. "Are you hurt? Did those men hurt you?"

Nicholas laughed bitterly. "I'm quite well, Miss Harcourt. It is you I worry about. You were flogged." His gaze rolled over her body, seeking any signs of pain.

"Oh..." She blushed, which despite her masculine attire still made her incredibly pretty. "It wasn't...he really didn't hurt me, much to my surprise." She bit her lip.

"So Dom told the truth?" He wasn't sure if he believed that or not.

"He did. I was scared at first, but it was no more than what an unruly child might receive. Which, I suppose, was a message in itself." She cleared her throat as though embarrassed. "Wait, you called the captain Dom..."

She deserved an answer to her unasked question. It was the only thing he could give her now. The knowledge of who the pirate captain truly was.

"I know him. The man who calls himself Captain Grey

is Dominic Greyville, the one-time future earl of Camden. He was once my dearest friend."

"DEAREST FRIEND?" ROBERTA COULDN'T BELIEVE WHAT he was telling her. "But how…?"

Nicholas sighed and nodded at a wooden crate close to him. Roberta took a seat, doing her best not to wince from the soreness, holding her breath as she listened to him.

"We were born two miles away from each other on the same day. Dom arrived into this world a mere three hours before me. We first met at two weeks old. Our mothers and fathers were old friends. Our bond as young children solidified into something greater over the years. We became inseparable." The hollow ache in Flynn's voice made Roberta's eyes mist with tears.

She had longed all her life to have a friend like that. But she'd never gotten along with the young women she met. There were those who were nice enough, but they were often not interested in the same things she was. It was hard to engage them in meaningful discourse and form lasting friendships.

"What happened between you?" she asked.

Flynn's eyes grew intense as he answered.

"I honestly don't know the truth of it, but I have my suspicions."

"I'm afraid I don't understand."

Flynn raked a hand through his golden hair. "We were fourteen when Dom disappeared. I bid him good night, and we both left for home. His father and mother said he was sent to bed without supper because they discovered he had been fighting."

"Wait, fighting? With whom?" Roberta leaned in closer to Flynn.

"Just a lad from a tavern. He'd slapped a pretty barmaid. Dom has a soft spot for damsels in distress."

An unladylike snort escaped Roberta's mouth. "If that were true, wouldn't he be more pleasant to me?"

The lieutenant shrugged. "That's part of the mystery. But as I was saying, he was in trouble for fighting and sent to his chambers. No one ever saw him again after that night."

Roberta put a hand to her mouth. "Oh, his poor parents. How frightened they must have been to find him gone."

"You cannot imagine, Miss Harcourt. Aaron was hard on Dom, but he loved him fiercely. He was never cruel, but he didn't let Dom run wild, which is something I'm sure you've sensed in him by now—wildness is in his blood." Flynn placed his palms on his knees and leaned back. "They never gave up. I have to get free at the next port and write to them. They must learn that Dom is still alive."

"Assuming the captain honors his word about letting us

go and we're allowed to leave in Tortuga..." She bit her lip. "We will both find a way between us to get to Port Royal and send his family the news."

"Thank you." Flynn smiled, but the broken expression made her heart hurt. "After everything that's happened to him, at least what I suspect, it will not be an easy or even a safe reunion."

"How so?"

"I cannot be sure, but my belief is that he was kidnapped. The slave trade does not only take Africans, but anyone who can be forced into it. Men have been known to raid the coastal towns of England, stealing away boys who won't be missed for indentured labor. The condition those boys live in are barely better than the poor Africans ripped from their homelands. Most kidnapped British lads end up in the company of pirates sooner or later. Pirates are, as I'm sure you've discovered, quite vicious. The abuse Dom must have suffered at such a young age, I cannot even fathom. I don't simply mean the whippings, either. Things happen on ships, especially to boys and young men."

Roberta tried not to think of what horrors a young, innocent Dominic would have faced, but her imagination was sometimes far more dangerous than reality. However, she had to admit that Dominic's crew were not the cutthroat sort of men she'd expected. He seemed to rule his ship in a far different manner than most pirates.

Despite this, she still wouldn't let her guard down in regards to him or his crew.

"What things?" she asked Flynn. She wasn't even sure what harm she was asking about, but her imagination provided a dark idea.

"When I tried to talk to him about his past, he shut me out. Only a man who's been through hell itself would close himself off to his best friend." Flynn's eyes grew overbright as he blinked rapidly and looked away from her.

"I failed him, Roberta." Flynn used her given name softly, the way a friend would. Roberta touched his arm, wanting to reassure him.

"You cannot fail someone like that. You were both children. And if you had been there, you might have been taken too."

Flynn sniffed and wiped his nose. "At least then we would have been together."

Roberta couldn't argue that, although it was sad to think about.

"I envy you the friendship you had. I've always been alone."

Flynn focused on her again. "It is easier for boys to form friendships. My little sister says the same as you. She feels alone most often. Only Josephine, Dom's little sister, gives her any comfort."

"Dom has a sister?"

"He does, and a brother. Josephine and Adrian are twins. They were only young babes when Dom was taken."

"He must miss them terribly." Roberta's heart ached for Dom and the wonderful life he had lost. It made his harsh, cold manner all the more understandable. She would have been bitter against the world as well if she had lost her family like that.

"But if we reunite him with his family—"

"That may be impossible," Flynn cut in. "Dominic has been pirating for over a decade. His reputation precedes him. The moment he sails into a port where the authorities recognize him, he will be put to death for piracy. He knows that, and it's why he wouldn't want us telling his family. If they came looking for him, it could get him killed." Flynn paused, as though to argue with himself. "But they must be told. They have to know after all this time."

"Yes, they do."

She was silent a moment and so was Flynn. It struck her that this was one of the few times she'd been alone with a man. She'd also been alone with Dominic, and the two experiences were so different. With Flynn she felt safe, even now with him as a prisoner. With Dominic? She felt just the opposite. He frightened her with his natural intensity, and yet that same intensity also drew her in like a moth to a flame.

Though it was a common expression, she had seen that happen once when a large black moth had dared to crawl into an oil lamp beside her bed. It had fluttered recklessly around the glowing steady burn of the fire, and then when it couldn't resist the light any longer, it dove into the flames. Its wings glowed like a firefly cast out of the pits of hell. And then in a fluttering, agonizing death, it spiraled down to the base of the lamp, perishing silently.

Is that to be my fate? If I stay too close to Captain Grey, will he burn me up until there's nothing left but ash and silence?

"You must take care, Roberta. I think the Dominic I knew as a boy is still inside him, but he's been a pirate for years now, at first to survive and now because he sees no other way. That part of him may be too strong." Flynn grasped her hands, and for a moment she was struck with the thought that this man, Nicholas Flynn, handsome, captivating, and far more noble than Dom, was the sort of man she should marry. But Dominic's flashing dark eyes full of midnight secrets and the feel of his hands on her body, his lips mastering her own...no one else could make her feel like that.

"I will be cautious," she assured Flynn.

"Good, I couldn't bear it if you were hurt, because I—"

Whatever he'd been about to say was silenced by a commotion from above. Reese threw open the cell door.

"On deck now, Robbie. A ship has been sighted." Roberta rushed out the door, leaving Flynn behind in his cell. She followed Reese up on deck. The sun had dipped below the horizon now, and the crew had lit lamps.

"It's the *Red Lady*!" one man clinging to the rigging far above on the mizzenmast shouted to them.

"What's the *Red Lady*?" Roberta asked Reese. They joined Dominic on the forecastle deck. Dominic's face was like stone as he looked to Reese, and both men ignored her question.

"We can't outrun him. The *Red Lady* is the only bloody ship that can catch up with us," Dominic growled.

"What's the *Red Lady*?" she asked again.

"The worst pirate ship to haunt the West Indies," Dominic finally answered, his eyes black as night in the gloom.

"He'll want to see you, won't he?" Reese asked, his face tight with worry.

Roberta could tell that there was something or someone on the *Red Lady* who was very, very bad. For an instant she saw a hint of fear in Dominic's face, before he buried it beneath cold defiance.

"He will. I'll have to let him or risk the lives of everyone on board." The decision made, he turned to her, grabbing her good arm.

"Robbie, find Luke and climb the rigging to the top crow's nest on the mainmast. Do not come down until I come for you. Do you understand? Don't disobey me this time or you will wish I had flogged you. The captain of that ship, *he's* the monster you should fear."

Roberta's throat constricted, and she swallowed hard.

"Yes, Captain," she replied, and meant it. She wouldn't

disobey. This wasn't a battle between them, not any longer. Obeying orders was truly a matter of life and death, and she would listen to him.

"Go, now," he ordered, his tone urgent. She fled down the deck stairs and headed into the belly of the ship to the galley.

Lee and Lucy were preparing the evening meal, and even under these dire circumstances, she was entranced by the aroma that wafted up from the pots on the stove. Lucy was instructing Lee on cooking.

"Then you add a bit of lemon. Lemon is important, you see. The admiral says it keeps scurvy away from the crew, and it adds a sharp flavor that most find pleasing to the roast chicken."

"Luke, we have to go," Roberta interrupted. Lee shot her a disapproving look.

"The boy is teaching me. Off with you, Robbie." Lee waved a hand as though to shoo Roberta away.

"Mr. Lee, we've been ordered by the captain to the crow's nest. The *Red Lady* is upon us."

Lee's eyes widened, and he muttered darkly about villainous bastards. "Go now. Stay out of sight." He tossed Lucy a loaf of bread and two apples. Roberta led Lucy back up on deck just in time to see the other ship pulling alongside.

"Climb, quick!" Roberta hissed. They were fortunate that the darkness covered much of their hasty ascent.

Roberta bit back a cry with every step of the rigging

she climbed. Between her rope-burned palms and her bad shoulder, she could barely manage, but Lucy helped her, supporting her with one arm around her waist until they reached the top and climbed over the wooden edge of the crow's nest. The wooden bucket-shaped design of the nest kept them safe from prying eyes. She hoped Lucy wouldn't become sick, given that the nest swayed quite a bit even on calmer seas.

"Why are we hiding?" Lucy whispered as she and Roberta sat down and split the bread and apples between them.

"The ship pulling up alongside us is called the *Red Lady*. The ship's captain frightens Dominic. That should be reason enough. Lucy, you should have seen his face—he was terrified."

Her maid stared at her in shock, her mouth agape, her apple held a few inches away from her lips. "He scared the captain? Oh heavens, my lady, we—"

"Hush," Roberta hissed as new voices carried upon the wind. French voices and Creole. She wanted to look now, but she knew she had to remain hidden.

"Dominic, it's been a long time, *mon ami*," a smooth, cold French voice called out.

"La Roux," Dominic answered.

Roberta closed her eyes, picturing Dominic standing on the waist deck, legs braced, showing off his hard, lean legs. He would have his arms crossed over his chest, and his face would be hard with only a facade of friendliness upon it. A pistol would be tucked in his belt and a saber hanging from a sheath on his hip. He would look every inch the deadly pirate he was. But whoever La Roux was, he must be a nightmare beyond imagining.

"We were about to dine in my cabin," said Dominic. "You're welcome to join us, but we're headed for Port Royal soon. I know you do not frequent there due to the English fleet visiting it so often." It was clear he was trying to chase La Roux off.

"Usually you are correct, old friend, but today I am tempted to visit it. I know you have a fondness for it and the ladies there. I believe we should join you for dinner."

"Very well." Dominic's voice grew softer as he moved from the waist deck down to the quarterdeck of the interior of the ship, until they could no longer be heard.

Roberta and Lucy held their breath until everything seemed quiet on deck, and then Roberta eased up on her knees and carefully risked peering over the edge into the neighboring ship. A few men moved about the lit decks of the *Red Lady*. They looked dirty and rough, not like the clean-cut appearance of the crew of the *Dragon*. In fact, for pirates, the *Dragon*'s crew was positively elegant in their manners and dress compared to those aboard the other ship. She watched two men break out into a fight over a bottle of rum, which soon escalated from fists to knives, and nobody else on board seemed to care. Roberta sank back down below the protection of the nest.

"Lucy, I fear it's going to be a long night."

11

Dominic's stomach knotted with dread and primal fear as he led Andre La Roux into his dining room. Lee had already set the table for Reese, Chibbs, Dominic, and three others. He must have guessed that La Roux would try to stay. Smart man. Even this little gesture would show La Roux that his men were on their toes.

La Roux waved at his two companions, his quartermaster, Blaise Robinson, a dangerous man with any weapon, and his bosun, Curtis Whalen. Blaise was strong and young like Reese, whereas Curtis was older and more rotund, but no less dangerous. Dominic wouldn't risk a fight while those two were on board. No matter how much he wanted to slit La Roux's throat, he wouldn't put his own men's lives at risk. Only a fool would think La Roux would be easily killed. Blaise and Curtis no doubt had some way to signal the *Red Lady* to prep their cannons.

Dominic eased stiffly down in his own chair only after La Roux was first seated. The rest of the men in the room waited briefly before following suit.

Lee brought plates of roasted chicken and biscuits and poured wine for every man. Dominic would never have tasted an enemy's wine, but La Roux was arrogant enough to assume no one would ever poison him. The idea had occurred to Dominic to take advantage of this, but he would have to ensure Curtis and Blaise drank as well, and they never did.

"Well now...this is a pleasant reunion, is it not, Dominic?" He caressed Dominic's name in a way that made his skin crawl. As La Roux spoke, he curled his lip in a sneer and his skin pulled tight, making his harsh features look even more bony and unearthly. La Roux was close to forty, but he had that ancient and ageless look only a devil could acquire.

While Andre was a thinner, more wiry version of his brother Gerard, their faces, voices, and attitudes were too similar not to revive the darkest memories of Dominic's time aboard that first ship. It had been Gerard who had hurt him, who had taken from him what no man should have. Andre had watched as Gerard took his pleasure on Dominic's much smaller body, and he'd said nothing. As far as Dominic was concerned, Andre was as vile and wretched as his brother.

Dominic tried to bury the gut-wrenching agony of those nightmare days, but even the scent of Andre's sweaty red brocade coat made bile rise in his throat.

"It is a pity that Gerard is no longer with us," Andre mused as he twisted his wine goblet between his thumb and forefinger.

"Indeed," Dominic muttered.

Neither man acknowledged the truth of Gerard's fate, though both knew it. Dominic because he'd been there, a week after his eighteenth birthday, a smoking pistol in his hand and his dead tormentor at his feet. Andre because he'd been told a week later, too late to catch Dominic's flight. Years had passed, and Andre had never come for his revenge, but Dominic knew it was only a matter of time. Even though his reputation as a pirate had only grown since he'd killed the bastard who first abused him, Dominic knew Andre wouldn't be intimidated and would eventually seek him out.

"Rumor has it you were chasing a prize from the coast of Spain," La Roux said before he sipped his wine.

"A prize from Spain? No, we left Spain, but not to go after any ship."

La Roux was the only man at the table who ate dinner. His silverware scraped against the china plate as he cut into the chicken, speared it with his fork, and chewed, confident and seemingly unthreatened. Dominic could feel Reese and Chibbs watching him, and their gazes darted back to La Roux.

"So, you didn't cross an English ship called the *Fortune?*"

"No, can't say that we have. Perhaps you have?" Dominic challenged the Frenchman.

La Roux chuckled. "If we had, we wouldn't have chased you. My crew would be enjoying the spoils of our victory in Tortuga."

Dominic calmly reached for his wine, taking one small taste. La Roux must have his own sources in Spain.

"I met such a lovely woman while in Spain recently. She told me of that ship. It's a pity what happened to her. Maria, I think was her name."

The wine turned to ash on Dominic's tongue.

"What happened to her?" He knew he shouldn't ask and betray that he knew the woman, but he had to.

"Oh, did you know her?" La Roux smiled, an edge to his gaze as he spared Dominic a glance before sawing into his dinner again. "She was a whore, you must know. In spirit if not in profession. And she died as a whore should...or so I hear." He delicately popped the morsel into his mouth, his eyes glittering into Dominic's. "Fell from a window after her husband learned she was unfaithful. Head cracked open on the cobblestones below like an overripe melon. *Crack*." Finished with his food, he smacked his lips, leaned forward, and smiled. "Awful way to die, wouldn't you agree?"

Reese shifted beside Dominic, the movement so natural that if Dominic hadn't known him very well, he would have thought nothing of it, but he knew Reese had just slipped a blade out from his vest under the table, just waiting for Dominic to give the word.

"That is a pity. I was acquainted with her." It took everything within Dominic to reach for his plate and take a bite of chicken as if the matter was of little concern. If La Roux knew that he could get to Dominic by killing innocent women, then more would no doubt meet that fate. The dark tension between them seemed to grow, making the air thin and the muscles of every man in the room knot tightly in anticipation of a fight.

"Well...I see the dinner company is not as enthusiastic as I expected. Perhaps I'll return to my ship after all." La Roux stood, walking a circle around the table, where he saw Gerard's old compass lying on a stack of papers. He picked it up, studying it with a slow smile before he set it back down and bowed deeply, hat in hand. "Your hospitality, as always, is most appreciated." Blaise and Curtis rose as well, though without the niceties, and followed him out of the room.

Dominic, Reese, and Chibbs all remained in the dining room, ready for anything that might happen. They were smart enough not to follow La Roux up on deck. If La Roux wanted blood tonight, he would start with the men in this room. It was better not to tempt him to violence until they were in a situation where Dominic was certain the *Dragon* and her crew had the advantage. Lee returned after a few minutes.

"They're gone, Captain. The *Red Lady* is pulling away."

"Thank you, Lee." Dominic slumped into his chair, his body shaking with relief.

Reese and Chibbs watched him closely.

"One of these days, I will kill him," Dominic vowed. "He'll join his brother in the cold depths of the sea."

"That day can't come soon enough," Reese added solemnly.

Dominic heard the *Red Lady* cast off, and he waited another half hour before he ventured up on deck. He stared out across the moonlit water to see if he could spot the other ship. It had already vanished. Dominic headed to the rigging at the mainmast and climbed up to the crow's nest. The moment he reached it, Roberta was on her feet with a slender cutlass aimed at his throat.

"Easy, Robbie," he crooned, but he remained still, giving her time to recognize him in the dark. "If you still want to slit my throat, at least wait until we're all safely back down on deck."

"Captain, I'm sorry, I thought..." Roberta lowered the weapon and backed away a few feet, as though expecting him to be furious with her.

"It is all right. Both of you can come back down. The *Red Lady* has cast off, and we're safe enough for now." He wouldn't tell the women that he would be sleeping with one eye open from now on.

Dominic helped the ladies make their way back down

the ropes. Once they were back on deck, Lucy rushed down to the kitchen to see if Lee needed her.

Dominic waved his bosun over. “Chibbs.”

“Captain?”

“See that the men have extra rum rations tonight. It will be quiet tonight, and we should all have a bit of drink to raise our spirits.”

Chibbs grinned. “My father used to say a pint a day keeps the doctor at bay.”

Dominic rolled his eyes, a small smile curving his lips. But unlike his men, he would have no relief tonight. He headed below deck and lay down on his bed, staring at the ceiling. The moonlight poured in through the cabin window, and the sea beyond flashed and sparkled in a way that made him think of Roberta’s eyes.

Everything seemed to make him think of Roberta now. The wind and the sails sounded like her soft sighs, and the rocking seemed to remind him of the peace he had found when he held her in his arms.

He tensed but didn’t move as his cabin door suddenly opened and Roberta appeared.

“I have your rum, Captain.” She came over, holding two cups. She handed him one as he sat up in his bed.

“You ever drink rum, Robbie?” he asked.

She looked down at her feet, suddenly bashful.

“You haven’t, have you?” He chuckled as he took his cup and downed the sweet burning fire in one long gulp. Then he set the cup aside on the floor.

"I had it once, actually. When I was fifteen. A cabin boy on a ship my father was serving let me have a taste."

"And?" he asked quietly, giving her a chance to relax.

She came deeper into the cabin and closed the door. "It was not to my liking." Her nose wrinkled as she seemed to try to recall tasting the liquor. "Though I'm told the taste grows on you."

"Well, to your liking or not, drink up. It will make your back hurt less."

She raised her cup to her lips and then tilted it back fast, swallowing a few times. Then she covered her mouth with her hand and gagged.

"Oh, that's...even worse than I remembered." She spat and wiped her sleeve across her mouth in a boyish manner, and her face reddened as she realized he was watching her rather unladylike display. "I'm sorry, I—"

"Don't apologize. You don't have to like something simply because others do."

"I know, but I wanted to fit in with the rest of the crew."

"Robbie, never do something to fit in. When you have occasion to stand out among the crowd, that's something to be proud of."

"I'm sorry," she said again.

"Stop bloody apologizing," he growled and got to his feet. She stepped back and collided with the wall opposite his bed. She winced again. He caught her by her good arm and turned her to face the wall. Her breath quickened.

"What are you doing?" she demanded, fear coloring her tone.

"I want to be sure you are all right." Dominic tugged her shirt out of her breeches and lifted it up to expose her back. Thick straps of cloth bound her breasts and had offered some protection from the flogger, but he still saw pale-pink lines along her lower back.

He traced a line just above her breeches. She didn't make a sound, but she trembled. And her trembling sent a wild fire racing beneath his skin. There was nothing sweeter than having a woman who was so sensitive when it came to her own body. She wouldn't be like the others, ones who saw sex as a transaction or a means to an end. With Robbie, it would be an act to join her heart and soul to a man's. The mere thought of that terrified and thrilled him.

"Does it hurt?" he asked. "Should I fetch Dr. Maynard?" He tried to keep his thoughts chaste, but he was fast finding it impossible.

"I… No. Don't bother him. It's tender, that's all." She tried to slide away from him, but he wouldn't let her.

"Robbie, you tempt me. You make me forget…" He closed his eyes as he leaned in close, inhaling the scent of her. Sweet, light, and feminine, mixed with rosewater. Reese was right.

"Make you forget?" Her breathless reply flooded him with arousal and visions of pulling her beneath him on the bed. What he wouldn't give to taste the creamy swells of her breasts and listen to her soft cries of pleasure mixed with the hushing sound of waves lapping against the *Dragon*'s wooden hull.

"Yes..." He lowered his face to her neck as he let her shirt drop back down.

He pressed his lips against the groove where her shoulder met her neck. He was not driven by urgency now. He was ready to take all night, with her in his arms and in his bed. Touching her, holding her like this, their bodies pressed close, her back to his front... He felt at peace, as though he could take his time exploring her. A quiver of longing—not just of the body but of the heart—rippled through him. How could this small slip of a woman give him such comfort simply by being here in his cabin?

She turned around but didn't pull away. "What do you want to forget?" Her eyes were bright, so full of trust and desire that he couldn't help but speak of the darkness that haunted him.

"What I've done." He cupped her face, brushing his thumb over her cheek and her lips. She was so sweetly yielding that it created a deep ache in his bones. "I have done things, Robbie, terrible things." The confession hurt even as it escaped his lips. He hadn't even meant to say that to her. He couldn't stand the idea that she'd take his words and condemn him with them, when she didn't even know why he might have committed them.

"Terrible things were done to you, but that doesn't make you terrible," she answered back just as gently, her tone so full of compassion that it was like a knife to his heart.

"How could you know...?" He hated his gruffness, but she didn't flinch and didn't pull away.

"It's in your eyes. So much pain." She lifted one hand to his cheek and then to his neck, stroking her fingers along the central spot at the base of his skull. His body tensed with fresh hunger, but it was tempered with something sweeter.

"Please," he begged softly, sounding almost like a little lost boy. "Help me forget...even if only for a little while." He didn't want her pity, and thankfully he saw none of it in her eyes.

Roberta stood on tiptoes, curling her fingers into his collar and pulling him down for a kiss. He felt wrapped in invisible warmth the moment their lips met. His senses spun, and he clutched her, pushing her against the wall so he could feel the length of his body against hers. He wanted to trap her there, make sure that she belonged only to him. His heart hammered as he savored the rum he tasted in their shared kiss. Her closeness to him was drugging, like an entire bottle of the best spiced rum.

He explored the soft lushness of her mouth with his while his hands roamed over her, gentle and questing. Her bottom filled his palms, and he couldn't resist squeezing. She whimpered against his lips, whether from soreness from the flogging or the desire that flooded her he wasn't sure, but her hands delved into his hair and held him for a deeper kiss.

Her small tongue played with his, and he smiled against her lips in delight. The lady learned quickly. One minute she kissed him with reckless abandon, and the next her lips brushed him in a whispering sweetness. She was the master of him in that moment, owning him until he forgot all else.

You are like the sea, he thought. *Deep, fathomless, full of fury, and yet capable of such soothing peace. I could die happy in your arms.*

The words stayed in his mind, but as foolish as it would be, he hoped he might whisper them to her while she slept. He brushed a hand up under her shirt to touch the bindings at her breasts, wanting to strip her bare and feast upon the tender peaks. He'd bite them, nuzzle them, suck them until she was screaming for mercy and for more. But he couldn't do that, not yet. So instead, he showed her mouth how to play with his, how to let her tongue explore his mouth while his hands roamed roughly over her.

When they broke the kiss, their panting breaths mingled in the still, quiet air of the cabin. For a second neither of them spoke. They simply held on to one another, their foreheads touching. She cleared her throat, her hands dropped from his body, and he reluctantly let go of her.

"I think I should rest, and you should as well,

Captain." She stepped around him to take up her position on the floor of the cabin. She wasn't angry with him, but damned if her putting distance between them didn't feel like a slap across his cheek.

Without a word of protest or a sound of discomfort, she lay down to sleep. He clenched his jaw as he fought off the desire to lift her up into his arms and carry her to his bed. But if he did, neither of them would sleep. The old Dominic would not have cared, but something inside him had changed. Like a rusted blade cast deep in the fire of a blacksmith's forge, he was melting down and slowly being reshaped into something new, perhaps something better. It scared the hell out of him because he did not know what tomorrow would bring. But he knew one truth now.

It was not only Nicholas Flynn he would follow to the farthest horizon.

12

Roberta awoke to the joyous shouts of "Land, ho!" from the upper deck. She sat up from her makeshift bed on the floor and glanced at Dominic's bed. It was empty, and the sheets were a mess. She sighed and with a rueful chuckle started to fix the bed. The sheets were still warm, and the lingering hint of where his body had been made her own body hum in response.

Last night she had almost asked him to take her. It had been there on the tip of her tongue. She had tasted such pain, such hurt upon his lips and felt the strong pirate almost tremble as he kissed her like they would not live to see the dawn. The dark pools of his eyes had revealed some of the secrets he held. The cold, dominating captain she thought she knew had vanished, replaced by a man she wanted to understand. A man she could love. She saw a man being reborn, like a phoenix stirring from the ashes.

She *was* falling in love with him. But he was trapped, living the life of a marauder at sea with no way to escape. All she wanted was to help him, to find a way to bring him back to the life he had been born to lead. But he was a wanted man, and men like her father would see him hanged without a thought as to his past.

Roberta finished tidying the room before she left the cabin and headed up on deck. She joined Chibbs, who was gazing out at the sea over the railing.

"Ah, Robbie, lad. Take a look." Chibbs pointed a thick finger toward an island that was fast approaching.

"Tortuga?" she asked.

"Aye," he echoed with a grin. "The men will be happy to spend their coin and stretch their legs and visit their lady folk there."

"Oh? Their wives must have missed them." Roberta grinned.

Chibbs coughed, his gray beard barely concealing the sudden ruddiness of his skin. "Wives? Er...no, not wives."

Roberta's face flushed. "You mean ladies who are free to...I see." She stared back at the island. "Does the captain have a lady he visits?"

"Does he?" Chibbs chuckled. "Quite a few. He never has to pay them, either."

A bitter taste settled upon Roberta's tongue. She imagined Dominic finding pleasure in the arms of another woman. That was something she never wanted to think about.

"Aye, Cap'n is a favorite on the island, but with those eyes of his, I can't blame the lassies. They flock like birds to the dock the moment the *Dragon* is sighted. Rumor is they think bedding the captain will draw more of the crew to their cathouse, but I think it's because they all fancy him."

Roberta scowled as their ship sailed into Tortuga. She was still scowling as the ropes were cast down over the sides to tie the ship in the shallow waters. She continued to scowl even when she and Lucy climbed into the longboat to row to shore. Sure enough, a whole group of women in brightly colored low-bodiced dresses were there to greet them. Dominic leapt onto the dock and grinned as all the women surrounded him. More than one stole a kiss or two from him before another woman shoved her aside.

Roberta's face flamed as she stared down at her boots in fury. Flynn was at her side and nudged her with an elbow. She looked up at him from beneath her lashes, which were coated with foolish tears.

"You've gone and fallen for him, haven't you?" Flynn's tone was neither harsh nor judgmental. Rather, his face was full of pity, and somehow that made it all the worse.

"Makes little sense. I must have lost all rationality," she whispered as the crew around them climbed onto the dock. Dominic set the women aside with teasing remarks that he had missed them but feared he would not be able to see them today. Many of the women took other crew members by the arm to escort them to a brothel nearby.

"Dom's always made me forget good sense as well. Do not judge yourself too harshly."

She took Nicholas's arm, squeezing it lightly. "Are you free to leave now? Will he let you go?"

"I believe so. But I must still find a ship to take me to Port Royal." Nicholas climbed out of the longboat, but as he was about to assist Roberta, Dominic was there, offering her his arm. She let him help her out but pulled away a little when he tried to put an arm around her waist.

"Upset with me already, Robbie?" Dominic challenged, flashing her a rare grin.

"Upset? No," she scoffed and turned to walk away, but Dominic caught up with her. Nicholas remained a respectful distance behind.

"Then what, pray tell, has you all riled?"

She spun on him. "I don't know—ask the hoard of ladies who were here to greet you on the dock."

"Those wenches?" Dominic burst out laughing so hard that he clutched his stomach. "Oh, Robbie, you're jealous. I like this side of you." He slid an arm around her waist again, and she had trouble extricating herself from it. Dominic leaned in to whisper in her ear. "I'll not touch another woman so long as you want me. Does that satisfy you, my little hellcat?"

It did, damn him. She answered with a curt nod, and he gave her hip a playful squeeze before letting her go.

Roberta turned her attention to the pirate haven of Tortuga. There were crowds of men in the streets, dusty and uncouth, some prancing about in tattered blockade outfits with hats festooned with large feathers. So many of the men she saw seemed to be playing a pirate, the way children would dress up to play soldiers. But Dominic stood out, a tall, handsome man with brown eyes that turned sable when passion aroused him. He didn't wear anything fancy. His gold-and-black brocade vest was his only adornment today. He had a cutlass and a pistol tucked into his belt, and his long dark hair flowed freely down his shoulders. He exuded danger. But he wasn't the only one.

Flynn, in his rumpled and unwashed naval uniform, looked almost as lethal. There was a new coldness to his gaze as he followed Dominic. Flynn knew he was among his enemies, men who would slit his throat if he showed weakness. She was flanked on either side by angels, one light and one dark.

Dominic stopped at a tavern with a rusted sign that said *The Siren*. Roberta and Nicholas followed him inside.

"Stay close," Dominic said to them both.

He pushed the tavern doors open, where a chaotic scene of men and women wildly carousing made Roberta's eyes widen like saucers. Men sang songs about faraway shores, lost ladies, and treasure as they swished their cups in the air, ale and rum splashing onto the floor. A man on a small stage in the corner played a violin to a fast-paced tune.

Roberta winced at the stale smells of sweat and alcohol that mixed with the scent of animals in the streets. This was certainly not how she had envisioned a grand life at sea. She was not so silly as to imagine that pirating was a noble venture, but this was not what she'd expected. They stopped at the bar, where Dominic spoke quietly to a man as he cleaned a set of brown mugs.

"Not what you had in mind?" Nicholas asked as they watched the animated behavior in the tavern.

"No, not at all," she admitted. Disappointment weighed her down, but she hoped Nicholas couldn't see that. Perhaps she'd envisioned men gathered to discuss the articles of the Brethren, not carousing.

Nicholas's lips curved into a small unguarded grin, not unlike the smile Dominic had given her when he'd helped her up onto the dock.

"What was it like to lose him?" she asked. "Sorry, I shouldn't pry."

Nicholas's eyes, so full of pain, tore at her heart. He smiled again, but this time it was a smile built upon broken dreams and lost childhood. "There was a grief inside me so powerful it paralyzed me. I couldn't think, couldn't breathe. It was nothing but endless pain, which dulled with time but never vanished." His expression changed to one of joy and despair. "And then I saw him on the deck of the *Fortune*."

"You love him," Roberta said softly.

He nodded. "He was a brother to me, a brother lost and now found. I let myself freeze in place all these years." He shook his head ruefully. "There was a woman once, one I could not have married without my brother at my side. I just felt unable to go on, to find joy."

"And now? Could you go back to her?"

Nicholas shook his head again. "I would, but she married another." They were quiet then for a long moment, the sounds of the tavern washing over them. "I know you have feelings for Dominic, but I urge you to be cautious. Where he goes now, only heartache will follow."

"I wish I could pretend that I didn't understand, but I do. He's gotten under my skin, and I can't..."

Nicholas chuckled. "You don't have to explain it to me. Just take care."

"I will," Roberta promised as Dominic returned to them.

"Flynn, there's a ship by the name of *India's Pride* at the far end of the port. It is headed to Port Royal and leaves at first light." Roberta watched the silent exchange that occurred between two men who'd been not only friends once but almost brothers.

"Dom," Nicholas whispered, the name full of agony, which made Roberta's eyes burn with tears.

"You should go, Nick. The captain will likely let you

board early." Dom held out his hand and Nicholas took it, which made both men seem for a moment like young boys again and the years that had passed between them vanished.

"You haven't changed. You're still the boy I knew." Nicholas's eyes were bright as he spoke the words that Roberta sensed Dominic needed to hear far more than he realized.

"As are you," Dominic replied. Then his gaze slid to Roberta. "And I've not forgotten my promise to you, Robbie. You have a choice now. Stay with me...or go with Flynn."

Roberta hadn't wanted to face this choice, not so soon. But it wasn't really a choice. She could have no life on the run with Dominic. The silly girlish infatuation she had for him would fade one day, it had to, and when it did, she would regret that she had no home to return to. She had to find her father in Port Royal and make the best of whatever life might cast her way.

"I...must go with Nicholas. M—my father..." She choked on the words.

Dominic gazed at her, acute misery so clear for a moment before he buried it with a smile.

"The ship doesn't leave until dawn. Stay and celebrate with the men here tonight." He waved at the boisterous rabble of the *Dragon*'s crew, who'd settled inside the tavern and were now singing a song about a wench from Wales who had a favorite sailor on every ship.

"Stay," Dominic pleaded softly. "Just the night. Drink with me, dance with me." He nodded toward a wooden platform where a few women were dancing a jig, to the delight of the sailors watching.

"You have time, Roberta," Flynn whispered. "I'll stay and wait until just before dawn, and we'll head to the ship together."

Roberta hugged Flynn and whispered back, "Thank you." Then she turned to Dominic and nodded.

"My lady," he teased and offered his arm as they took a table near the stage. A woman with a low-cut bodice and attractive features and unnaturally red hair paused at their table.

"Anything to drink, my love?" she asked Roberta and winked at her.

Roberta blinked. "Er..."

Dominic laughed. "We'll take a bottle of your stoutest rum."

"Of course," the woman purred, still focused on Roberta.

"What the devil is wrong with her?" she muttered as the waitress finally left them alone.

"I think she's wanting you to bed her."

"What?"

Dominic burst out laughing. "Robbie, love, you make a very fine-looking young man. Many of the wenches here would happily take you to bed, but they'd be sadly surprised to find that you are in fact *not* a man."

"Oh!" Roberta's face flamed with mortification. "Do I really look that...manly?" She almost choked on the word. She'd almost forgotten that she was supposed to be masquerading as a cabin boy. She'd settled into ship life so easily that she'd forgotten she was acting the part of a man.

Dominic snorted. "Not in the slightest. You look far too delicate and feminine. Some women like that, is all. You're a fresh, sweet face compared to the smelly, unkempt louts in the room."

She couldn't disagree with that.

When the woman returned with a bottle of rum and some glasses, Roberta accepted her glass once Dominic poured it because, despite her dislike for rum, she desperately wanted something to calm her nerves. This was her last night with Dominic, the last night that she would truly be free.

"Easy there," Dominic warned as she drained the pint.

"May we dance?" she asked, deciding that she did indeed want to frolic about the room. She'd never get another chance after tonight.

Dominic escorted her to the platform and tossed a few coins to the man holding the violin.

"Play us a jig!" he called out.

The man grinned and nodded, testing out a few notes on his violin before he began. The tune was light and fast paced. Roberta couldn't help but smile as Dominic started to dance. Her heart sang with delight as the dark, handsome pirate transformed before her eyes. He moved his feet swift and sure as he danced for her, and the crowds cheered, clapping to the beat each time he struck up a steady rhythm upon the wooden boards.

Roberta was amazed. Dominic laughed, the carefree sound seeming both foreign and completely natural to him. And then she was spinning as he caught her by the waist and dragged her into the dance with him.

They didn't speak, they only laughed and smiled as they whirled around and around, their feet moving in time together while the musician continued to play. Never in her life had Roberta ever felt like this, as though the night would never end and the hour hands upon the clock had ceased to move. She was caught in a spell, dizzy with her own joy.

"Nick, come join us!" Dominic shouted at his friend.

Nicholas finished his glass of rum and came up on stage. Roberta moved back a little as the two men squared off, as though they meant to fight, but then suddenly, Nicholas began to dance, fast, hard, his feet moving wildly. He paused, breathing slightly harder than before as Dominic started to dance back. It was clear that the two men were competing as they each copied the other before adding on a new move. Roberta giggled as their moves became more and more complex, until both men finally had to stop, their faces red and their wide grins perfect mirrors of one another.

"Nick, you can still dance better than I ever could." Dominic slapped Nicholas's back.

"Unlike you, I actually paid attention in our dance lessons. Remember when you put the toads in the ballroom to avoid dancing? The maids were chasing those down for a week."

Dominic chuckled, but there was a bittersweet look to him now as he gazed at Roberta and held out his hand. She reacted without thinking and put her hand in his. The violinist began a slow, sweet tune, and Nicholas began singing from somewhere behind them.

Fare thee well, my lovely Dinah,
A thousand times adieu.
We are bound away from the Holy Ground
And the girls we love so true.
We'll sail the salt seas over
And we'll return once more,
And still I live in hope to see
The Holy Ground once more.
You're still the girl that I adore,
And still I live in hope to see
The Holy Ground once more.

As Nicholas sang, his deep, melodic voice carried across the tavern, and as Roberta and Dominic danced, she saw many a man wipe a tear from his dirt-stained cheeks.

Now when we're out a-sailing
And you are far behind
Fine letters will I write to you
With the secrets of my mind,
The secrets of my mind, my girl,
You're the girl that I adore,
And still I live in hope to see
The Holy Ground once more.

Dominic pulled her body in close to his in a way that was less dancing and more swaying. The intimate hold of his body around hers sent her heart skittering madly. It was foolish to be dancing like this while she pretended to be a boy, but Dominic didn't seem to care. He started humming and then joined in with Nicholas, and the harmonies of their two voices sent her to a secret heaven.

Oh now the storm is raging
And we are far from shore;
The poor old ship she's sinking fast
And the riggings they are tore.
The night is dark and dreary,
We can scarcely see the moon,
But still I live in hope to see
The Holy Ground once more.

His lips brushed Roberta's ear as he nuzzled her temple, and she inhaled his scent, losing herself in the feel of his tall, warm body against hers. She'd never thought she'd been alone or even lonely until this man held her. She realized then what she'd been longing for, this other piece of something deep inside. Her other half. This man, this renegade was a mate to her own soul. She clung to him tightly as he and Nicholas finished the song.

It's now the storm is over
And we are safe on shore
We'll drink a toast to the Holy Ground
And the girls that we adore.
We'll drink strong ale and porter
And we'll make the taproom roar,
And when our money is all spent
We'll go to sea once more.
You're girl that I adore,
And still I live in hope to see
The Holy Ground once more.

Dominic drew back from her, and she wiped away a tear. She tried to smile up at him.

"You all right, love?" he asked.

She answered with a jerky nod. "I...know I must leave tomorrow at first light, but I don't wish to leave you," she whispered. His soft, sweet chuckle only made her heart ache worse.

"And I'm just enough of a gentleman still to let you go." He sighed, closing his eyes for a second, and then he stared down at her, a sudden heat in his gaze. In his eyes was a question that she knew the answer to.

"Yes," she said.

He tilted his head slightly. "Yes?"

"Yes." She twined her fingers in his hand and gave a gentle squeeze. He knew what she was asking now, and she wanted it, wanted *him*.

"Nicholas..." Roberta turned to face the handsome lieutenant.

"I'll be here, waiting for you," he promised them. His smile was a melancholy echo of her own as he seated himself at a table to listen to the violinist play another tune.

Tonight was a night of goodbyes, and she wasn't going to waste another second of what little time she had left with Dominic.

✠ 13 ✠

Dominic took her elbow in his palm and guided her up the stairs to a hall of bedrooms. He chose a room at random and opened the door. It was empty. He ushered her inside, then shut the door and leaned back against it.

"I don't want to leave you," Roberta said. She faced him bravely, despite the rending of her heart.

"But you will. And you should." Dominic's large frame should have been imposing, but she wanted nothing more than to curl up against him and hold him close. How had this man become so important to her in the last few days?

"Let us make this a night to remember for the rest of our lives." His tone was rough with emotion, and she trembled as she came to him. Misery so acute welled up in her that it stole her breath as she threw herself into his arms.

Their mouths met in desperate hunger, each moment searing like summer lightning strikes and calm skies. Dominic gathered her against him, his warm breath fanning her face as he brushed tears from her cheeks. She sank into him, opening her mouth for him, her tongue playing with his as a slow heat built within her. This man awakened something inside her, and for an instant she saw herself standing on the edge of a cliff, holding her breath.

"Please, Dominic, show me what you promised. If I could have you but once..." She buried her face against his throat, still kissing him.

He chuckled, but the sound was raw. "Just once? Robbie, you don't know what you're asking."

She pulled away and stared at him. "But I do. If I have to live the rest of my life without you, I want this one memory to cling to. *Please*."

He closed his eyes and sighed. When his eyes opened, there was a piratical gleam to them. He moved fast, pulling at her clothes and his. She toppled back onto the small bed, and he was on top of her, kissing her with a savage need that made wetness pool between her thighs.

His lips, teeth, and tongue explored her body with kisses and gentle nibbles. He bared her breasts, nuzzled and kneaded them. She moaned as he sucked one tender peak and then the other. She dropped her hand and dragged her fingers through his hair, clutching his head to her breasts as he tortured her with such fiery sweetness that she thought she would die. He ravished her mouth again before moving down her body. Dominic flicked his tongue along her belly and spread her thighs, bracing his shoulders against her legs to keep her open. She blushed wildly as he gazed at her.

"You are beautiful, Robbie, the most beautiful woman I have ever seen." He lowered his mouth to her folds, and she clasped the sheets as his tongue licked against the most sensitive part of her. She whimpered and bit her lip as he sucked at the small bud of pleasure on her mound. Waves of ecstasy began to build, each new one crushing against the last, tossing her about in a storm of pleasure.

Dominic moved up her body and settled in the cradle of her thighs. He nuzzled her nose with his as he whispered a sweet apology. Before she could ask him why, she felt him shift above her and thrust into her. She cried out at the searing pain and wrapped her arms around his neck, holding on to him as the pain slowly ebbed.

"Kiss me, love," he moaned, and their mouths crashed together in another violent kiss. His lips demanded that she forget the pain, and when he started to move again she did. All she could think about was the feel of him surging in and out of her, like the sea and the shore playing with each other without end.

Tears escaped her eyes as she gazed up at his face. She had never imagined she would feel like this, like the world was only in this room, only between them. Her breasts rubbed against his chest and their breaths mingled together, and Roberta knew she would never want anyone else the way she wanted him. She cupped his face, stroking the dark beard along his jaw, and she couldn't help but wonder what he would look like if he were clean-shaven. He would look so different that he'd be another man, but he would still belong to her.

Dominic rolled his hips over and over, his thrusts deepening, and she cried out as the pleasure grew until it was too great. She gasped as her entire body flooded with a shivering, pulsating ecstasy. Was she dying? It felt like she was.

"Dom." She whimpered his name, and a second later he shouted hers back—Roberta, not Robbie—and then he collapsed on top of her. Their bodies melted in a tangle of sweat-soaked limbs. They were silent a long while, simply holding one another as they slept lightly, waking only to make love again and again. A few hours later, Dom cleared his throat. She could sense the hours passing too quickly. Their time together wasn't going to be enough.

"We cannot delay any longer. Dawn will be here soon. You, Nick, and Lucy need to reach the ship before it leaves." He extricated himself from her arms, and she already missed him. But she didn't speak as she donned her clothes. Then they headed back downstairs. Nicholas was leaning against the bar, but he straightened as he saw them. His eyes took in their rumpled appearance, but he said nothing.

"Take care of her for me, Nick," Dominic said quietly, his eyes distant.

Roberta's lip trembled, but she dared not say anything for fear of making this parting worse.

Suddenly the tavern doors burst open, and a group of men entered. The entire tavern went still.

"Well, Captain Grey, we meet again. And so soon! I thought you were destined for Port Royal." The familiar French voice of Andre La Roux burned through Roberta's insides.

Dominic tensed and spoke softly to Nicholas. "Get Robbie out of here and don't look back."

Nicholas didn't move. "Dominic, we can't leave. You need help to fight him."

He shook his head. "I need to know you're both safe."

Roberta bit her lip, knowing that if she dared speak, she would only say something foolish.

Nicholas cast a glance toward La Roux. "You can't face him alone. I have to stay."

"Nick, you made a vow once. Do not break it now."

"A vow to *stay* with you," Nicholas growled.

"To the farthest horizon," Dominic said. He looked upon Roberta, his tone suddenly gentle. "She's my farthest horizon now. Protect her, Nick."

Nicholas's face paled, and he nodded to his old friend. Before Roberta could protest, Nicholas grabbed her by the waist and ran. A second later, the tavern erupted in chaos. Pistols cracked, men shouted, and women scrambled for cover, screaming.

Roberta had but one chance to look back before she

and Nicholas escaped out a back door. Dominic had his cutlass out and his pistol aimed at La Roux. One or both would die tonight, and she couldn't bear the thought of losing Dom.

Nicholas didn't let her stay to see the bloody end—he spared her that fate. But her heart broke apart like a ship upon a reef during a hurricane. She would never recover, never survive this night.

DOMINIC LAUGHED AS HE FOUGHT, A STRANGE WILDNESS to his movements, making him more deadly than ever. The second he saw La Roux enter the tavern, he had known now was the time to finish this fight. He would force La Roux into it if he had to. The distance they had kept from each other after Dominic had killed Andre's brother had finally come to an end, and in a way he was glad. La Roux would haunt him no longer after tonight.

"La Roux!" He bellowed the name so fiercely that the roof timbers of the tavern shook.

Eyes still fixed on Dominic, Andre stabbed the pirate nearest to him. It was one of Dominic's crew, but he wasn't sure Andre cared either way. The man's limp body fell to the ground. All around them, men were fighting, the clang of sabers, cutlasses, and knives ringing like discordant bells.

"Captain!" Reese vaulted over one of the nearest tables

to join Dominic as he pressed through the melee. Reese protected his back as Dominic headed for La Roux.

The French pirate was merciless, now wielding two blades in his hands, a short sword in one and a cutlass in the other. Anyone in his path was parried, countered, and quickly cut down. Chibbs was battling with two men from La Roux's crew, and La Roux headed straight for him.

"Chibbs! Duck!" Dominic shouted.

His bosun heard the warning in time and dropped to his knees a mere second before La Roux would have skewered him from behind. Chibbs rolled into a somersault beneath the nearest table and slashed at the knees of the two men closest to him.

"You want me, La Roux?" Dominic shouted. "Come and get me!"

Andre's dark eyes flashed with fire as he headed for Dominic.

Reese now joined the fight, trying to get close to La Roux.

"Where's Luke?" Dominic called out.

Reese had been watching over the young lady's maid since early that evening. "Safe at the *India's Pride*. Where's Robbie?"

"On her way with Flynn." Dominic didn't want to think about Roberta. Right now, he needed to be a cold, heartless pirate. It was the only way he could end this.

Men scrambled out of the way as Dominic and La Roux got within a sword's reach of one another. Andre's eyes were full of fire, and the faded red waistcoat he wore was splattered with the blood of his men, his long hair still pulled back immaculately and tied with a black ribbon. He looked too much like Gerard, too much like the man who had robbed Dominic of his innocence and stolen his future by forcing him into piracy.

Andre and Dominic circled each other, each man wielding a blade. Dominic moved with practiced ease, almost dancing as he lunged toward Andre, but Andre had the flair of a dancer as well and parried and thrust back. Neither man spoke at first, the heat of the battle too intense between them for words. But when La Roux finally taunted him, his words turned Dominic's blood to ice.

"Pretty little cabin boy you had with you. I knew my brother chose well in you. It seems you have the same tastes in pleasure."

Dominic snarled as he countered La Roux's thrust. "Your brother was a madman and a cruel bastard." He swung his sword wildly at Andre, trying to force him back.

"You speak ill of him even after everything he gave you? And then you murdered him? I know what a sniveling little coward you are, Dominic Grey. I remember how you cried for your dear mama every night."

A red haze descended over Dominic's vision as he dove at Andre. Andre moved fast, expecting his move, slicing Dominic's left arm. Dominic was still in motion, the pain momentarily ignored as he spun and swung his blade. He caught Andre in the side. The man stumbled back, clutching the light wound, but a smile was still on his face.

"You forgot to mention while dining the other night that you were host to an English admiral's daughter. I stole a glance at the *Fortune*'s manifest during dinner. There were two female passengers listed." La Roux was still smiling. "She wasn't on the longboats. We saw the men from our spyglasses as they headed to Port Royal. That means you kept her on board...dressed as a cabin boy, *perhaps*?"

Dominic said nothing as he lunched for Andre, but the man raised his sword, deflecting the blow.

"'Twould be a damned shame if some harm befell the pretty creature, wouldn't it? Accidents do tend to follow those you love."

"I will slit your throat from ear to bloody ear!" Dominic charged him again, this time less watchful, and he almost missed the glint of triumph in Andre's eyes.

"Dom, behind you!" Reese shouted.

Dominic whirled in time to block what would have been a deadly blow from one of La Roux's crew. He forced the man's arm back and stabbed him with his cutlass, causing him to clutch his belly and fall over. When Dominic turned back to face Andre, there was no sign of him. Andre's sudden disappearance sent his men scurrying out of the tavern and into the night.

Reese rushed to Dominic's side. "Captain..."

"I'm all right, Reese. Get our men back on board now.

He knows about Robbie. We have to make sure she's safe." He'd wanted to kill La Roux, but he'd lost the chance.

"But that means..."

"The one port full of English ships currently hunting for us. Port Royal."

14

Roberta joined Nicholas on the gangplank leading down from the *India's Pride* at the docks of Port Royal. They'd been surprisingly silent for most of the journey. Neither of them had felt like speaking after leaving Dominic behind.

"You'll be glad to see your father," Nicholas said, trying to start a conversation.

"I will," she agreed, but her heart was still broken. "What if..." She halted, turning to face Nicholas. "What if he is gone?"

The pain that showed on his face echoed her own.

"You mustn't think about that. Dom's a cat with nine lives. But we'll likely never see him again, and that's for the best. He's at risk if he comes too close to a place like this. Better that he slip away to some small port and remain safe."

They both started down the slatted wooden walkway. Halfway down, the men waiting on the dock jerked to attention at the sight of Nicholas in his rumpled uniform. Roberta recognized the men from the *Fortune*.

"Lieutenant Flynn!" one young midshipman called out. He rushed over to them, followed by the others.

"How are you, Charlie?" Nicholas looked over the crew. "How did you all fare after the *Fortune* was sunk?"

"Well enough. The captain was upset to lose his ship, to say the least." Charlie's face reddened. "Did you find Miss Harcourt and her maid? The captain and the rear admiral have been sending out sloops to look for the pirates."

Roberta spoke up. "I'm here." Lucy came behind her on the gangplank, also wearing her cabin boy clothes.

"Miss Harcourt!" The midshipman blushed and bowed low. "We must notify your father at once." He raced away with the exuberance of a young puppy, and for a moment she and Nicholas shared a smile. Nicholas offered her his arm and led her onto the docks. Within a few minutes, Charlie returned, an elegant carriage following behind. When it rolled to a stop, her father came out, frantically searching for her.

"Roberta!"

Seeing her father after so many days broke the last bit of her resolve to stay strong. She ran to him, throwing herself into his embrace. He stroked her hair, comforting her.

"There, there, my dear, dry your eyes."

Roberta held on to him, inhaling the strong scent of tobacco. She slowly pulled back to look at him. "Are you hurt? I heard—"

"I'm fine, my dear. I was wounded during the battle, but it is all healed now." He pointed to a scab on his brow, but his eyes were dark with concern. "Roberta, what happened? Are you well, my dear? Do we need to fetch a doctor? When I learned you were still on board with those pirates, I was so afraid they would..." Her father swallowed hard.

She didn't want to lie to him, so she altered the truth as best she could. "Lucy and I posed as cabin boys. They let Lieutenant Flynn and me go when we were able to get passage on the *India's Pride*."

Her father cupped her face, brushing the tears from her eyes. "You can tell me anything, you know that, don't you?" He stroked her hair again, and Roberta swallowed the lump in her throat.

"I know, Papa. I'm fine, truly. You mustn't worry about me."

A wry chuckle escaped him. "A man who has a daughter always worries. It's the nature of fatherhood, a divine duty to be forever worried." He kissed the top of her head, and she embraced him again.

Her father called out to Nicholas. "Lieutenant."

Nicholas, who had been keeping a polite distance during the reunion, now approached.

"How did you fare with the pirates?" her father asked.

"I'm no worse for wear. I was imprisoned in the brig most of the voyage."

"Where did they release you? We may be able to catch them." Roberta's father's eyes grew hard with the need for vengeance. Roberta's stomach turned at the thought of him sending men to capture and hang Dominic and the crew of the *Dragon*.

"They left us at Tortuga, but it is no use to chase them. They are long gone by now. They were headed north to the colonies."

"Ah..." Her father pursed his lips. "Well, perhaps they'll be foolish enough to come back to the West Indies."

"I very much doubt it. I overheard the captain was most interested in sailing north as far as Boston."

"Blast. I wish I could see the man dance on the gallows. Did you learn his name? I never heard. I confess, I was in a fair amount of pain while we were being put onto the longboat."

Nicholas glanced only an instant at Roberta before replying smoothly. "It was Fernando Montez, I believe, a Spanish fellow. But he goes by the surname Grey." If Roberta hadn't spent time aboard the *Dragon*, she might have actually believed Flynn's lie.

"Montez, eh? I'll make a note of it." Her father cleared his throat. "Now, you both must be exhausted. I have secured lodging with a good man here. He was away on business until this morning, but when he heard of what happened to the *Fortune* and that I was living in a hotel by the docks, he sent word for me to stay at his home. The estate I planned to acquire isn't ready for us to move in as of yet. So I took my new friend up on his offer. He's a tea planter, nice fellow by the name of Aaron King. His plantation, King's Landing, is extensive, and the house is magnificent. The Crown is indebted to him for all that he's done for us. Come, we'll take his coach back."

Exhausted and heartbroken, Roberta followed them to the carriage. The carriage had lovely black velvet cushions and gold French tassels hanging down from the curtains. Understated elegance that spoke clearly of money. But that was no surprise. The islands were full of rich merchants who'd built fortunes on tobacco and tea. Fortunes often created upon the backs of slave labor. Roberta's stomach turned as she wondered what sort of man King was to live luxuriously at the expense of others.

A pretty pair of white horses pulled the coach, with black manes and tails. If she had to guess, they might even be Arabians. Roberta suspected he was the exact sort of man that her father would wish her to marry. The thought soured her stomach. She did not want to be paraded around for any other man. She wanted Dominic and no one else.

"How is Captain Huntington?" Nicholas asked her father.

"Well enough, but by the devil, that man has a temper." Her father looked away, his brows drawn together. "I misjudged the man, Roberta. You were quite right to refuse him. He complained most of the way to Port Royal. I think a few of the midshipmen considered mutiny at one point. He's a selfish man if I ever met one."

"As much as I don't wish to speak ill of any man, I will agree that he is more of a fair-weather officer," Nicholas added carefully.

Her father harrumphed in agreement, taking no offense at the remark.

Roberta looked out the carriage window, barely listening to Nicholas and her father talk. Instead, she took in the streets and the colorful flowers overflowing in the window boxes of the nicer residences they passed. The humid air was thick with the smell of the ocean and a host of other exotic scents she had never smelled before, part floral, part fruity in nature. Brightly feathered birds occupied the branches of tall willowy trees as the carriage turned up the lane to pass through two white pillars that marked the entrance to King's Landing.

Roberta steeled herself for meeting the tea planter and tried to push away all thoughts of Dominic. But the moment she closed her eyes, all she could see was him, all she could feel was his hands on her body, his lips on her skin, and the sensation of the two of them tangled together.

I will never forget you, Dominic, or one moment of what happened between us. Wherever you are, I hope you won't forget me.

The coach rolled to a stop, and she climbed out with the assistance of a servant. For the first time in days, she felt out of place wearing the clothes of a man.

The butler met them at the base of the stairs to the grand manor house. "Welcome to King's Landing." Roberta blushed as the butler stared a moment too long at her clothing before he cleared his throat. "The master's attending to business just now but would like to see you in a few hours for dinner."

Roberta and Lucy were shown into a lavish bedroom on the second floor. A dark mahogany four-poster with pale-blue and cream silk curtains paired well with the champagne-colored chairs and couch by the fireplace. Roberta couldn't imagine ever being cold enough here to need a fireplace, but the elegance of the room was undeniable.

"Why don't you rest while I have a bath drawn?" Lucy offered gently. "It would give me a chance to change out of these clothes."

"Yes...I could do with a bit of rest." Roberta crawled onto the bed, still wearing her filthy boyish rags as sleep claimed her.

She was awakened gently an hour later by Lucy announcing the bath was ready. She led Roberta to an adjoining room where a large copper tub was steaming in the corner. Roberta stripped out of her clothes and climbed into the tub with a weary sigh. The hot water felt good on her skin and her aching muscles. The last few days aboard Dominic's ship had pushed her to her physical limits, using muscles she hadn't even known she possessed. Lucy collected the clothes Roberta had dropped onto the floor and then put them away to be washed.

Roberta tucked her knees up under her chin and sat in the hot water until it began to cool. The weight of the last few days finally seemed to be settling in past the shock, and she couldn't stop the silent sobs that shook her hard enough to leave her body aching. Finally, she wiped away slowly falling tears before she climbed out of the tub. Lucy held out a red robe of soft cotton, which she wrapped around Roberta.

"Mr. King had some clothing delivered for you from one of the modistes in Port Royal."

"Oh?" Roberta let Lucy dress her and fix her hair. The *robe à la française* was brocaded with lovely rich gold and midnight blue colors. She admired the coral pattern sewn into the stomacher. It made her think of all the trunks of her clothes that were still in the belly of the *Emerald Dragon*. She gazed at the fine gown in the tall mirror nearby the bed and felt empty in a way she'd never felt before.

Brushing her hands over the skirts, watching the fine embroidery shimmer and the way the gown billowed out over the pannier hoops on her hips, she looked ready to attend the French court. Such a thing in the past would have delighted her, but now she longed for the freedom of breeches and the wind blowing against her face as she moved about the deck of a ship.

A cool breeze teased the filmy white curtains of the veranda doors, catching her attention. She walked out onto the balcony of her room and stared at the sunset. The gold light seemed to illuminate everything in its path, even her. She leaned against the white painted railing and caught a glimpse of the gardens below.

Nicholas stood alone, not fifteen feet below her, his legs braced slightly apart, his hands behind his back in the military position she had seen so often while they had voyaged together. His gaze, like hers, was fixed on the sunset over the farthest edge of the island.

In that moment she and Nicholas mourned Dominic, each in their own way. Not knowing his fate was the worst of it. She would never know if he was dead or if he was just within sailing distance but forever out of reach.

Lucy interrupted Roberta's grim ruminations. "My lady, it's time for dinner. I just heard the gong."

Roberta turned away from the veranda and allowed Lucy to put a pearl bracelet on her wrist and a matching choker around her neck.

She touched the pearls, which warmed on her skin just above her collarbone. They weren't hers. "Whose are these?"

"They're a welcome gift from Mr. King. I've heard the servants say he's anxious to meet you. He has never had a lady come to stay with him before. He's a confirmed bachelor, or so they thought, but now that you're here, his staff is hoping you might find him amiable."

Roberta placed a hand over her stomach, a sudden knot of anxiety making her sick.

"Lucy, I don't think I can go to dinner." Just then she heard laughter in the hall, deep, rich male laughter. It reminded her how much she'd liked to hear Dominic laugh and how she hadn't heard that sound nearly enough. Was she doomed to long for Dominic in even the smallest ways now that she had lost him?

"Go on down and have a good dinner. It will make you feel better." Lucy nudged her out of the bedchamber and closed the door behind her, preventing her from retreating back into the room.

She walked down the carpeted hall to the top of the stairs. A servant was lighting lamps in the hall, and he bowed respectfully as she passed by. She started down the stairs, lifting her skirts with one hand, and her other hand held her steady on the gleaming wooden banister as she summoned the courage to face Mr. King and whoever else would be at dinner. Two men stood at the base of the stairs. One was her father, the other a tall well-built man with his back to her. The confirmed bachelor Mr. King, no doubt. At least he had excellent taste in gowns.

Her father said something to the man, who threw his head back and laughed again. She was halfway down the stairs when her father called up to her.

"Ah, Roberta, come down to meet our benefactor."

The man in front of her turned around, and Roberta's heart stopped. Dark sable eyes met hers, and sensual lips curved up into a grin. A typical gentleman, and yet so... No, it wasn't possible. Roberta's head spun, and before she knew what was happening, she began to fall.

"I've got you." Strong arms banded around her, and she was eased the rest of the way down the stairs by the dark-haired stranger who looked like...

But it couldn't be. Surely not.

His hair was short and pulled back into a queue at the nape of his neck, bound with a black ribbon. He was clean-shaven, no rugged beard or mustache, and no unruly black hair. This man had all the appearance of a gentleman, but...

She inhaled deeply as he set her carefully on her feet. That dark, exotic scent that was uniquely Dominic's was there, buried beneath a light layer of French cologne.

She raised her eyes to his, her hands clutching at his chest and neck as she tried to make sense of what she was seeing. Dominic was here in Port Royal. But he did not look like the pirate she'd come to love. Yet he was no less handsome, no less dangerously attractive to her. He was a stranger with familiar eyes.

"It's a pleasure to meet you, Miss Harcourt," Dominic greeted gently. "Your father speaks highly of you." All traces of the hardened pirate were gone, except for the lingering hold of his arms as he let go of her.

"I'm so sorry. I must have taken a bad step. Thank you. You are...?"

"Mr. King," Dominic replied. "Aaron King."

Aaron, like his father back in England. Roberta made the connection and regained most of her breath as she leaned on the banister for support. Somehow he had made it here before her, escaped or defeated Andre La Roux and the fiends of the *Red Lady*.

"It's a pleasure to meet you as well, Mr. King." She gave Dominic a slow nod. He winked at her when her father turned to greet Nicholas.

"Lieutenant Flynn, come and meet our host."

Nicholas, wearing a freshly pressed officer's uniform, strode into the hall but halted at the sight of Dominic. The color drained from his face for an instant before he recovered himself and shook Dominic's offered hand.

"Lieutenant Flynn, is it?" Dominic asked politely, as though they'd never met before.

"Pleasure," Nicholas replied. Concern clouded his stormy blue eyes, and she could understand why. What game was Dominic playing? How could he put his life at risk like this? Surely her father and Huntington would recognize him. But perhaps they would be lucky and the memory of a man they'd seen for only a few minutes on a ship days ago would not be strong enough for either of the two men to remember.

"Shall we adjourn to dinner?" Dominic offered his arm

to Roberta, leading her ahead of her father and Nicholas into the dining room.

Her father was momentarily distracted by Nicholas, and Dominic took the opportunity to whisper in her ear as he helped her into her seat. "I will come to you tonight." His lips brushed her cheek, unseen by her father, and then he moved to sit at the head of the fine rosewood table.

Mr. Lee, the *Dragon*'s cook, now came into the dining room dressed in fine clothes as he delivered dishes along with Griffin. Griffin saw her and winked, which got a disapproving scowl from Dominic.

"Thank you again for letting us stay with you, Mr. King. England is in your debt. I must admit, these are far better accommodations than the hotel by the docks."

"You are quite welcome. I'm sorry not to have been here when you first arrived. My business has kept me detained." Dominic sipped his wine, and Roberta remained quiet, studying the transformation of him from pirate to aristocrat.

It was astonishing. He had cut and styled his hair according to the current fashion and without the beard and mustache. He looked younger, more boyish, though the firm, masculine cut of his features did not lend him any feminine traits. It was possible he was more attractive now than ever, but the ferocity that belonged to him was still there, hidden in the curve of his smile and the glint of danger in his eyes.

"How long have you lived in Port Royal?" Nicholas asked. The seemingly innocent question was full of silent demand.

"Ten years. I landed here when I was eighteen. I worked my way up from a penniless lad to a tea merchant. I bought this land when I turned twenty-three and have built my home and business here." Dominic leaned back in his chair as the second course was served, lobster bisque and quail. Lee and Griffin set the plates down and left. Roberta wondered how many others of the *Dragon*'s crew worked here at King's Landing. Perhaps he didn't employ slaves as she'd feared. The Dominic she'd come to love took pleasure in hunting down slaver ships and setting men free.

"That sounds lucrative," Roberta added, quietly challenging him to speak the truth. Why hadn't he told her of this place? Why hadn't he mentioned he might come here? More importantly, she wanted to know why Dominic had continued to pirate all these years after finding work in an honest trade. If he left pirating, they could be together, couldn't they?

"Tea can indeed be lucrative, so long as one has the necessary financial backing."

He must have used his gains from piracy to establish his tea trade. And yet he clearly refused to leave his pirating behind. Did she matter so little to him that she wasn't worth telling about this secret life of his?

"I assume now you stand on firm ground, with the tea

trade?" She pushed the question at him, making it sound innocent, but she saw him raise one dark brow.

"I do, but it can be a tedious endeavor, so I often find other things to entertain me."

His words felt like a slap. Was she just a dalliance to entertain him or just another tedious endeavor? Not wanting to know the answer, Roberta cast her gaze down at her food.

"Mr. King, I understand you have the ear of the governor in Kingston?" her father asked.

"I do," Dominic replied.

"I should like to arrange a meeting with him about the matter of pirates. They are hunting these fine waters far too much." Thankfully, her father seemed oblivious to the tensions present at the table.

"I would be happy to arrange that."

"Excellent." Her father tucked into his food, unaware of Roberta and Nicholas's silence.

The moment the meal was over, Roberta returned to her room, while the men stayed and drank port and smoked cigars. The sweet scent of the smoke lingered in the hall outside as Roberta paced in her bedchamber, wondering when Dominic would come to her and what on earth she would say to the man who had just broken her heart.

15

The smoke of the cigars drifted lazily in the air as Rear Admiral Harcourt bid good night to Dominic and Nicholas.

Once they were alone, Dominic puffed on his cigar, then released a breath, forming a smoke circle that traversed the space between him and his old friend, until it grew so large it seemed to frame Nicholas's head.

Nicholas leaned forward in his chair, his eyes intense. Doves from outside the open windows cooed, and the cries of Jamaican monkeys could be heard from deep in the jungle beyond the windows. Dominic finally allowed himself to relax. He'd been worried about his reunion with Roberta and Nicholas and how they might react. Had they accidentally betrayed his identity, he could have ended up on the wrong end of a hangman's noose.

"Happy to see me?" he said to Nicholas.

"How the bloody hell did you end up here? What about La Roux? How did you manage this charade?" Nicholas waved a hand around at their opulent surroundings.

Dominic chuckled and snubbed his cigar in a nearby tray and got to his feet. "This is no charade," he answered. "Not in the way you mean it. I truly do own this place. I bought the land as I said, and I built this place—every brick, every beam of wood—with my own hands. The crew of my ship helped me. I employ every man and woman on the land by paying fair wages—I have no slaves."

He admitted he'd enjoyed successfully hoodwinking the admiral and the other officers from the *Fortune* who'd seen him up close on their ship and still didn't recognize him even now. He collected Nicholas's empty glass and refilled it with more port, then handed it back. Nicholas took it and drank a large gulp.

"And La Roux?"

"La Roux escaped. I was close to finishing him off, but he got away. I wouldn't have come here, not until Huntington left, but La Roux knows."

"Knows what?" Nicholas asked.

"About Roberta. He knows she is the admiral's daughter and that I have a fondness for her. He threatened her. I couldn't let you and Roberta face him alone, not when he'll attack you at the moment you least suspect. I know how he thinks, so I had to risk coming here."

Dominic turned to face his friend. "This is my home. It has been for a long time, and when the harbor is empty of English naval vessels, I return here and become the man you see now."

Nicholas half smiled. "It's quite the transformation."

"It is, isn't it?"

"You look like the man I always thought you'd become." Nicholas set his empty glass aside and came to stand by him at the fireplace. How long had it been since he and Nicholas had been like this? How long had he dreamed they would have lives like this, friends drinking port after dinner, discussing the future and all its possibilities? This moment would never happen again, and the thought made him shudder.

"Nick, I'm sorry for putting you in irons before. I..." His throat constricted as words momentarily failed him.

Nicholas placed a hand on his shoulder. "You don't need to say it."

"Don't I? I owe you an apology, Nick. We were friends once, and I should have honored that, not treated you as my prisoner."

Nicholas's lips twitched as though he fought off a smile. "We are friends. Years and changing circumstances haven't stopped that. But I'd have done the same thing had I been in your position, at least until I knew you were still the man I remembered."

His friend's words made that ache in his chest only deepen.

"Nick, I've done things. Things you might never forgive me for. I have killed men, I have sunk ships. I've..." His voice broke as he met Nicholas's eyes. Everything seemed so clear in that instant.

"I know, Dom. I know what men like La Roux do to the boys they take. I know the unspeakable pain and rage that blinds you to all else. I *know*."

Nicholas's words broke down the fortress Dominic had built around himself. He couldn't stop it now, couldn't keep Nicholas at bay. The tears he'd refused to shed all those years ago came now, running down his cheeks. It was good that Nicholas kept his hand on Dominic's shoulder, otherwise he might have drifted away on dark tides.

"Let's have another drink." Nicholas poured him a fresh glass, and they drank together in silence, a full silence that a man could only have with a friend he trusted.

"We should turn in. Tomorrow we have to talk about La Roux," Nicholas finally said. Before he could leave the room, Dominic held out his hand.

"Thank you for not giving up on me, Nick." He hoped Nick could hear the unspoken love he had for him, the trust and loyalty he knew he didn't deserve, yet somehow Nicholas had kept it for him anyway.

Nicholas smiled a little. "You would've done the same for me. Do try to get some rest...after you see to Roberta."

Dominic laughed. The weight on his chest eased. "I

will." He watched Nicholas leave, and he took a moment longer in the room alone, gathering his thoughts.

Roberta was here in his home, wearing the fine gowns he had ready for her and the jewelry he had purchased years ago with his first sale of tea from the plantation. He'd hoped to present them to a woman who held his heart someday, but he'd given up that dream until he'd met Roberta. The thought of watching her descend the stairs in such feminine glory set his blood humming. Yet he would never forget her as his feisty cabin boy. The way her face lit up as she watched the sea, how her little bottom fit in his hands as he cupped her backside. How free he had felt with her on his ship. Chibbs would say that a woman on board was a curse, but she had been nothing but a blessing.

Dominic left his study and headed upstairs. Lamps had been extinguished in the upper hall for the night. He trod quietly on the carpeted floors. Roberta had been given the room next to his, which also happened to be the farthest room from her father's. As he reached Roberta's bedchamber, he tried the door handle. It gave easily, and he slipped into her room. He expected her to be waiting for him on the bed, but she was out on the veranda, her dark silhouette already captivating him.

The Caribbean moonlight bathed the balcony and the white sandy beaches of the bay below. He moved quietly, coming up behind her. He caged her body from behind, placing his hands on either side of her as they stared out at the view below. Fireflies danced in the gardens, soft green lights and enchanting play of glowing color. As he stood there with her, he felt the deepest sense of peace wash over him. This woman was such a mystery to him, how she could both arouse and calm him in the same moment.

"I thought I'd never see you again, yet here you are." Her voice was soft, so full of something he was almost afraid and yet desperate to hear. He leaned in and nuzzled her ear, feathering his lips against the sensitive shell. She sucked in a breath, and the fabric of her dress whispered against the marble floor of the veranda.

"I didn't think I would see you again either," he said.

Roberta turned her head slightly toward him. "What happened to La Roux?"

"We fought, but he escaped. I came after you because he knows—he saw the passenger manifest from the *Fortune* and saw you weren't on the longboats." He swallowed hard. He had braved battles at sea and escaped the gallows more than once, but speaking to this woman about his feelings and his fears was far more dangerous than anything he had yet faced, on or off the seas.

"Why does it matter? I don't mean anything to him." Roberta turned in his arms, and he marveled at how small she was, a tiny creature of delicate curves, yet she was also lean and strong. And now she was adorned in the finest fabrics he could buy.

The pearls around her throat shone like condensed moonlight against her golden skin. She'd spent so much time on deck with him earning her place like any man that she had acquired a tan. He knew that most men preferred the milky-white skin of ladies who never set foot outside, but he adored Roberta because she was no trophy to earn and display. She was a woman who could keep up with him and his men.

"He knows I have an attachment to you. He has set his sights on you. I had to make sure you were safe. So I risked coming here, even while Huntington and your father were present. I tend to stay away from Port Royal when naval ships are prowling around my harbor. But I had to protect you, no matter the cost. I don't think he's foolish enough to risk coming after you here, but I cannot be sure."

Roberta's eyes searched his face, and he wondered what it was she was looking for.

"And after I'm safe?" she asked.

"I will confess, I don't know. Regardless of what I want, there's no way in which..." His tongue felt like lead as he tried to explain. "I'm not a man a good woman should settle down with. I'm a pirate. I run a crew from a pirate haven. I doubt I could stop now. Too many pirates know me and would sell my identity here if they could make coin from it. Life with me would mean life on the run for both of us."

Roberta reached up to cup his face. Her hands were warm, and her touch held a mixture of comfort and sensuality as her fingers traced the line of his lips. He had done that to dozens of women, but none had ever touched him back in that way. He closed his eyes, letting her fingertips wander.

"Let's not think about tomorrow, then," she said, and he tightened his hold on her arms.

"We were rushed earlier. I won't rush now. Not this time," he promised.

ROBERTA GRASPED DOMINIC'S HAND AND LED HIM BACK inside. The few candles that lit the room were burning low, and their flames would soon extinguish. All the better for her to explore him in the shadows and not worry about him seeing her blush. She stopped next to the bed, slipped out of the satin mule slippers she wore, and reached for his waistcoat. He remained still as she threaded the buttons through their slits, opened the waistcoat wide and slid it off his shoulders.

They took turns undressing each other, taking their time. Her gown came next, as his fingers slipped through the laces at the back until the gown collapsed in a blue-and-gold puddle at her feet.

Next came Dominic's shirt. Roberta touched his waist, tugging the long white shirt from his breeches. He pulled it over his head and tossed it to the floor. She placed her palms on his chest, sliding them over the rigid muscles of his abdomen and to his strong chest. She circled a fingertip around one flat nipple, and his breath hitched. Emboldened by his response, she leaned in and covered his now erect nipple with her mouth, flicking her tongue gently against his skin. She gripped his arms as she sucked at him, and a soft moan escaped his lips.

Dominic hissed as she moved to the other side of his chest, then trailed kisses up to his neck, where she playfully nipped him. Roberta giggled as she paused to look up at him.

"You little minx," he growled, his tone full of playfulness.

"I've never had the chance to explore a man's body. Pardon me if I wish to take my time."

Dominic's eyes glowed. "You are pardoned. And I think I should have the same chance." He stroked a finger down her collarbone and along the tops of her breasts, which swelled tight against her stays. He unfastened the laces until the stiff fabric collapsed on top of her dress. Now she wore only a filmy chemise, and her nipples pebbled against the unexpected chill.

Dominic gently lifted the chemise up and off her body. She was tempted to cover her nakedness, but in the moonlight she was not embarrassed.

"It's as though I dreamt you up," he murmured as he brushed the backs of his fingers over her breast. "The perfect woman."

"Perfect?" She laughed ruefully. "I would hardly think so. I'm—"

"Shhhh..." Dominic pressed a finger to her lips, then lifted one of her hands and opened her palm. The rope burns had healed into scabs, and soon they would be nothing more than faint scars. He held her hand up for her to see as he stroked her flesh, being careful not to hurt her.

"You see this? This to me is perfection. A woman unafraid to live, to rise up to challenges, to cross over the edge. You are not simply a woman with nothing but a body to claim. You are..." He paused, drawing a step closer as their bodies touched. "*Infinitely* more."

She was startled by his words. "I am?" She had always known she wasn't like other young ladies her age, but she had thought her differences to be flaws, not assets.

"Oh yes." Dominic's chest rubbed against her breasts as he pulled at the ribbons in her hair so he could run his fingers through the freed strands.

His hands in her hair felt wonderful. She shivered as one of his palms swept down her back to cover her bottom. He squeezed gently, his hold playful and yet possessive in a way that thrilled her. She giggled, feeling suddenly dizzy at the thought of standing before him in only her stockings.

"You are brave and brilliant. You took a lashing from a cruel pirate."

She leaned in to kiss his jaw. "The pirate wasn't that cruel, and the lashing was not so harsh a punishment," she replied. But she had shown him that she was indeed brave.

Brave enough to share tonight with him when neither of them knew what tomorrow would bring.

Dominic lifted her up and set her on the bed. He rolled her stockings down her legs one by one, kissing each inch of her skin that he bared before he rose to stand between her parted thighs. She trembled, remembering the feel of him inside her last time with that initial uncomfortable invasion. But she wanted him too much to let her trepidation rule her.

His eyes glowed in the firelight of the single candle still burning on the table. He removed his shoes, stockings, and breeches, and she had the chance to truly look at him, to see the dark trail of hair from his navel down to his erect shaft and his strong muscular thighs. Her belly quivered in wild excitement, but he didn't take her now like he had in the tavern. He climbed up on the bed beside her and with tender hands pulled her on top of him so she straddled him, the way she would have sat atop the tallest beam aboard the *Dragon*.

"Take me when you're ready," he murmured, and then he pulled her down on top of him to kiss her.

She was mesmerized by the feel of their bodies pressed close as the cool island breeze drifted through the curtains from the open veranda. Caribbean doves called out a sweet symphony, mixing with her kisses and exhalations as she and Dominic explored each other. She learned every scar upon his skin, each one earning a kiss of tenderness before she discovered a new one to tend.

"Who hurt you?" she asked in a whisper. "Was it always La Roux?"

"Most of the time it was Gerard La Roux, Andre's brother. His crew feared him, and he was savage to the young boys he brought on board. He paid for men on shore to kidnap them and bring them to his ship to work for their freedom in labor and piracy. Had it just been working off one's debt, life aboard his ship would have been bearable. But the man was a monster. He liked to break them, as he put it, before putting them to work." Dominic hesitated, and she kissed away the distant frown upon his brow.

"And his brother?"

"Andre knew what his brother did—sometimes he watched. I've seen men who have done dark and terrible things, but it haunts them when they sleep. They know they are damned, and it lies heavy upon them. But not Andre. There's nothing but darkness within him, a vast void lacking light and hope, let alone mercy. He took pleasure in watching Gerard hurt me. As I grew older, I knew one day I would be a match for Gerard, but not Andre. I waited until Andre was off chasing another prize on his ship. Once Gerard was deep in his cups, and he demanded that I fight for my freedom. I took my chance. I killed him. Shot him through his black heart with his own pistol, and then I stole a compass and a longboat and sailed three days without food or water until I reached Port Royal. I started my life over."

Roberta kissed his cheeks and tasted the delicate salt of his tears. "I wish you had never suffered, that you were never taken like that." She kissed his trembling mouth, blackening out the entire world around them.

He cupped her face, and their gazes locked. "If I hadn't, I might never have met you. I'm not sure I can fully regret the path my life took, since it led me here." The honesty in his eyes rocked her to the core. "I would do it all over again, suffer everything to know this one night would belong to me, that I would have this single memory to carry with me always."

"I love you, Dominic Greyville." She spoke his true name, wanting him to know that she loved him now as he was—beautiful, vulnerable, and entirely hers.

"I love you, Robbie." His sensual mouth pulled up in a boyish smirk that made her giggle.

"You didn't call me Roberta," she chided him.

"That's because I like remembering how I first met you. Roberta, while lovely, is far too serious a name for a pirate. You're a true member of the *Dragon*'s crew now, and you deserve to keep your nickname."

She rolled her eyes and then sighed in longing as he kissed her deeply. She tugged on his shoulders, her need for him too strong to deny a moment longer.

"I'm ready. I want you." She gasped as he rolled them over and pinned her against the soft feather mattress.

His hips slid between her parted thighs, and he sank into her. They shared a moan as he filled her, stretched her, and claimed her fully. There was no pain this time. Only delicious need that built up higher and higher as he rocked against her. Dominic gripped the bedframe above her head with one hand, leveraging his body to deepen his thrusts. She clung to his hips, gasping each time he pushed into her. The soft curves of her body molded to the hard lines of his. Pleasure burst between them, and she cried out before he silenced her with a kiss. He thrust deep a dozen more times, letting her ride out wave after wave of pleasure until she couldn't stand it anymore.

She lay limp beneath him, drunk with passion spent, as he finally came, his face twisting into a look of wonder and surprise as he gazed down upon her. There was no stopping this rush of emotion that poured from her body and soul into his. Whatever they would face tomorrow, they had this night, this beautiful moment, to hold on to forever.

Dominic collapsed next to her and pulled the bedsheets up around them. She burrowed into him, exhaustion creeping in. She placed a palm on his chest, stroking her fingers over his chest.

"You know, when I was little, I thought I could trap light, like one would trap an insect in a jar. I was always putting jars on my windowsill in the morning. My father didn't have the heart to tell me it wasn't possible. When I cried over my darkened jars, he would hold me close and whisper, *'You cannot catch the purest of lights, my dear. It cannot remain there. It becomes a part of you instead. Can you feel it,*

Roberta? That glowing warmth deep inside your heart?' And I would feel it. I felt my love for him, my love for life, my love for myself—it was all within me, glowing like the sun, bright and bold."

Dominic smiled. Perhaps he was picturing her as a child thinking and feeling these things.

"When I grew older, it became harder to find that light. But now you've chased all the shadows from my heart." She pressed a long, lingering kiss to his mouth, hoping he could feel the warmth, the love inside himself now.

Dominic answered with an earnest, desperate kiss of his own that softened into a thousand silent pledges of love and loyalty. How had she ever doubted him or his feelings for her? They mirrored her own.

They made love long into the night, their bodies creating symphonies of pleasure until the sunlight began to illuminate the skies outside.

Dawn had arrived, and they would face whatever came together.

ANDRE LA ROUX TWIRLED THE CRYSTAL GOBLET IN HIS palms as he gazed out upon the vast ocean from the windows in his dining cabin. Dawn colored the water a brilliant gold. He knew the sight was stunning, but it inspired no love in him. He'd only loved one person, his brother, and that man was dead. Dead because Dominic had killed him. Andre had been biding his time, seeking an opportune moment. Now it had finally come in the form of the admiral's daughter.

The look of fear on Dominic's face when he had shouted for the girl to run had told Andre all that he needed to know. The girl meant something to Dominic, so Andre would take her. Once he had the woman in his grasp, he would torture her and kill her, and then he'd find a way to set Dominic up for her death and have him hung. Andre would stand at the base of the gallows and watch his brother's killer's neck snap and his feet jerk in the wind.

Pleasure oozed through Andre's veins at the thought of destroying the thing that Dominic loved most. It would be as good as his memories of watching Gerard hurt the boy all those years ago, but it wasn't enough to sate his need for more. That hunger for the pain of others would never be fully satisfied.

Andre threw the glass across the room so hard it shattered against the wall. Pieces fell to the floor, and the sun coming in off the dining room windows shimmered.

But all Andre saw was red.

16

Dominic followed Roberta into the back gardens of his estate the following afternoon, watching the way the train of her cream-and-rose-colored gown trailed along the lush green lawn. Every few seconds he would catch up to her, brush a hand along her waist. Each time, his blood would hum with a sweet delirium when she would turn and show him those flashing eyes. Then he'd gently tug a loose curl of her hair or catch his fingers in the expensive silk of her skirts and pull her back against him to feather his lips upon her neck, and all too soon he had to let her go lest her father see. This game of catch-and-release was going to kill him, but the pleasure of finally tumbling into each other on the nearest flat surface away from prying eyes was only a matter of time.

The rear admiral was walking farther ahead. His

animated discussion with Nicholas carried across the air through an island breeze. Thanks to the admiral's influence, Nick had been given special permission to remain here rather than aboard a new ship in the port with Huntington and the rest of the royal navy sailors from the *Fortune*.

Dominic was only half listening to Roberta's father, because he was far more interested in Roberta and the way her hips swayed as she moved. The view was quite tempting, but bits and pieces of the admiral's conversation still managed to break through his sensual daydreams about pulling Roberta down into the grass and having his wicked way with her.

"We know the pirates frequent Tortuga and Cartagena, so I think it's time we have man-of-war ships patrol those ports far more frequently," the admiral suggested.

Roberta paused to study a line of English rosebushes. She bent over to cup one well-grown bloom, and she smiled as she brushed the soft petals against her lips. A flash of envy surged through him. He was jealous of a flower, a bloody flower. He wanted her lips on *his* skin, brushing softly over his scars the way she had before, making him feel like a whole man, not a broken one.

She looked toward him, her gaze holding his for a long moment. Hunger and longing shot through him in equal measure. Lord, when had a woman ever looked at him like that before? As though he'd caught the moon and handed it to her. That was how he felt about her, that she was the one who'd grant every dream in his heart, even the ones he'd thought had perished long ago.

"I'm afraid there will always be pirates in some form or fashion," Nicholas said. "Men have been raiding ships and coastlines for centuries. That won't change, not unless you could find a way to have ships cover every inch of the sea."

Roberta caught Dominic's eye and gave him a suggestive little wink as her father and Nicholas started to go on farther ahead of them.

As soon as the admiral and Nicholas turned the corner around a row of hedges that dwarfed the two men in height by a few feet, Dominic didn't wait another moment. He rushed to Roberta and pulled her into his arms. She accidentally plucked the rose that she'd been holding as he pulled her to him, and the petals scattered as she wrapped her arms around his neck. Their lips met in a sweet explosion. The tangle of her red hair covered his hand as he gently gripped the back of her neck and massaged the stiff muscles. Her responding moan delighted him.

They were fools for taking such a risk, but he couldn't hide what he felt for her. Her words last night had changed him forever, banishing almost all of the darkness inside him. She was his warmth, his jar full of light. When he was with her now, like this, the last fourteen years seemed to fade away. He could pretend that they were secretly engaged, that soon he would ask the admiral for her hand and that they would stand side by side in a church, making their vows to one another and planning names for their future children.

He suddenly froze, realizing that they had made love half a dozen times in the last two days, and there was every chance she could be with child now. His child. *Their* child.

Lord, he prayed the child would be more like Roberta than him. Their lips parted, and he held her face in his hands, memorizing her every feature.

"What is it?" she asked, reading his concern. It was becoming harder and harder to hide his feelings from her.

He blew out a slow breath before he spoke. "I've been a fool. I haven't been careful with you."

"Careful?" Her eyes were filled with innocent confusion.

"I mean children. You could be with child because... because I could not restrain myself." He did not want to explain the details and hoped she understood enough. "I have been selfish in my pleasure." He closed his eyes, trying not to panic. What could she do if she was indeed in the family way?

"Dom, I've known from the first time the risks we took. I didn't ask you to be careful because I was open to the outcome." She seemed to want him to respond, but it took him a moment to find the words.

"You want the child, our child, even if I cannot marry you? You would be ruined. You might be forced to give up the—"

"Hush." She kissed him again. "My father would never take my child from me, and I would face any future so long as I had a part of you to carry with me."

Dom's throat tightened, and he closed his eyes again. This woman was a beautiful miracle, and she was killing him with the power of her love.

She pulled away from him. "I hear my father coming back." She quickly stepped back far enough to be considered respectable.

She was once again admiring the cultivated roses he'd grown in honor of his mother. He knew his family was alive and well, and once a year he sent one of his crew to check on them in secret.

The reports assured him that his younger brother, Adrian, was capable, with a good head on his shoulders. Adrian's twin, Josephine, was a beauty like their mother, with a quick wit. He imagined his mother was as stunning as ever, though his men were not foolish enough to wax poetic over her looks, merely informing him of her movements. And his father. He didn't need the reports to know that his father was still a powerful man in politics, with the king's favor bestowed on him, which he used to help the lower classes whenever possible. They were, altogether, better off without him.

"Sir?" Griffin approached and stopped a few feet away. "Captain Huntington is here to see the rear admiral."

"Ah..." Dominic knew it was only a matter of time before Huntington came to call.

"Orders, sir?" Griffin prompted.

"Show him out to the gardens."

"Yes, sir." Griffin retreated.

Dominic glanced at Roberta. "Your darling fiancé is on his way. Should I have him tossed into the bay?" He couldn't resist teasing her, but he kept a solemn expression on his face to let her believe he still thought she was engaged to that oaf. He had resisted mentioning Huntington after Nicholas had assured him the engagement had never existed, but now was his chance to set his darling lady's temper on fire in just the right way.

"Oh...Dom, we were never actually engaged. I only said that to make you cautious with me and my maid." She started toward him, panic lighting her eyes. He held up a palm, reminding her to keep her distance as her father and Nicholas reappeared from around the corner of the hedges.

"Captain," the admiral greeted as the captain walked briskly down the steps from the house leading to the garden.

"Admiral, I received your message about Miss Harcourt's safe return." The captain's gaze shot past Dominic and straight to Roberta. Relief colored the man's face as he came up to her and clasped one of her hands, bringing it to his lips.

Dominic bit back a growl as Huntington continued to touch his woman. He hadn't paid much attention to the man when he'd tossed him into a longboat, but now he had a chance to study the fellow. Huntington was tall, with a decent build, and the man no doubt had been classically trained to fence and box. Not like Dominic, whose body had been forged in the fires of hell as he'd tried to survive on the high seas under the cruelest conditions. A man either adapted and grew strong or perished. Huntington would lose to him in seconds in an actual fight, but in Huntington's favor, he had the Royal Navy and the law on his side.

But that didn't stop Dominic from imagining throwing the fellow into another boat, this time much farther from Port Royal.

"I'm so relieved to find you safe and well, Miss Harcourt."

Roberta flushed, but she kept her behavior polite. "I'm quite fine. Lieutenant Flynn came to my rescue and helped me and my maid escape the pirate ship when we landed in Tortuga."

"Is that so?" Huntington's focus shifted to Flynn, and jealousy burned in his eyes. Dominic was amazed that Huntington had simply walked right past him, the master of the house he was visiting, and hadn't even noticed Dominic bearing a passing resemblance to the pirate who had made a fool of him and sunk his ship.

"I hope that Flynn truly did perform his duties as you said." It was clear to everyone that he didn't care for Flynn and would jump at any excuse to reprimand him if possible.

"The lieutenant performed admirably," Roberta's father cut in. "My daughter is not some silly creature. If she states her rescue was at Flynn's hands, then she speaks true. I would advise you not to challenge my daughter again. Am I clear, Captain?" The tone from the rear admiral drew Dominic's admiration. He saw the value the man held in his daughter. That was good. She deserved a parent to defend her against men like Huntington.

"Well, I'm glad to hear that," Huntington said, but there was still a bite to his outwardly polite tone. He straightened up, tweaking his uniform and lifting his chin imperiously.

Finally, the captain turned his way. "And you must be Mr. King?" His assessing stare didn't threaten Dominic.

He smiled politely and held out his hand. "Aaron King. Welcome to King's Landing."

"Thank you." The captain's gaze drifted to the large plantation home behind Dominic. "Lovely home, very lovely. You are a merchant, I hear?"

"Yes, tea mostly." Dominic waited to see how deeply the captain would look into his story.

"Hmmm," Huntington answered with a polite sound and then turned back to Roberta. "I would like to invite you to dine with me this evening at my lodgings in town. I was hoping we could revisit our conversation about the future."

By the way Roberta's eyes darkened, Dominic could guess what the subject of that conversation might be.

"I don't think we have anything further to discuss. But I do thank you for the invitation. I wish I could accept, but—"

"Regrettably, she has already accepted my dinner invitation here. You are invited as well, of course, Captain." Dominic took a secret pleasure in seeing Huntington squirm, trying to control his temper. It was utterly delightful.

"I wish I could accept, Mr. King. It's most gracious of you, but I have accepted dinner in town this evening." The naval captain looked ready to stab Dominic through the heart with the nearest sharp object.

"A pity. Perhaps another time, then? I will leave you all to enjoy the garden while I discuss tonight's menu with my cook." Dominic headed back, but he paused at the top of the stairs to see how things played out. Huntington tried once again to talk to Roberta, but she carefully planted herself between Nicholas and her father.

Dominic grinned, but all too soon that smile faded. He would have to say his farewells and see that Roberta was safely on her way back to England soon.

When Roberta came back in from the garden, Dominic was waiting for her, and he pulled her away from the parlor and into the hall.

"Come with me."

She lifted her skirts with her free hand as he led her away. "Where are we going?"

He said nothing until they were in her bedchamber.

Dominic pointed to a stack of clothes Lucy was laying out on the bed per his earlier instructions. "Dress in these and meet me outside in a few minutes." The maid's eyes turned to Dominic.

"How is Mr. Lee?" she asked.

"Grumbling a storm because you aren't on the *Dragon*," Dominic answered with a grin. He had noticed that the little maid had taken to his reluctant cook. Lee, like Reese, had discovered Luke was in fact Lucy only a day into the voyage to Tortuga and had seemed quite captivated by the woman. If there had been more time, there might have been a future between them, one that would have proven beneficial to the bellies of the *Dragon*'s crew.

"Is he to return here soon?"

"He had to return to the ship to see to the men there. But I could try to have him return tonight for supper." He'd had Lee and Griffin come up to cook a few meals when they'd first arrived but then he'd worried about the rest of his crew and their lack of decent food while they hid on board his ship awaiting for orders.

Lucy's smile faltered, but she mastered control of herself. "I hope so. Thank you, Mr. King."

Roberta lifted up the brown riding trousers, which had been tailored to her size. "Breeches?"

"Yes, we're taking the horses out this afternoon, and a riding habit would be too stifling. Besides, I had a feeling you would prefer them. I'll be downstairs."

Dominic left Roberta to change, and he called for his

groom to ready his best stallion and his finest gelding. As he paced the front hall, Nicholas came to join him. His friend cast a glance about to be sure they wouldn't be overheard.

"The admiral is determined to find the *Dragon* and its crew. You're not concerned?"

"The ship is moored offshore in a small cove that the Royal Navy frigates do not sail into because of the reefs."

Nicholas sighed. "They can't stay hidden forever."

"Once I'm able to leave, we will head for Spain, or perhaps north Africa, until Huntington gives up the search."

"Huntington has arranged for a ship to leave tomorrow for England. He is escorting Roberta back before he returns to his duties aboard a new vessel. The admiral has decided it's not safe for her to remain here, not when she's unmarried without a husband to protect her."

Dominic's body tightened as panic gripped him. "So soon? I thought he wished to move her here." He had secretly hoped it would take the admiral a few more days to find a ship headed back to England and to make arrangements. A new sense of urgency drove him to steal what moments he could with Roberta, even if it was but a brief kiss amid the English roses.

"I know—it is far sooner than we'd hoped," Nicholas said. "But the admiral has changed his mind. He doesn't feel he can keep her safe here. Your capture of the *Fortune* has him greatly concerned and he won't let her stay. I promise to protect her the entire voyage home. He's asked me to sail with her because he believes I kept her safe aboard a pirate ship. You have my word no harm will come to her." He touched Dominic's shoulder and gave it a gentle squeeze before he went in search of the admiral.

Dominic forced a smile upon his lips as Roberta rushed down the stairs with coltish energy.

"You were right—I do prefer breeches. How do I look?" She spun in a circle before him, and he laughed at her open delight.

"You know you look radiant," he chuckled.

She had pulled her hair back into an elegant queue bound up with a green ribbon. A few stray wisps of hair had curled against her neck. Dominic took in the sight of her, the afternoon sunlight from the windows lighting up her face. She was the single most beautiful thing he had ever seen. Better than a thousand moonlit bays or Caribbean sunsets, better than the colorful array of coral and fish beneath cerulean blue waters. She was the answer to every question that had ever mattered to him. And he was about to lose her forever for a second time.

"Ready to go?" He choked out the words past the lump in his throat. She nodded eagerly.

Dominic took her arm, and they walked down the front steps to the pair of waiting horses. He would not miss one more minute of his time with her. And then, he would do the right thing and allow her to leave. She would be safe in England.

Far from him. Far from La Roux.

ROBERTA COULD FEEL THE TENSION COMING FROM Dominic. His rigid posture astride his black stallion made her certain something was amiss. She steered her mount closer to his, hoping to examine his face more clearly. The road they were on was thickly forested, and the horses' hooves created a steady thumping on the moist brown dirt. Exotic birds flitted in the trees above, and sunlight intermittently cut through the shelter of the foliage. Roberta felt like she had stumbled into an enchanted wood, ruled by some ancient wood god. At any other moment she would have embraced the magical feel of this place, but right now she was too worried about Dominic's silence.

She reached across the space between them and touched his hand. "Dominic, what's wrong?" It was too warm for gloves, and the skin-to-skin contact gave her some small reassurance as he gently squeezed her palm.

"Nicholas said you are to leave tomorrow." His words were gruff, but she didn't feel he was upset with her, but rather regretful that they would soon be parted. She was doing her best to forget it herself.

"I don't wish to leave. I could stay...I *would*...if you asked me to." And she would, without hesitation. She would risk ruination and live with him, even if he would not marry her.

Dominic led them off the main road and deeper into the woods down a narrow path. After a while, the woods gave way to a white sandy beach. Waves crashed into the shore, and the pure blue water kissed a soft blue sky.

Roberta followed him as he dismounted and tied his horse to a nearby tree. He caught her in his arms as she slid out of her saddle and held her close, his lips touching her forehead in a faint kiss before he stepped back. She placed her hand in his, and they walked to the pale sand, which shimmered in the sunlight. Dominic knelt, removing his boots and stockings. Roberta smiled a little as she did the same. They splashed in the shallows together, playing like children for what felt like hours, until she was exhausted and collapsed back onto the sand. He joined her, stretching his lean body alongside hers, and folded his arms behind his head.

"Dom, please, can we discuss this?" she asked.

He pulled a small but beautiful oyster shell out of his pocket and brushed the pad of his thumb over it before giving it to her.

"For you," he said. "I found this when I first visited this stretch of beach ten years ago. I keep it in my study at King's Landing as a way to remind me of my chance to build a life here in this paradise. I want you to take it back with you to England."

Roberta could almost hear his unspoken words that he

wished for her to take what little of him that she could. It was an infinitesimal comfort in a vast landscape of pain.

She accepted the shell, and her lips suddenly quivered. "Dom, we have to talk."

He abruptly got to his feet and started walking down the beach. She chased after him and grabbed his arm, jerking him to a halt.

"Please...speak to me," she begged, her voice catching.

Dominic faced her, and she saw the emotions he had been so desperate to hide. Pain and grief etched his handsome features, making him look years older than he was.

"I would give *anything* to keep you, Robbie, anything to make you mine, but it isn't possible."

"Why not?" she demanded and furiously wiped tears from her cheeks.

"Because La Roux won't stop until either he or I am dead, and he will find you and kill you first to make me suffer. I won't risk your life for any reason. He's too smart to pursue you on the water when you're heavily guarded, but he might try here on the island. I don't trust that you'll be safe if you stay. You will sail to England tomorrow. Once you're there, you will live a safe and happy life and never look back. You must."

A few days ago Roberta might have believed that was possible, but she had tasted true happiness with Dominic and refused to believe she could abandon it simply for her safety.

"La Roux wouldn't dare come here. Not with the navy looking for pirates."

"He might," Dominic replied darkly. "If he felt the prize was worth the risk."

Dominic walked back up the beach and sat down on the sand beneath the shade of some palm trees. He bent his legs and rested his forearms on his knees. Roberta joined him after a long moment. She leaned her head on his shoulder, and he placed his cheek against her head. Ahead of them, the waves crashed in a ceaseless rhythm. Roberta drew some comfort from it, but not enough. Her heart was sore with a bone-deep ache as she faced the truth. Dominic wouldn't let her stay.

"What if you kill La Roux? I could come back. I"

"Even if it were easy to find him and kill him, that isn't the only reason you should return to England. Roberta, you deserve a full life. Even if I stopped pirating tomorrow, there are men out there whose lives I spared who could identify me or my men. Someone someday will learn that I am also Captain Grey. I am a man of numbered days."

"We all have numbered days," she answered in a whisper.

"But if I'm hung for piracy, the Crown would take everything—my home, my fortune, even the things I have lawfully earned. It would leave you penniless and without a home. I cannot do that to you, or any children we might have."

She wanted to tell him she didn't care, but in truth she did. Not for herself. She could survive somehow, but their child, if she was carrying one, would depend on her for protection. She could not let her selfish thoughts take over.

"We should return soon," Dominic murmured.

"If we must," she sighed and cupped his face. "You will come to me tonight, won't you?"

"Nothing could keep me away." He bent his head to kiss her, stealing the last bit of her heart that she'd tried to keep safe.

THE *RED LADY* SAILED INTO A DISTANT DOCK ON THE opposite side of the island of Jamaica from Port Royal just as midnight passed. The crew were quiet and cautious as they secured the boat to the dock. Andre La Roux left his men and descended the gangplank, walking down the wooden walkways that led from his ship back to the shore. The moon's glow was so white that it almost burned his eyes as he stared up at it.

Now he had to wait. Patience was one of his many gifts. Tonight he sensed he would be lucky. Fifteen minutes later, one of his men met him at the dock.

"What news do you bring me?" Andre asked the man.

"When the *India's Pride* docked, the cabin boy and the

navy officer were met by an admiral. He called the lad Roberta."

"So I was correct, the boy is the admiral's daughter."

"Yes. It was as you suspected when you glimpsed her listed on the *Fortune*'s passenger manifest. They were escorted to a tea merchant's home. A man called Aaron King. I got as close as I could, and it was as you suspected. Dominic Grey makes his home here under a different name. Word on the island is that he makes money on a legitimate tea trade, separate from his pirate prizes."

Andre considered this. What a fool Dominic was to keep a life here, one that could be ripped away by someone like him. It provided so many opportunities to hurt him. Take the woman, take the plantation, take his tea trade. What would cause him the most pain?

"He took the woman out riding today, alone. They were embracing on the shore when I last saw them."

"Embracing?" Andre turned the word over and over. He had seen Dominic's affection for the girl back in Tortuga and had played with Dominic, challenging him over his fear of losing her, but he knew Dominic well. Any woman was safe with that fool because Dominic had a soft heart for the fairer sex. What Andre wished to know was whether Dominic loved this admiral's daughter.

"Yes," the man replied. "I know little of love, but I would hazard that Grey may in fact be in love with this woman. I overheard a bit of their conversation as it carried on the wind. They were speaking of marriage and a life together."

"And you're sure she's the admiral's daughter?" It would make her a difficult bird to catch, but all the more powerful when caught. Leaving her dead and laying the blame at Dominic's feet could see Dominic facing the noose. What a sweet turn of events that would be indeed if he could set things in motion.

The man nodded. "I was able to discern that they leave for England tomorrow. The admiral has decided it's too dangerous for her to remain here. He plans to escort her home tomorrow aboard the *Majesty's Falcon*."

Andre grinned. The tide of war between him and Dominic had finally turned. He held out a leather pouch with coins and tossed it to the man, who slipped back into the shadows of the small dockside port. Andre returned to his ship, issuing orders to make sail again by dawn.

"Blaise!" he snapped at his quartermaster. The young man came over to him, a wary look in his eyes.

"Yes, Captain?"

"I have a special task for you."

Andre had decided what would cause Dominic the most pain, and he would soon take his revenge.

17

"Mr. King. A word, if you please," the admiral said to Dominic after the servants cleared away dinner. Roberta and Flynn had gathered near the pianoforte, speaking softly and smiling. Dominic felt comforted that Roberta liked Nicholas. In another life, he would have been overjoyed to see his woman and the man he once called his brother getting along so well.

"Yes?" He brought his attention back to the admiral as they stepped into the hall.

"I know I may seem to be a preoccupied man, but when it comes to my daughter, I'm quite observant. You have tried to hide your intentions, but I'm no fool."

Dominic tensed as he met the man's gaze. The admiral was in his late fifties, but Dominic suspected the man could put up quite a fight, if properly motivated.

"I'm not sure I follow," he answered carefully. What exactly did the man know? That he was bedding Roberta, or that he was the pirate who had taken the *Fortune*?

The admiral's face softened. "You are attentive to Roberta, and dare I say you are forming an attachment."

Dominic relaxed ever so slightly. "I may indeed," he admitted carefully.

"As you know, I'm sailing to England tomorrow to escort her home, but if I was given a reason to feel that it would be safe to leave her here…say under the protection of a new husband…"

It took everything in Dominic's power not to say that he would like nothing more, that he wanted Roberta as his wife. But as long as Andre La Roux drew breath, Roberta would never be safe in the West Indies.

"As much as I wish to, I cannot provide a reason. Pirates are an ever-present threat. Not just in the water, but also on shore. As the daughter of an admiral, she would be a prize to any number of seafaring rogues to take and use to hurt you. It would be best if she returned to England." The words crushed him like a boulder.

"Then I was mistaken? You are not overly attached to her?" Disappointment in the older man's face was so evident that Dominic's stomach knotted in answering sorrow.

"On the contrary. I'm *too* attached, and it is taking all of my strength to remind myself that her safety should come first. I feel as though I've known her for years, possibly in another life, and it is because of that depth of feeling I must insist she is returned to England where no harm can come to her." He was surprised at himself for sharing his feelings with this man, but he felt that after everything that had happened he owed him the truth.

Charles's face lit with understanding. "She is capable, as capable as any man in most ways. Despite her small size, she is fierce. I know perhaps a father ought not to discuss his daughter like this, but she is no wilting lily. She is as stalwart as a tree, hardy and clever and unafraid. Does that make a difference?"

Dominic's hands clenched as he struggled to keep his emotions in check.

"I am all too aware of those attributes in her. They have only strengthened my esteem and affection for her, but consequently, it puts her in even more danger. She would not hesitate to put herself in danger to save someone she loves, including myself."

The admiral smiled ruefully. "Ah. I was so hoping you and she might..." He trailed off. "I could not bear to see her marry a man like Huntington. I thought at first he was a good match, but now that I've seen him for who he truly is, I cannot. Roberta deserves to be with a man who values her, one who wishes to partner his life with hers, not to cage and display her like a pretty toy and only free her when the mood suits him."

"Any man who truly values her should always put her safety before his own."

Charles clasped his hands behind his back and sighed. "Right you are." It was a weary sound that reminded Dominic so much of his own father, but this was a sound of defeat rather than frustration.

"After her mother died, I was at a loss as to how to raise her. But I couldn't leave her with a governess, not when I was always at sea. It didn't feel right to be apart from her. It felt like I had left a part of myself in England—one I couldn't live without. So I chose to break with tradition and bring her with me on all my voyages. It has given her a taste of the world most ladies will never have, but I do not regret it, even if it has made it harder for her to settle down."

"I believe you did the right thing. She is the finest woman I have ever known." Dominic meant it. He would never find a woman to equal Roberta.

"Well, I shouldn't trouble you further with talk of marriage." The look of defeat on the man's face threatened to break down Dominic's defenses. He wished more than anything that he could tell the admiral who he really was and that he was madly in love with the man's daughter, but he'd only end up getting hanged.

Dominic chuckled wryly. "Why don't we drown our mutual sorrows in a glass of port?"

"That would be good, I think." Roberta's father

followed him to the study. Dominic wished to dull the pain inside him in a way he hadn't in years.

ROBERTA GLANCED ABOUT THE LIBRARY AND REALIZED that her father and Dominic were gone. She turned back to Nicholas, who stood by the pianoforte. He pressed down on a single key and chuckled at the rich sound the note made.

"Dom never was one for music, yet here he has a fine instrument kept well in tune. Did he learn to play this? Sometimes I wonder if too much time has passed between us. Do I know him at all?"

Roberta's throat tightened. She didn't know what to say. Nicholas leaned back against the pianoforte and looked at her intently.

"You would marry him if you could, wouldn't you?" There was no censure in his tone but rather hope. "A good woman could save him, I think..." He trailed off, his face turning a ruddy hue.

"Andre La Roux saw me at the tavern. He knows Dominic cares about me. It's too dangerous. I would brave anything for Dominic...but he won't let me have that choice. I've never seen a man so afraid, Nicholas. He was terrified for me. I love him too much to put him through that fear over and over."

Nicholas adjusted his neckcloth and straightened. "I would give anything, even my own life, to go back and undo what was done to him. To give him back his life…and to have him back as my friend without fear of our opposing occupations tearing us apart." Nicholas's blue eyes were bright and so full of pain. Roberta touched his arm, trying to offer comfort.

"You've been a good friend to him. You never lost hope."

Nicholas sighed. "I wonder what I will do now. My commission ends in a year. I only ever went to sea in the vague hope of finding him. Do not misunderstand me, I love the sea, always have, but the way Dominic lives upon her waves and the way I have under the flag of the Royal Navy…we've two very different lives. I harbor no love for the life of an officer. The cruelties and disciplines leave little for a man to love about a life at sea."

"You could come back here. Keep watch over Dominic for me." She swallowed hard. "We could write to each other, and you could tell me how he fares?"

The lieutenant grinned, but it was bittersweet. "I suppose I could. I don't believe I could partake in his lifestyle, but perhaps I could help him manage his estate here, the tea shipments and such."

"You should. If I cannot look out for him, you can."

"Then that's what I'll do after I escort you back to England." He put her hand to his lips and kissed her knuckles before he left her alone with her thoughts in the library.

Roberta lingered a moment longer, examining the books and gently playing a few notes on the pianoforte. This could have been her new home, her new life, only...

She turned away and left her sorrow behind as she headed up to her room. Tonight she wanted to be happy, just one last time, with Dominic. She entered her bedchamber, startled by the darkness. The lamps had all been extinguished.

"Lucy?" she whispered. There was no answer from her maid. She must still be in the servants' quarters.

"Dom?" she called out, wondering if he had crept inside to surprise her. But she was met with only silence. The veranda doors were open, so she walked out onto the balcony to feel the cool breeze upon her face.

A sudden whiff of a familiar acrid stench hit her nose. The smell of a man who had been long at sea and rarely bathed. She choked at the smell as she realized the danger she was in, but by then it was too late. Far too late.

BLAISE CARRIED THE SMALL WOMAN OVER HIS SHOULDER. Her voluminous skirts and petticoats proved frustrating as he descended the house at King's Landing, but thankfully the woman was unconscious. She'd put up a fight, one he hadn't expected, and his bollocks still stung from a well-placed kick, but he couldn't afford to lose any more time.

He had to be back on board the *Red Lady* with the woman in his arms by dawn.

Once Dominic Grey discovered his pretty little bird was gone, he would scour every inch of the island before setting sail, and by then the *Red Lady* would be long gone. Witnesses would see the ship leaving the port flying the colors of the *Emerald Dragon*, which would set Dominic up to take the blame when the woman died. La Roux would have his revenge, and all would be well on board. But until then, La Roux would continue to take his temper out on the crew. Blaise prided himself on being a loyal man, but he had his limits.

The woman stirred as he placed her on the back of a horse and tied her down, but she didn't fully wake. For that he was glad because he didn't want to hit her again. He didn't much care for striking women. They fucked better when they weren't unhappy, and hitting a woman tended to make her sour. He'd learned long ago that charm was the key to bedding a wench. He felt a brief flicker of guilt, knowing that La Roux would most likely torture her before finally killing her, but that was the cost of being a lover of La Roux's enemy.

When Blaise reached the *Red Lady*, La Roux was waiting at the gangplank, his eyes shining in the moonlight like black coals lit with flames as he watched Blaise approach.

"Well done, Quartermaster, well done. Take her to my quarters."

"Aye, Cap'n." Blaise descended to the quarterdeck, eager to be rid of the wench and to get himself far away from the captain's quarters. Then he would find the nearest bottle of rum and try to ignore the screams that would soon echo across the ship.

DOMINIC MOVED SOUNDLESSLY DOWN THE HALL, HIS heart burning deep with longing as he opened Roberta's bedchamber door. Darkness drew him inside as he searched for where she might be. Her bed was empty. The dressing room was empty as well. There was no sign of Lucy, but that wasn't surprising. He had summoned Lee to come to visit her from the *Dragon*. But where was Roberta? One of his crew from the *Dragon* working as a footman had assured him that she'd gone from the library up to her rooms.

"Robbie?" he whispered.

Silence settled upon him, and that sense that something was terribly wrong grew stronger. That instinct had served him well over the years, and each time he had barely survived the events that followed by the skin of his teeth.

His skin prickled, and the hairs on the back of his neck stood up on end. Someone else had been here. There was a faint smell, something sour...like an unwashed body. Someone who'd been at sea would have a stench like this, but everyone who had transferred from the *Dragon* would have scrubbed up first thing.

His heart pounded as he rushed out onto the balcony and skidded to a stop as he noticed dark drops on the ground. He trailed his fingertip through it and lifted his finger up to his nose. The coppery smell of blood was unmistakable, despite the scents drifting up from the flowers below the balcony.

She had been attacked—*taken*. Dominic dashed from her bedroom and into the hall, bellowing for Nicholas and Charles. Nicholas was out of his room in an instant and the admiral a moment later.

"What's the matter, Mr. King?" the admiral asked.

"Roberta has been kidnapped. Someone attacked her and took her from her room. I found blood on her balcony."

"Taken?" Charles echoed, his face as pale as the moon that shone outside.

"Nick, escort the admiral to the harbor. Take my horse. Wake that fool Huntington and have him commandeer the fastest ship in port. I'll take my ship."

"What's he talking about?" Charles demanded as Nicholas rushed downstairs to catch up with Dominic.

"Dom, wait. If you sail the *Dragon* out there and Huntington sees you, he'll learn who you really are. He won't stop until he hangs you from the gallows."

Dominic retrieved two pistols from a drawer of the

rosewood side table by the front door and handed them to Nick.

"Nick, I would do anything for her."

"Even hang?" Nicholas whispered as Charles joined them.

"Even hang," he answered calmly. He would die for her —there was no question of that. He had to make sure she was safe from La Roux forever. He'd face the consequences of his decision later. All that mattered was getting to her before La Roux could hurt her. Even the strongest man could not survive more than a few hours when Andre had his mind set to cause pain.

"Where are you going, King?" Charles asked as he pulled on his coat.

"I have another ship. You and Nicholas will have Huntington take the fastest ship here, and I will search with my own."

"But...I still don't understand. Who's taken her?"

"A pirate by the name of Andre La Roux," Nicholas explained. "He learned of your daughter being here in Port Royal and saw it as a personal challenge to take her."

"What?" Charles roared.

Dominic didn't want to hear Nicholas try to explain La Roux while omitting any mention of Dominic being a pirate as well. He ran to the stables and helped his groom saddle his horse.

"Prepare two more horses for Flynn and the admiral," he

shouted at the young man as he mounted and raced past him. He rode hard down the dirt path that led deep into the island to another beach where his ship was waiting in a nearby inlet.

"Hold on, Robbie. I'm coming for you." He prayed that she would be unharmed when he caught up with her and put a bullet through La Roux's black heart.

18

Roberta woke to the taste of blood in her mouth. She groaned when her stiff muscles protested as she sat up. She blinked in a daze as she took in the sight of the luxurious cabin. She lay in a narrow bed that was unfamiliar. This wasn't King's Landing, and the gentle sway beneath her warned her that she was no longer on land. The gilt-frame bed and writing desk nearby spoke of wealth, and she would wager it was ill-begotten wealth at that.

"Awake at last," a cold, silky voice said. "I was worried my quartermaster might have been a bit heavy-handed with you."

Roberta saw the shadow of a man seated in the corner. He leaned forward, letting the lamplight bathe him in its glow. Andrc La Roux. Shc was in his cabin aboard the *Red Lady*.

"What, no screams? No pleas for mercy?" He chuckled.

Terror rippled through her, but she focused on being still and calm. "Is that what you desire? Fear? You will not earn that from me."

"Oh, I think I will...in time. No need to rush matters." He rested his chin in his palm, gazing at her the way a lover might. There was an intimacy, a fascination, even an obsessive nature to his stare. Had Dominic looked at her like that it would have given her wings to fly, but this man? His intense stare crashed her into the darkest pits of despair. This was the look of a man who enjoyed killing and planned to kill her. Eventually.

Roberta stared back at him, hoping to keep her shaking hands hidden in her skirts.

He stroked the thin dark beard along his jaw, drawing her focus to the sharp, angular planes of his face. "Do you know why I brought you here?" He wasn't unattractive, it had to be said, but the coldness of his heart dampened his fair looks.

She clenched her jaw. "Because of Dominic."

"I have waited ten years for this, acting as though I considered my brother's death to be simply the risks one took with our occupation. Ten years I've pretended that, while there was no love lost between us, I did not have my sights set on my brother's murderer. Ten years I've waited to find something he loved more than his own skin. Something he would be foolish enough to fight for."

"He won't come after me." Her words came out with surprising firmness, almost as if she believed them.

"Oh, but he will, *ma petite*. Because he knows what I will do to you. And when he does, he'll find you in pieces. And the Royal Navy will be on his heels. You see, when I left the harbor with you on board, we raised a flag that is identical to the *Dragon*'s. Those English officers will take him and hang him for your death." La Roux removed a small cutlass from his belt. He ran the edge of it along his finger, drawing a faint cut on his own skin.

"Cuts so smooth, like a knife into fresh butter," he said, licking the wound almost seductively. "You won't feel the first cut, perhaps not even the second. Only as you start to bleed will you feel the pain, and by then you'll be too breathless to scream, in too much agony to do more than gasp like a fish flopping on the deck." He swished the cutlass in the air playfully, and her heart jumped into her throat. She didn't want to think about what he was going to do to her with that.

Terror squeezed her heart, but she didn't dare move. She had to keep him talking. Find a way to delay him. She knew Dominic would come, and she would have to keep herself alive or else he would lose the fight to La Roux. It was exactly what the bastard in front of her wanted, so she wouldn't give him the satisfaction.

"You are really scared of him, aren't you? You won't fight him on even ground."

She saw a brief flicker of hate in La Roux's eyes before he shuttered his emotions.

"I don't need the fight to be in my favor, but I do so enjoy watching him suffer. He was always a brat. My brother, Gerard, seemed to like breaking that trait out of him."

"You were a coward to let your brother hurt a child," Roberta challenged him.

"Coward? No. A man who likes to see others hurt? Yes. I am a man who *enjoys* pain for pain's sake, *ma petite*. The pleasure I get from the pain of others, it is exquisite." La Roux sighed almost dreamily. "When my brother brought Dominic aboard fourteen years ago, I saw such strength in him. He did not cry or snivel like most of the little brats. Gerard liked his playthings as much as I do, but he preferred molestation to torture, you see. When Dominic realized what my brother enjoyed, he offered himself to Gerard willingly to save the others. Gerard was very pleased." La Roux smiled. "I can still see his face, even after all this time. He even shook Dominic's hand, agreeing to the bargain. For four years, I watched my brother use him like a whore. Gerard took pleasure in finding ways to make him scream, whatever it took. He even destroyed the boy's pride, just to see him break. It was a thing of beauty."

Horror descended on Roberta as she tried to comprehend the depth of La Roux's words. Dominic's abuse had been so much worse than she had feared. But Dominic had dragged himself out of the darkness and into the light.

"You're wrong. Your brother failed to break him," she reminded La Roux. "He suffered, yes. But Dominic was biding his time until he saw an opportunity, and then he killed him." She was shaking now, though not with fear. Fury rolled through her, building like a hurricane, the winds of rage aimed at the man in front of her. "Dominic won't need to kill you," she said.

She moved a hand into the slim pocket of her skirts, feeling the small bit of metal she had learned long ago to always keep with her. Her fingers closed around the mother-of-pearl handle of the tiny knife. Dawn slowly crept across the room as they stared at each other.

"He won't?" La Roux replied with a dark smirk.

"No, because I will." She removed the dagger from her dress and threw it as swiftly as she could. It embedded itself into the wall an inch away from his shoulder, and would have struck his black heart if La Roux hadn't leapt out of the way.

"Your mistake was throwing away your only weapon." La Roux calmly pulled the knife from the wall and started to walk toward her. The measured pace of his steps and the gleam of patient delight in his eyes sent fear slicing through her. She dove out of the way and had just a second to glimpse a set of white sails on the blue horizon. Could it be someone giving chase?

Roberta grabbed a chair and smashed it into La Roux. "This room is full of weapons!"

He staggered back in pain, and she took the chance to escape. She threw the door to his cabin open and saw the ugly bosun's face staring down at her. It was clear he'd been standing guard and hadn't expected the door to open.

"He's hurt! You must help him!" She pointed behind her, hoping the man was as stupid as he looked.

He was. The heavy man lumbered into the room, and she shot past him in a flutter of blue and gold satin. She raced up the stairs and onto the waist deck. Men stood all around her, seeing to the ship. A number of them stopped abruptly to stare at her. Roberta had but an instant to decide what to do. She couldn't jump overboard. Even without the weight of her dress, she was nowhere near land. Her only option was to climb. She wished she could rip her skirts up the middle to give her legs more freedom but the fabric was too thick and she'd lost her knife. With a deep breath, she hoisted up her skirts in one hand to keep them out of the way and rushed toward the mainmast. She was halfway up the rigging when she heard La Roux shouting from below. She chanced one look down and saw him standing there below her, hands on his hips.

"You have nowhere to go, *ma petite*."

Roberta turned her back on him and resumed her climb. The crow's nest was only another fifteen feet up. If she could get there, she might be able to defend her position until that distant ship arrived, if it was indeed coming for them. The wind whipped at her, slowing her ascent more than she wished, and she couldn't afford to be caught on the rigging by any of La Roux's men.

"After her!" La Roux shouted.

Roberta reached the nest and glanced down again. Another man was on the ropes now, climbing his way up toward her. He had a dagger between his teeth. Roberta cursed and struggled up over the side of the nest, landing in the large wooden bucket. She wished she was back in her breeches and unhampered by skirts. It would make it hard to fight.

"'ere, poppet," a pirate teased as he reached the crow's nest. "Come along and I won't have to cut ye." The instant the man's face appeared over the wooden lip of the nest, Roberta braced herself against the wall of the nest behind her and kicked him in the face. Not expecting the blow, the pirate swallowed a shout of surprise and fell like a dead weight straight down to the deck twenty-five feet below.

Roberta closed her eyes as his body collided with the deck in a sickening crunch. A roar of anger came up from the crew below.

"Go, all of you!" La Roux shouted. "She's just one bloody girl!"

Roberta winced. She couldn't fight off the entire crew. She looked back at the distant ship she'd seen before. It was gaining on them! Relief made her limbs shake as she tried to assess how long it would take for the vessel to reach them. Her climb to the crow's nest had slowed down the *Red Lady*. The sails flapped uselessly in the wind because the sailors had stopped working when she'd emerged on deck. The ship was now drifting, and the vessel that had been chasing them on the edge of the horizon was now close enough for her to see.

It was the *Emerald Dragon*.

Dominic was coming.

"WHAT DO YOU SEE, CHIBBS?" DOMINIC DEMANDED AS the *Dragon* closed the distance to La Roux's ship. They had caught up too easily. Why had La Roux slowed down, or was that part of his plan?

"Bloody bastard is flying our colors!" the bosun snarled.

Dominic glared at the ship in the distance. La Roux must intend to frame him for whatever he planned to do to Roberta. His fists clenched. When he'd taken the *Dragon* out to chase her down, he'd had his crew run up the Union Jack because today they weren't pirates. They were men of England chasing down seafaring scum.

"What else do you see, Chibbs?"

Chibbs pressed a spyglass to his eye again, his expression baffled. "I ain't so sure of what I'm seeing, Cap'n."

"Give it to me." Reese stole the spyglass from the bosun and looked through it himself. He suddenly chuckled and handed it over to Dominic. "You'll want to see this, Captain."

Dominic peered through the lens, and his mouth fell open. Almost all of the *Red Lady*'s crew were trying to climb the rigging. The weight of so many men had broken several bits of the sea-salt-weakened ropes. Dominic shifted the spyglass's view higher up to see what the reason was for such dangerous activity. There in the crow's nest was Roberta. Her hair blowing wildly in the wind, she was fighting off men with her bare hands. It seemed they didn't expect a fine lady to punch them square in the face. Each time they reached her, Dominic could see another body falling to the deck below her. Four men lay unmoving, likely dead from the fall.

"Chibbs, ready the cannons. We need to give those men another distraction so Robbie won't be hurt. Aim for the deck. Aim for La Roux." Dominic pointed to the distant figure on the forecastle deck, dressed in red.

"Captain, an English ship has caught up with us. I see Huntington, the rear admiral, and Flynn on deck."

"Signal to Flynn to circle around the *Red Lady* on the other side. We aim to sink her."

"Aye, Cap'n." Reese rushed away, leaving Dominic to check that his pistols and his sword were tucked securely in his belt as Chibbs gave the order for the *Dragon* to fire. The explosive report of cannon fire deafened him, and seconds later the answering guns of the English ship responded. Wood splintered across the *Red Lady*'s decks, and Dominic searched for La Roux. He saw Andre climbing the rigging, well out of harm's way from the cannon fire. What the bloody hell was he doing there? Only one thought came to mind.

"Reese!" Dominic bellowed. "I have to board! He's going after Robbie."

He grabbed the nearest free rope and, once the two ships drifted within range, swung across. He barely made it across, landing with a thud on the deck. The *Dragon* ceased fire as she passed and circled for another run, while the *Red Lady* desperately returned fire. Having only the aft side to aim at, they seemed to do little damage. Shouts from the *Dragon* and the English vessel surrounded him as men from both sides moved in to board the *Red Lady*.

"On your left!" Flynn's voice came from slightly behind him as Dominic surged to his feet and started running.

Dominic leapt onto the rigging, his gaze fixed on La Roux above him, just as La Roux reached the crow's nest.

"La Roux!" Dominic hoped to warn Robbie and catch La Roux's attention at the same time.

La Roux shot a look down at him and grinned. "Better catch up, boy, or you'll miss me cut her to ribbons." La Roux reached the nest and hopped over. Robbie screamed. Dominic rushed up the last ten feet of rigging and tried to climb into the nest.

"Dom, watch out!" Roberta shouted. He ducked just as La Roux swung a short sword where his head had been.

La Roux cursed and snarled, "Little bitch!"

Seeing his chance, Dominic crawled over the wooden railing and dropped into the nest. La Roux now had Robbie pinned against the opposite side, a dagger pressed into her bodice just above her heart, which Robbie tried to keep at bay with one hand. Her other hand was balled up in a useless fist, trapped against the nest by La Roux's left hand. It wouldn't take long for Andre to overpower her.

Below them the clang of steel and the crack of pistols created an unholy symphony, and for the first time in years, the sound made his stomach turn. He had once loved the sound of war, the cries of men in battle, but no longer. That part of his life was over now.

"La Roux, it's me you want. Let's finish this," Dominic snarled and drew his short sword. It was too risky to use a pistol this close, and with the crow's nest swaying, he could hurt Robbie.

Much to the surprise of both of them, Roberta reared her head back and slammed it into La Roux's head. He cursed, clutching his head and staggering back a step. Roberta sprang away as Dominic rushed in, but La Roux recovered quickly, blocking Dominic's initial thrust. Their swords clashed, sending sparks shooting off the metal like angry fireflies.

"You won't kill me that easily, *boy*."

Dominic glared at La Roux, the hatred of so many years swelling like a vast, mighty storm deep in the middle of the Atlantic. The rage was so pure, it was almost blinding.

"You are a foul stain upon this earth," he growled through gritted teeth. La Roux spat into his eyes, and Dominic blinked. It was all La Roux needed. He swung his blade down and clipped Dominic's side, causing him to howl in pain.

"No!" Roberta threw herself at La Roux, leaping onto his back and curling one arm around his neck to try to choke him. He roared and slammed his body backward, smashing her against the nest. She slumped to the ground, semiconscious.

Dominic surged forward, striking at La Roux and winning a blow to the man's arm. But his strength began to wane as he held his hand to his side to stem the flow of blood. La Roux kicked at Dominic, forcing him back. He struggled for breath as La Roux turned and lifted Roberta's limp body up, leaning her over the edge of the nest by her neck. She struggled against him, clawing at his hand around her throat.

"Such a pretty little bird. Let's see if she can fly."

And with that he tossed her over the side.

Dominic's roar was deafening. He ran at La Roux and thrust his blade deep into the man's stomach. Icy tendrils of dread stabbed his heart, but he tried not to think past killing La Roux.

Don't think. Finish it.

He twisted the blade buried in La Roux's gut. "This is

for Robbie and for me," he said. "You will never hurt another soul. You will be forgotten. Your ship and your body will sink into the depths with only sharks for company."

La Roux's eyes widened as fear replaced hate. Then that fear bled out into confusion as he gasped for air. Blood bubbled from his lips as he tried to speak. Whatever last curse he wished to utter was lost upon the wind as he sank to his knees and fell over. Dominic kicked his body, but La Roux didn't move.

Only then did Dominic allow the crushing despair to sink in. Roberta was *gone*. He remembered the look on her face as La Roux let go of her. In an instant, everything that had held meaning in his world seemed to fade away. There was no point to any of it anymore. His legs began to shake beneath him, and he knew he'd collapse any second, but a sudden cry from close by sent him running to the edge.

"Bloody Christ!" he gasped at the sight of Roberta clinging to some torn rigging a few feet below him. Alive... his sweet Robbie was alive!

Adrenaline shot through him as he climbed over the nest and worked his way down. "Hold on!"

She reached out for him, and he caught her, drawing her safely to the more stable part of the rigging he held on to. He pulled her close, burrowing his face into her hair. She smelled like heaven, and the feel of her body, warm and alive next to his, brought tears to his eyes.

"I thought I'd lost you," he choked out. His emotions had robbed him of his self-control.

"I thought you had too," she answered, trembling in his arms. He pressed his forehead to hers, their noses brushing as he held her. Then he winced as fresh pain in his side forced him to adjust his grip.

"You're hurt."

"'Tis a scratch," he muttered.

Her face paled. "Don't be daft. It's a fair bit more than that. We must get Dr. Maynard to see you at once."

He didn't argue with her. The drip of blood down his left leg warned him she was right. He wouldn't stay on his feet much longer.

"I can climb down on my own," she said. Instead of him helping her, she helped him climb down.

They started down together, but he froze when he saw the group of English officers waiting below. Several pistols were aimed at Dominic. Huntington watched him with a gleam of triumph.

"Dom, you mustn't go down." Robbie started to cry as she glimpsed the officers waiting below.

"I knew the risks when I came after you, love."

"Can't you escape to the *Dragon*?" She pointed to Reese and the rest of the crew who had returned to their ship, but they were watching him anxiously.

"I can't get across like this. Too far," Dominic murmured.

He stared at his ship, watching the *Emerald Dragon* roll

on the waves. The ship had brought him good fortune, friends, and...Roberta. He hated to think he'd never stand on her decks again and chase the setting sun.

Dominic met Reese's gaze across the short distance and called out one last order.

"Cast off, Captain. She's yours now."

Reese nodded solemnly in understanding. He would be a good and fair captain. The *Dragon*'s sails unfurled, and the ship drifted away. Huntington didn't focus on them—he had his prize. That was one small measure of relief. His friends aboard the *Dragon* would live to fight another day.

"Dom, I'm so sorry. I never meant for any of this to happen." Roberta pressed her face into his neck, shaking. He curled an arm around her, holding her close, ignoring the pain in his side as best he could.

"Robbie, I regret nothing. Not one moment I had with you. No matter what happens next," Dominic whispered before he stole one last kiss. Her sweet soft lips trembled beneath his as he savored one last taste of her before he let go of her and climbed down to surrender to Huntington.

"Mr. King," Huntington said coolly as Dominic and Roberta landed on the deck.

Dominic bowed his head respectfully. "Captain."

The admiral rushed to his daughter, gripping her in a fierce hug. Flynn stood next to Huntington, his blue eyes dark and full of pain. He was the only officer not to have a weapon aimed at Dominic. That act might not go unpunished, but it made Dominic's chest flood with warmth at his friend's show of loyalty.

Huntington struck out, clipping Dominic's head with the butt of his pistol. Dominic fell to his knees with the force of the blow and clutched his head. Everything around him began to spin in dizzying circles.

"You think I'm a fool? I thought you looked familiar, *Captain Grey*," Huntington said, close enough so only Dominic could hear. Then he shouted to the two nearest soldiers, "Clap him in irons!"

Dominic was cuffed and dragged off. He heard Roberta cry out for them to stop, but her scream came to nothing. Dominic was led below deck to the brig. Soon he would face a hangman's noose.

19

"Mr. King...is a pirate?"

Roberta looked from Flynn to her father and nodded. The three of them were inside a cabin aboard Huntington's commandeered vessel. "He's the one who attacked the *Fortune*, it's true. But he's a good man. He saved my life. Twice." Roberta recounted the great storm and how Dominic had risked his life to save hers.

"But he's also Mr. King?" her father asked in confusion.

Flynn cleared his throat. "In truth, he's Dominic Greyville. Rightfully, the future Earl of Camden."

"Aaron Greyville's son? I know the man quite well. He's made many inquiries about pirate vessels over the last ten years. I didn't know he was trying to find his son. Good God..." He soon put the pieces of the puzzle together. "The boy was kidnapped, wasn't he? That was the rumor, but I always assumed the boy had run off to sea. Many young lads do."

Roberta covered her father's hands with hers. "We have to help him, Papa. Dominic was forced into piracy at fourteen. He had no choice. He was taken from the docks by his home against his will. And by the time he won his freedom, the life he once knew was forfeit."

"She's right, sir," Flynn said. "I grew up with Dominic as a boy. He's a good man, but he's been dealt a tough blow."

Charles sighed and rubbed his closed eyes with his thumb and forefinger. "I wish I could help, but my hands are tied. Huntington saw him take the *Fortune* and sink it. He has all the proof and witnesses he needs. I cannot refute that. He knowingly committed acts of piracy."

Roberta stifled a sob. They had to find a way to help Dom. They had to.

"Please, Papa, I love him. I..." She closed her eyes as tears streamed down her face.

"Hush, my dear." Her father curled an arm around her shoulders. "I wish I could save him for you, I do..."

But there was nothing to be done, she knew that. Huntington was her only hope.

She fled the cabin and headed up on deck. Huntington and one of his lieutenants were conversing about changing course due to the drifting tides. When the captain saw her, he dismissed his subordinate.

"Miss Harcourt, how are you feeling after your little

adventure?" Huntington inquired politely, but he didn't look at her the same way he had before. He was cold to her, and that didn't bode well.

Roberta knew she ought to be more tactful, but she was exhausted and anxious.

"Captain, if I agree to marry you, would you let Dominic go free?"

Huntington looked at her in surprise, and then his lips twisted into a sneer.

"That's how I am to win you over? In exchange for a pirate's life?" He laughed coldly. "You are fetching, but there are dozens of girls prettier than you who would be happy to be my wife. You are no more remarkable than the rest. *Respectfully*"—he spoke the word sarcastically—"I decline your offer."

Whatever hope Roberta had clung to withered away. She had offered Huntington her life, her freedom, and he had laughed and called her unremarkable.

"He will hang tomorrow," Huntington called out after her with a harsh laugh.

Roberta returned belowdecks and met Flynn. He caught her by the shoulders, holding her in place before she could run to her cabin and cry like a foolish girl. She should have known Huntington's pride was stronger than his desires, and she'd always known deep down that she was not a great beauty. Only Helen of Troy could have convinced Huntington not to claim Dominic's neck.

Flynn studied her in concern. "You offered yourself to

save him, didn't you?" It wasn't a question, but she nodded mutely in answer. "Foolish, but noble. Come with me."

Flynn escorted her down to the brig. A single man stood guard, and when Flynn gave a jerk of his head, he left his station to wait outside.

Dominic lay on a cot on the floor of the cell. The ship's doctor had stitched up the cut on his side. Huntington wanted to hang his prize alive and well.

Dominic moved slowly into a sitting position and stood up. "How close are we to port?"

Flynn placed his hands on the iron bars of the cell, his head bowed. "We'll make berth in a few hours. You are to hang at dawn."

Dominic chuckled. "I thought Huntington would try to do it sooner. He seems awfully eager to stretch my neck."

Roberta leaned against the bars next to Flynn. "Dom! Please don't make light of this." She couldn't take him teasing at a moment like this—not when she felt as if she were the one about to die.

Dominic came over. He reached through the bars and clasped one of her shaking hands, bringing it to his lips. The feel of his warm breath and soft lips was a comfort she would never get to feel again.

"I'm sorry, my heart, but sometimes a man finds solace in gallows humor."

Misery so acute that it caused a physical pain inside her made her eyes burn with tears.

"Don't cry, *please*. I cannot bear it," Dominic begged. "I'm a black-hearted pirate, love. There's no reason to mourn me. No reason to waste your tears." He cupped her chin and brushed the pad of his thumb over her quivering lip. She'd always believed herself brave and fearless, but facing losing this man—not to the winds of fate, but to the hangman's noose—was too much to bear.

"It's not true," Roberta sniffed and tried to compose herself, but no one had ever taught her how to do that with a shattered heart.

"She's right," Flynn whispered hoarsely. "You're a good man. Even a pirate can have a heart of gold." Flynn touched Dominic's arm, and the three of them were silent for a time, a strange unity of love flowing between them.

"Don't come tomorrow, Robbie. Let Nicholas take you riding into the hills." She shook her head, but he continued, speaking softly, almost as though in a dream. "I'd like to imagine myself with you, the dappled light upon your face and the exotic flowers blooming around you as we ride to a distant shore. Will you do that for me? Give me one last moment of peace before I go?"

Roberta's heart was bleeding. She could feel it pooling inside her chest, making it hard to breathe. "Dom, I don't—" She cut herself off, uncertain what she should do. Leave him to die alone...or be there to see the light vanish from his eyes. She felt damned either way.

Dominic cupped her face in both of his hands. "*Please*, my love." In that moment, she could deny him nothing.

The longing and the heartbreak in his eyes matched her own. They were one in their suffering. If he didn't want her to see him die, then she would grant him that final request.

"I will go with Nicholas," she finally said.

"Good." He swallowed hard. "Give me a moment with Nick?" Roberta nodded, glad to have time alone to mourn the only man she would ever love.

NICHOLAS WAS STILL HOLDING DOMINIC'S ARM, AND Dominic was glad for it. It reminded him of their years as boys, of simpler times hunting in the woods with rabbit snares or carrying fishing poles to the lake behind his home.

"I need you to do something else for me, Nick"

Nicholas shook his head. "Wait, just bloody *wait*." He glanced around the empty brig as though to make sure he couldn't be overheard. "I could steal the keys to let you out. I could have a boat ready. You could be long gone before we reach Port Royal."

Dominic sought his friend's churning gaze. "Thank you, old friend. But I can't do that. You'd hang for helping me escape. Huntington is no fool. It's too late for me, and I'm weary of running, weary of looking over my shoulder. I may not have chosen this life, but I've lived it, and now that judgment has been made, it's time I face my end."

"Dom... Please. I cannot lose you again. Roberta cannot lose you." Nicholas's blue eyes were bright, and his voice broke as he implored Dominic. "I made a vow to bring you home."

"You will. I'm only sorry I won't be alive to see it."

"So is that it? I am to bring your body home? Break your mother's heart? Your siblings' hearts? What about your father? He never gave up hope of finding you."

Dominic tried to swallow down the anguish his friend's words stirred inside him. "Running away like a coward... I cannot do that. Just tell them that I died with honor, saving the woman I loved. Even my father couldn't find fault with that."

Nicholas gripped the bars of the cell, his face red and his knuckles white as though he sought to destroy the bars between them. "This isn't bloody fair, Dom, and you know it."

Dominic shrugged. "Life has never been fair. All we can do is make the best of the time we have. Take care of Roberta. She may need you if she is with child."

"What?" Nicholas looked stunned. "You...and now you'll just leave her? By God, Dom, you can't do this to her!"

"Marry her. Love her in the ways I couldn't."

Nicholas stared at him with haunted eyes. "You think our hearts would mend by marriage to each other? Every day we would look upon each other and we'd remember who we've lost."

Dominic had no words to ease his friend's suffering. "Consider it a dying man's final request."

His friend bit his lip and then closed his eyes briefly, nodding once to show he understood. "I will offer, and do my all for her should she agree."

"Don't let her come back here, Nick. The sooner she forgets about me the better."

His friend chuckled, though there was little humor in it. "Forget a man like you?" Nicholas's voice roughened, and he struggled to speak. "Neither she nor I will ever forget. You are and have been my best friend, Dominic. The years apart have not changed that." Nicholas drew in a deep breath as though if he didn't, he might perish on the spot. Dominic knew the feeling all too well.

"Tomorrow I sail for the farthest horizon without you," Dominic said, his voice barely above a whisper. "I'll wait for her and for you there. Someday..."

"Someday...," Nicholas echoed.

Dominic swallowed, and it felt like broken glass tearing at his throat. Who knew that goodbyes could cause one's heart to break so completely?

He collapsed back on the cot as Nicholas left. In more ways than one, he was already dead, his soul miles ahead of his body. He closed his eyes and tried to find one moment of peace, but he knew there would be none.

Dawn arrived, and Dominic now stood at the base of the steps leading up to the scaffold in the center of Port Royal's main square. His gaze drifted up to the noose hanging from a wooden beam. The cheers and shouts of the excited crowd seemed oddly distant as he focused on that ominous length of rope. Two soldiers in red uniforms stood behind him, preventing any escape.

Huntington appeared in front of him, just short of the steps of the scaffold. "Mr. Grey."

Dominic smiled at him. "Here to celebrate?" He felt blessedly empty. It was easier than he imagined to summon a cheery smile.

"Indeed. It is a joyous day when a pirate dances in the wind, and you *will* dance." Huntington wiggled his fingers as though they were legs kicking in the air. "It's almost funny to think that Miss Harcourt offered herself to me in order to let you go. Did you know that? But I turned her down. Marriage to such a willful, rebellious creature isn't worth the chance."

Dominic's heart suddenly gave a wild, erratic beat. Roberta had tried to save him by giving herself to this wretched man? In his attempt to pour salt on Dominic's wound, Huntington had unwittingly given him something wonderful instead: the knowledge of just how much Roberta had been willing to sacrifice for him.

"Then you're a bigger fool than I thought, Huntington. You aren't fit to breathe the same air as a lady like her."

Huntington's eyes lit with icy rage. "And neither are you."

On that, Dominic agreed. He would never be worthy of Roberta.

"Take him up," Huntington barked.

The soldiers on either side of Dominic jolted into action, marching him up the steps until he stood over the wooden trapdoor. The planks beneath him creaked ominously. He looked up again at the noose as another uniformed man slid the circle of rope down over his head.

Dominic stared out across the sea of faces watching him and lifted his gaze beyond the buildings of the town. To the forests and the white sandy beaches of the place he'd called home for the last ten years. Somewhere out there Roberta and Nick were riding away, yet if he closed his eyes, he could see himself there with them. See the way Roberta's red hair gleamed like fire, and hear her laughter mixed with his as he and Nicholas shared stories of their youth to make her smile.

I've done many bad things, he thought silently. *But loving her wasn't one of them.*

The rattle of the military snare drums forced his eyes open. He couldn't stop the sudden spike of fear as he knew he had only seconds left to draw breath. His eyes darted around the crowd. He sucked in a breath as he saw Roberta pushing through the throngs of people, with Nicholas behind her.

Damned fools. They were supposed to stay away. He didn't want their last memories of him to be like this.

"Any last words?" Huntington asked.

Roberta was a dozen feet away now, wearing the finest gown ever created. The bodice was decorated with seahorses, and her gold skirts billowed out with the breeze. She was the loveliest thing he had ever seen. Perhaps it was a good thing she was here to see him, so that he might die with her in his eyes.

Huntington grew impatient. "No? Very well." He nodded to the hangman. Only then did Dominic realize what he'd been asked.

"Robbie, I love y—"

The trapdoor beneath him sprang away, and he fell fast. The world blurred, there was a sudden jarring yank on his neck, and the air whooshed out of his lungs. He closed his eyes and welcomed death, because he'd had one last glimpse of her.

ROBERTA SCREAMED THE SECOND DOMINIC DROPPED.

"His neck didn't break," one of the guards on the platform shouted to Huntington. "Should we pull his legs?" The man started to hop off the scaffold to go below the platform.

Huntington waved the guard away. "No. Let him dance."

Roberta covered her mouth. "Oh God..." She was going to be sick. The crowd around her grew silent as Dominic swayed, his legs still jerking.

Then suddenly there was a mighty shout, and a man charged through the crowd on the back of a black stallion. People screamed and dove out of the way as he rode toward the scaffold. He jerked the horse to a halt, and then, in a feat that stunned Roberta, he stood on the horse's back and leapt nimbly to the wooden platform. He charged the soldiers, waving a deadly-looking saber, forcing them back. Then he shoved Huntington so hard with his free hand that the stunned captain fell onto his back. With a bellow, the man swung his saber and severed the rope holding Dominic up. He crashed to the ground, still twitching. People backed away in fear as reinforcements came running, muskets raised.

"Who on earth is *that*?" Roberta tried to make sense of what was happening as Nicholas shoved through the crowd to reach Dominic beneath the trapdoor. He grasped the noose and jerked it loose and free of Dominic's head.

"Breathe, damn you!" He pressed his hands down on Dominic's chest, repeating the motion over and over until Dominic jerked and suddenly gasped for air.

"What's the meaning of this?" Huntington bellowed to the man who'd cut the rope. "That man was a condemned pirate. By interfering with his execution, you face the same fate."

Roberta now rushed to Dominic, cradling his head in her lap.

"You have no authority over Dominic Grey," Dominic's rescuer announced from atop the platform.

"Enough of this foolishness!" Huntington snarled above them. "Seize him!"

Scuffling boots above sent dust dancing down over Roberta's head, and she shielded Dominic's face. He blinked slowly, his dark eyes full of confused wonder.

"Should have known heaven would have you waiting for me," Dominic murmured to Roberta.

Nicholas and Roberta shared a glance of relief, but the struggle above caught their attention again, as did the dozen armed redcoats who surrounded the gallows, guns raised.

"Halt! By order of the king, you have no right to the pirate called Dominic Grey. I have a royal pardon here," the man above them informed Huntington.

"Dom, you need to try to stand," Nicholas urged. He and Roberta struggled to get him to his feet.

"A royal pardon?" Huntington snapped. "Let me see."

Dominic, Roberta, and Nicholas cautiously stepped out from under the scaffolding and for the first time got a decent look at the man who had saved Dominic's life. He was tall and well built. A bit of gray hair streaked from his temples into the darker brown strands.

"And just who the bloody hell are you?" Huntington handed the man back a roll of parchment.

The man turned to look down at Dominic, his eyes suddenly soft. There was no mistaking the resemblance between them.

"I am the Earl of Camden, his father."

Dominic went limp all over again. Roberta and Nicholas struggled to keep him on his feet.

"Father?" Dominic whispered, a boyish look of hope on his face.

"*Father?*" Huntington stared down at them in stupefaction. "Are you telling me that damned pirate is a peer of the realm?"

The Earl of Camden smiled down at his son. "Yes, and it's time for him to come home."

☙ 20 ❧

Two months later

Dominic sat nervously in an elegant coach bearing the crest of the Earl of Camden. He and Roberta and his father drove down the long drive to his old childhood home in Cornwall. He still couldn't believe he was back in England, or that he was alive.

His father had heard rumors of a pirate called Captain Grey some months before and had called in every favor he had with the king to secure a royal pardon.

As it turned out, his father had landed in Port Royal just hours before Dominic had been escorted off Huntington's ship, but he hadn't heard about the hanging until just before the actual event.

With a pardon in hand, Huntington had been unable to have his public execution of Dominic and had to content himself with executing the remaining crew of the

Red Lady. Roberta, Nicholas, Charles, and Dominic's father had all returned to King's Landing for a few days. Charles had seen to it that Huntington was assigned to a new vessel and sent to the American colonies for a bit. Dominic had happily said good riddance to that bastard.

He and his father had talked long into the night before they'd agreed that he should return to England along with Roberta and her father. Nicholas, under Charles's command now, was assigned to accompany them all home.

Dominic and his father had spoken a little on the voyage home to England, but not as much as each might have liked. There was still a distance between them, a tension that Dominic was certain was his fault. He'd called his father a coward, and now he understood what his father had meant. That sometimes *not* fighting was the right course. He'd given up the fight to save Roberta's future, and he hadn't regretted the choice. But he wasn't sure how to tell his father that he'd been right all those years ago and that Dominic was sorry for all of the pain his foolhardy decision to leave the house that night had caused everyone.

As the coach stopped at Camden House, Dominic started to shake. In contrast to him, his family home had barely changed. Roberta placed a hand on his thigh, and he covered her hand with his. If he survived today, he planned to ask her to be his wife, but he was too nervous to consider that possibility until he'd faced his family for the first time in fourteen years.

He climbed out of the coach after his father and helped Roberta down. Then he ascended the stairs and went through the open doors into the grand hall. It still smelled of wildflowers, his mother's favorites. Tears pricked at his eyes as he gazed around. He stared around at the old familiar portraits of his ancestors and the way the sunlight from the high windows illuminated the gleaming wooden banisters he'd ridden down so often as a child. He wanted to call out for his mother, to see her, but a part of him feared how she would react. When they had left Jamaica, they hadn't had time to send a letter ahead of them. She had no idea he was alive or that he was here. His father had warned him that she knew only that he'd set sail with a pardon for a man he'd hoped might be Dominic, but he hadn't been sure.

"Father?" A young man dressed in a fine waistcoat and breeches rushed downstairs to meet them. He halted at the sight of Dominic. His smile faltered, and his eyes widened. He looked so much like Dominic's father.

"Adrian?" Dominic spoke the name quietly, as if the young man before him were a ghost. He heard his father and Roberta come inside the house behind him. Adrian's lips parted in shock, but he didn't speak. His throat worked as he tried to swallow while he gazed at Dominic.

"Adrian? Who is it? Has Papa returned?" A dark-haired beauty who looked like their mother came down the stairs in a flurry of purple satin. She stopped just beside Adrian as she took in the sight.

The young woman threw her arms around Dominic, hugging him and squealing in joy. "He's home!" She hadn't needed to hear him say anything—she'd just embraced him without another word.

"Josie." Dominic choked on her name as he clutched her back. The twins had grown up into fine young people. He'd missed almost their entire lives, and knowing he'd lost so many years, hurt him beyond words. He finally released her, only to be snared by Adrian in a fierce hug next.

"Thank God, he found you. We've been searching for years, brother." Adrian's words made the tears in Dominic's eyes start to spill over, but he managed to keep them at bay...until he saw his mother.

She stood at the opposite end of the hall, her face pale as a sheet.

"Dominic? Is it truly you?"

He rushed to her as she started to sink, catching her in his arms before she hit the floor, whispering a thousand apologies for every moment he had not been there for her.

"I'm so sorry, Mother," he breathed. "But I'm home now. I'm here."

"You found him, *mi amor*?" she asked her husband.

Aaron clasped a hand on Dominic's shoulder. "I did. From what I hear, our son is quite the hero."

"Hardly," Dominic said, heat rushing to his face. He wasn't used to praise from his father.

"From what Miss Harcourt tells me, you've become

the finest man she's ever known." His father chuckled. "You had best marry her before she changes her mind."

Dominic lifted his mother up, and his father curled an arm around her waist, holding her steady.

"You're truly here? I'm not dreaming?" His mother cupped his face, her eyes searching his for any hint that this was not real.

Dominic placed one of her hands against his chest. "I'm here, Mother."

"Tell me everything."

"Everything? Well...that might take a while." He chuckled as he began to tell his mother a palatable retelling of his kidnapping, how he'd survived, his life at sea, the *Emerald Dragon*, the men who sailed with him, and how he'd met the love of his life.

ROBERTA STOOD AT THE EDGE OF THE ROOM, WATCHING Dominic tell his mother and his siblings all about life at sea after Adrian and Josephine had introduced themselves to her. Aaron came over and pulled her gently away, asking his children for a moment alone.

"Miss Harcourt, since my son has not told me all of what he went through these last few years, could I prevail upon you for more answers?"

Roberta nodded. "He suffered much, my lord. I think it's fair that such truths not be hidden from you. He was captured by a cruel man. One who hurt young boys." She couldn't speak the words, but she saw the pain in Aaron's eyes and knew that he understood.

"My son..."

She nodded. "He was brave. He spared the other boys pain by suffering it himself. And when the time came, he put an end to that man, since no one else could. He is the strongest, bravest man I've ever known. He is a man to be proud of. The past pains him greatly, but I believe with time he will be able to let it go, so long as his family is beside him to love and support him."

"We will be...and, I hope, so will you."

Roberta blushed. "I hope so, but now that he's home, he has many marriage prospects. I would be no competition to such ladies worthy of him." She knew Dominic wanted her, but his father might have other ideas about who an earl should marry. She was, after all, only a naval officer's daughter, not a lady with a title or any great wealth to offer.

The older man's charming smile showed her that Dominic had some of his father in him after all. Not all of his fiery blood was from his mother's side. The thought made Roberta's face even redder.

"You, my dear, are the only woman he will ever want. I've seen that look before—it's how I feel every day when I look upon my wife. Trust me, he will want no one but you and I have no intention of convincing him otherwise."

Roberta smiled back as she and Aaron turned their focus back on Dominic and his family's reunion.

Sometime later, Roberta escaped to the gardens in front of Camden house. She'd been debating whether to return to the docks where her father and Nicholas were arranging to return to Port Royal in a few months' time.

She reasoned that Dominic would need time to adjust to being back home, and she should give him space to think about how he wanted to live his life now that he'd returned. In the last two months aboard the ship back to England, he'd kept a polite distance, only stealing a few kisses in the dark alcoves of the ship, and she'd begun to fear that he had changed his mind about her. She also needed time to think, to worry. The free life she'd always dreamed of had been within reach at King's Landing, but she was back in England now. What if she married Dominic and faced the fate she'd feared with Huntington? H is peerage duties would call him away and she'd be left alone, trapped in a parlor and so very far from the sea and the man she'd fallen in love with.

"Robbie!" Dominic called out the nickname that made her heart race with longing and desire.

She turned in time to be caught in his arms, and he kissed her, hard, hungry, then melting into the most tender of kisses. She curled her arms around his neck, leaning into him. There was nothing more magical than being held by him like this. The universe seemed to shrink to just the two of them, yet she could sense a world of infinite possibilities all around them. The whirling doubts that had assailed her moments ago seemed to evaporate.

When their lips broke apart, Dominic offered her that rare boyish grin that reminded her he hadn't always been a pirate.

"Trying to sail away so soon?" he teased. "These skirts make poor sails to your lovely ship." He playfully gripped the pale rose-colored fabric of her gown.

"I wanted you to have some time with your family," she said. "And..." She glanced away, too embarrassed to admit that she was worried about how they would go on now, whether they would marry, whether she would become caged inside the life she'd always feared would be her fate.

"And?" He cupped her chin, forcing her to look up at him.

"And I thought perhaps you needed time. I don't wish to force myself into your life. You have other choices now, and I honestly don't know where I would fit in."

Dominic gazed at her with such intensity that she felt vulnerable, almost naked in his arms. "You think I would choose another woman?"

"I don't know. I'm not exactly suited to be a countess. I can't live a life trapped on an estate, playing a perfect wife. You know me, you know my love for the sea, the need to be...*free*."

"I'm not exactly suited to be an earl. And I haven't forgotten how much of the sea is within you, my heart.

'Tis one of the best things about you among a long and glorious list of things that I adore you for."

Driven by some wild need to make her point, she continued, even knowing she sounded like she was trying to convince him to walk away.

"But you could make a better match than me." Huntington's words still haunted her. She was unremarkable, unworthy of a future earl. She hoped...no, *needed* to hear him tell her how he truly felt, that he wanted her and only her and that they would live a free life...together.

"What other woman would chase the stars with me? What other woman would watch the sunset from the crow's nest or brave a hurricane? When I stood up on that scaffold, thinking I'd never see you again, I was ready to die knowing that I'd been fortunate enough to have but the briefest, purest joy I've ever known, which was to love you. There is only one woman who could go with me to seek the farthest horizon."

He got down upon one knee and held her hand in his. Her heart pounded in her chest.

"Roberta, there is but one greatest adventure, one purest treasure that even pirates like me could secretly dream of." His warm brown eyes melted her heart, and she drew in a sharp breath. "Would you do me the honor of becoming my wife? Become my greatest adventure and purest treasure?"

She couldn't speak, she could only nod as tears streamed down her face.

He grasped her waist as he stood and twirled her around before pulling her close and kissing her.

Bliss rolled through her in mighty waves, and she embraced it, letting it overwhelm her. She leaned up on her tiptoes to whisper against his lips, "You really are a pirate with a heart of gold."

His rich laugh rang in her ears as he spun her again. And as she whirled in his arms, she glimpsed a brilliant horizon just beyond.

EPILOGUE

Nicholas Flynn stood at the entrance to the large military garrison in Port Royal. He wore a pair of dark-brown breeches and a sensible waistcoat of red silk. He looked like any man off the street rather than the naval officer he was. He drew in a steadying breath as he entered the barracks and found Charles Harcourt waiting for him. The rear admiral gave him a small nod to follow him, and they entered his office.

Harcourt took a seat, and Nicholas joined him, taking a chair opposite the admiral's desk.

"You sent me a letter to come out of uniform," Nicholas said quietly, wondering what assignment the admiral had for him.

"Yes, thank you for doing so. We have just captured a young man who we believe knows the whereabouts of the pirate Thomas Buck. He's what the men call a pirate king, of all things. Runs several crews here in the West Indies, and he's been destroying our trade routes."

Nicholas leaned forward in interest. "And the man you have in custody?"

"He was set to hang, but another prisoner, hoping to stay his own sentence, informed one of the guards that the man is Buck's right-hand fellow."

"Ah." Nicholas could see now what the admiral might have in mind. "You want me to gain his trust, find out what he knows?"

"Quite. We would have you share his cell and find out all you can. Once we know enough to catch Buck, we'll have the man's sentence carried out." Harcourt said this with a bit of sorrow in his eyes. In the last few months of working with Roberta's father in Port Royal, Nicholas had learned the man had a soft heart. He didn't like executions, even of pirates, but the law was the law. Perhaps having a son-in-law who was a former pirate had opened the admiral's eyes to the fact that not every pirate case was such an easy a thing to decide. Not every man was evil. More than one of them had been brought into piracy by force, and it turned Nicholas's stomach to think that they were hanging victims rather than perpetrators.

"When am I to start?" Nicholas inquired.

"This very moment." Harcourt stood, and Nicholas followed. Harcourt held out his hand. "I know this is a difficult task, but you would be helping all of us. If we are able to stop the source of piracy, we will stop the men taking the young boys from our shores and return the crown it's source of revenue. We could put an end to all of it."

Nicholas shook his hand and nodded. He'd meet this prisoner and do what he must in order to help stop a greater evil at work in the world. Harcourt showed Nicholas out of his office, and two young red-coated officers came over to them.

"Escort Mr. Flynn to Mr. Holland's cell. Act a bit rough once you're in earshot of him."

"Yes, sir," the men replied in unison. With an apologetic look to Nicholas, they grasped his arms and escorted him away. Once at the back of the garrison, they half dragged him toward the cells. Flynn feigned a struggle when he sensed they were getting close to the last cell in the prison block.

"Let go of me, you bloody bastards," he snarled, putting up a good show for whoever this Mr. Holland was. The first officer opened the last cell door.

"Shut up and get inside!" The second officer kicked him hard in the back, and he stumbled into the cell, tripping on the uneven stones of the floor and falling to his knees with a curse. The cell door clanged shut behind him, and he was sealed in semidarkness. The only window faced opposite the sun, and since noon had passed, that meant he would be trapped in a dim room for the rest of the day.

"Who the devil are you?" a quiet voice demanded from the corner.

"Me? Who I am is of no importance to you," Flynn grumbled as he got to his feet. He noticed the two cots on each side of the cell. He eased down onto his, as though pained and stiff from being treated poorly by the officers.

"It damned well is if we are to share a cell." The voice was bolder now, and a young man leaned into the faint light from the window. "I'm Bryan Holland." He held out a tentative hand.

Nicholas eyed the man's hand for a long second, letting him see his distrust before he slowly accepted the handshake.

"Flynn. Nicholas Flynn."

The man's hand was small, almost too small. And the closer Nicholas looked upon the man, he realized he was a boy, a young boy, no more than seventeen. He would be hanged for piracy, a boy who was likely once as innocent as Dominic had been.

"What are you in for, Flynn?" the boy asked.

"Piracy. Got a bit drunk when my ship docked in port, flapped my mouth to the wrong people. Damned redcoats were on me before I knew what happened. Bastards," he muttered.

"Bastards," the boy agreed. "They caught me stealing from the marketplace." He wrinkled his nose. "Threw me in here and left me to rot, I suppose."

Nicholas studied the boy, who now stood up on his cot

and looked out the small barred window. Nicholas blinked, and then his lips parted as he realized that something wasn't quite right.

Bryan Holland wasn't a man, wasn't even a boy. Holland was a *woman*.

What the devil was she doing here? And why was she believed to be consorting with pirates? Her delicate profile was obviously female, but since when did most men see anything other than what they wished to? They were looking for a pirate, and so they found one. Dominic had fooled Harcourt and Huntington quite easily simply because they weren't looking for one. A short crop of blonde hair and masculine clothes combined with a coltish young body made her appear boyish, certainly, but Nicholas had long ago trained himself to see what other men did not.

Bloody hell. He had been sent to betray this woman and help hang her for piracy. All he could do in that moment, as she turned to look at him and smiled, was think of how much he suddenly wanted to pull her into his lap and taste those soft, curving lips. The selfish, lustful thought made him cringe. This woman would lose her life, a life that might have been full of happiness if she hadn't gotten tangled up with pirates.

She started to softly hum a song he recognized, "The Ballad of Captain Kidd," and she sang the words as she dropped back down onto her cot opposite him.

To the execution dock I must go, I must go,
To the execution dock I must go.
To the execution dock, while many thousands flock,
But I must bear the shock, and I must die.
Take a warning now by me, I must die, I must die,
Take a warning now by me, for I must die,
Take a warning now by me, and shun bad company,
Lest you come to hell with me, for I must die.

NICHOLAS STARED AT THE YOUNG WOMAN, WHO SEEMED so carefree in that moment as she sang of death. What the devil was he going to do? He couldn't just let her die.

Nicholas cursed silently as he made up his mind. He'd get the information he needed, and then he would save her.

Somehow.

THANK YOU SO MUCH FOR READING DOMINIC AND Roberta's story! The next in the series is all about our darling Nicholas Flynn as he falls in love with a lady pirate headed for the gallows in *In like Flynn*! Get it HERE!

Made in the USA
Middletown, DE
26 September 2025

18145505R00188